DA
THE DEAD

DAWN *and Dave* OF THE DEAD

DAVID WAKE

WATLEDGE BOOKS

First published in Great Britain by
Watledge Books
Copyright © 2023 David Wake
All rights reserved

This paperback edition 2023
2

ISBN: 978-1835300015

For

Everyone of Us
In These Interesting Times

The End of the World is Nigh.

Sandwich-board man
Villa Park, 1973

Screeching, eye-watering smells, shouts, cries, people everywhere, closely packed, breathing on one another...

Li Chaoxiang stumbled and almost dropped his case.

"Xiǎoxīn!" he said, but the fishmonger had moved on.

Li shouldered his bag and jostled through the crowds. He held his hand in front of his face. The rendezvous was set for noon. It was nearly time, so he hurried on through the Daveet, slipping on dung, rotting vegetables and discarded fast food wrappers.

He reached the clock with two minutes to spare.

This pleased him.

He would buy his wife a dress, he thought. Something nice, embroidered with gold thread as well as a few treats for himself, a new phone, a games console, perhaps even a Western car. His job at the research laboratory paid little and he only ever had a few yuan left at the end of the month.

He didn't like it here.

There were bats in cages above his head, animals and reptiles in boxes and a fish tank full of insects. It was unsanitary. He liked the research laboratory with its steel surfaces gleaming, its aroma of disinfectant and everyone dressed in white. He could hide behind his mask and goggles there.

He wished they had chosen somewhere better to meet. Starbucks, for example; he only needed a few more stamps to claim a latte.

The case, held against his chest so hard that he could feel his heart beating, would change the world. The greatest medical breakthrough of all time should be shared amongst all nine billion people and not sold to greedy rich capitalists. Li Chaoxiang believed in this despite working for the exploiters. But where else would the funding come from?

But think of it, he thought, longer life, as long as you wanted, just as soon as they could iron out one or two little, minor, tiny, barely worth mentioning, niggling trifles.

A bat screeched.

A pangolin jumped against its cage.

Startled, Li Chaoxiang dropped the case. The sound of breaking glass froze his blood.

Thank Chairman Mao's ghost, he thought, that he wasn't dead.

He'd have to take it back and unpack it in the isolation–

"Li?"

"Hao xiansheng nin hao," Li Chaoxiang said.

The man took the case and his colleague shoved a packet of notes into his hand.

They turned to go.

"Hao xiansheng, deng deng!"

Mister Hao paused, "Ni bù yìng gai bànyan shàngdì."

Li Chaoxiang watched them as they barged through the crowds until the men were swallowed by the bustle and jostle of the living.

He had been going to buy a new smartphone, an Xbox or a PlayStation, a BMW – and a dress – but now he was going to buy a one-way ticket to as far away from China as possible. If the research translated from rhesus monkeys to humans, then people would live forever and he certainly didn't want to be around when that happened.

He could get the metro to Wuhan's Tianhe International Airport and there'd be a plane going somewhere... anywhere.

As he fled the lively market, he wondered about Mister Hao's fate. It was odd that an honoured comrade of an atheist organisation should mention a deity, but he supposed Mister Hao was right.

They should not play God.

1

It was not so much the End of Days
as the Middling of Days.

Dexter Harding

The End of the World was over.

Phew.

We were saved.

Thank goodness.

It had all been a bit much, rather too touch-and-go for anyone's liking. Much like a referee's decision going to VAR.

To be fair, zombie hordes still overran everywhere, the infrastructure had collapsed, supplies were scarce and workplaces deserted. The un-death toll outnumbered the death toll. Mental health was important too.

Birmingham had been hit just as hard as the rest of the world and its leafy suburbs had become a prison. House prices had collapsed, so moving anywhere was impossible.

However, the latest variant was a shambler, things can be repaired, there were fewer people wanting supplies and working from home had been a great success. It was a shame, but, despite the unlife, life went on.

And there was Pimm's, which passed the time during the endless months of Sundays.

It actually was a Sunday – there was a thing.

Dave sat in the garden, half-hidden by the long grass, drinking Pimm's. It had everything: strawberries, apple, slices of orange, cucumber and carrot, all floating amongst the bubbles. The Pimm's itself had been carelessly conjured from gin, apple juice, parsley, the last of the vodka and a sticky bottle of something that began with 'J'. The syrupy nature of that last liqueur had long ago dribbled gunk over the label. This Pimm's tasted much better than some of the earlier experiments. Kosher Pimm's itself had become somewhat rare – almost as precious as flour and pasta – so beggars couldn't be choosers.

The Prime Minister had explained the current situation in his inimitable style.

"It is not the end of the end, it is not even the middle of the end, but it is, perhaps, the beginning of the middle of the end, if not the middle of the end's beginning."

And that made perfect sense.

The Acting Emergency Minister, Fenton-Briggs, MP, had recently assured everyone that they might even be as far along as the end's middle middle.

During the apocalypse, everyone had retreated to their computer as a diversion from what was happening outside. The virtual world was so much more fun than the real one. Even work had been a video game. Last month's sales figures (low to very low) were a welcome distraction from the mayhem in the streets. Not that everything had gone smoothly – for example, sales of *shoot 'em up* video games had tanked.

But it was over.

Phew, etcetera.

The bright, great and wonderful uplands of the New Normal beckoned with the promise of growth, growth, growth, which was something to look forward to. Pensions were down, down, down, but inheritance was up, up, up. There'd be work, work, work. For example, solicitors found new billing opportunities arguing for legacies from the recently undead and insurance had become a complicated endeavour. And there would be plenty of openings, apparently, even in the field of advertising.

These opportunities would extend even to people like Dave, who had, after all, come up with the witty and important '*Keep up appearances and act like everything's fine*' slogan.

So, as Ends of the World went, this one wasn't too bad.

Not that Dave had had much experience. This was his first apocalypse. It was everyone's first apocalypse and for many, it had been their last.

Dave flapped his hand to discourage a buzzing thing.

"Do you remember Notre Dame cathedral burning down?" Dexter asked. Dave's housemate sat on the other deck chair in his pyjamas and hoodie.

"Er..."

"Of course not, but it was a sign." Dexter held his hands up, his open palms seemed large and all encompassing. "It was the first of the seven biblical plagues."

"Biblical plagues... like Moses and–"

"Revelations!"

"Oh, the four horsemen, six-six-six and–"

"There was the destruction of the cathedral, a plague of locusts in Africa, fire in Australia, hurricane, flood and now, zombies."

"I see."

"The end of the world is nigh."

"Nigh? It's here."

"Put this hat on."

Dave looked dubiously at the crumpled tin foil. It looked more like a false nose than a hat.

"It's why they pretend that the world is round," Dexter continued. "If we run on a round world, then we'll be running towards the zombies, but on a flat world–"

"We'd reach the edge and be trapped."

"Backs against the ice wall."

"Hmm... how do you explain Australia and New Zealand?"

"We could move to New Zealand. No zombies there."

"We'd have to quarantine!"

"We'd have to take a plane."

"Or a boat."

Dexter shook his head. "Remember the cruise ships?"

"Hmm..."

At the start, or as the PM would have put it, the beginning of the beginning of the beginning, Dave had suspected something was wrong. He'd popped into the local supermarket for supplies, and, as he'd gone up and down the aisles – bread, beer, bagels, the essential three Bs – he'd come to a sudden halt.

In between fabric conditioners and soothing balm tissues, there was a gap like a missing tooth.

No loo roll.

There was that expression, 'shit scared', but seriously? Anyone who had ever played a video game knew that you didn't panic-buy quilted, double-ply; you stocked up on guns, ammunition, explosives and... well, not in England, of course, but that was the principle.

And, in video games, there were also special abilities, magic items and cheat codes, which would have been handy in this real-life situation.

He'd stood there in aisle five stunned, looking at the vivid space. Other trolley pilots, their wheeled cargo pods piled high, had had to weave around him. The entire section was devoid of stock, an empty hole in the shelving for household goods. Everything else was there, so it was – he shrugged – probably fine.

He did buy more tins than he'd planned.

Back home, Dave hadn't paid much attention to the news either. Whatever it was, it wasn't a thing and it would soon blow over. They'd said so on the telly.

He'd sat on the sofa, eating spaghetti hoops on toast with a bagel burning in the toaster and a beer in his hand, while a government spokesman had been very reassuring, very anti-alarmist, and very... but the footie had been on the other channel, so Dave had missed the actual specifics of what he hadn't needed to worry about.

The next week, the supermarket had run out of pasta, bread, Pimm's and anything frozen. Dave had been forced to buy fruit and vegetables. The fruit did come in handy for the non-existent Pimm's, so it hadn't been a completely wasted trip.

And two days later, he'd been furloughed.

'Furloughed' hadn't been a word in anyone's vocabulary, but it turned out to mean a yellow card and a sit down on the subs bench.

So, feet up in the garden, Dave was well into the swing of learning cocktails, and attempting to cook carrots so that they looked like tagliatelle and cabbage so that it resembled toast.

When the apocalypse proper arrived, the change had been rapid.

People wandering around, shambling really, with only a vague and distracted awareness of their surroundings, their eyes bloodshot and glazed over from staring at their smartphones, were all too quickly replaced by the screaming and desperate running, and then by zombies.

Everyone hid indoors: stay indoors, stay calm, stay sane... save yourself, save the NHS, save power, save loo roll, save lives.

They had all lived in a bubble.

Three weeks later someone discovered Zoom and it was back to work from the sofa. So far as that went, it hadn't worked for his back. The office had promised to send out proper ergonomic chairs with tilt and lumbar support, but these had never arrived. In the end, he'd switched to the kitchen table and pretended that the software for his laptop camera hadn't been installed properly.

Friday night down the pub was cancelled as was Saturday at the match and Sunday league football. With all the extra time, Dave had expected to play a lot more Fifa on his PlayStation, but he never quite felt in the mood.

"Sitting on the patio drinking Pimm's is actually nice," Dexter said.

"It's one way to use the fruit before it goes off," Dave agreed.

"Bats."

"Eh?" Dave grunted. He could feel some ludicrous game coming on. The garden Olympics had been, at best, a mild success until the ball had zinged over the fence onto next door's decking. The suggestion of playing *Dodge Mrs Hoskins* to get it back hadn't been taken seriously.

"Bats biting people," Dexter continued. "The venom of the bat is well known for raising the dead."

"As vampires."

"And zombies."

"No, I refer you to *Dracula* and *Buffy*."

"Those are just myths," Dexter insisted. "You see, real vampires in Transylvania weren't the upper classes, but peasants – hence, zombies."

"Then why don't they say that on the news?"

"They're keeping it quiet."

"What for?"

Dexter leaned closer and tapped his nose.

"Well?" Dave said.

"It's all a conspiracy by satanists to control people." Dexter nodded knowingly and then poured himself yet another Pimm's. "This is growing on me."

"It's an acquired taste," Dave agreed.

"That I'm acquiring."

They sat for a while in their own thoughts, mellow in the sunshine. Large white clouds alternated the patio between heat and shade as the gentle breeze up in the cumulus wafted the weather east towards the forecast of overcast later. No contrails crisscrossed the sky, which might explain why Dexter hadn't mentioned the world government's plan to indoctrinate the population with chemicals.

Dave closed his eyes to enjoy the peace and quiet.

"Listen," Dexter said, "you can hear the birds."

"I can't."

"No, shhh... listen."

Dave joined Dexter, craning his neck to concentrate. Yes, there! Slipped into the silence between the gunshots, sirens, screams and the ever-present moaning of the undead, Dave could just make out the *tweet-tweet-tweet* of birdsong.

He searched for the right word and found it despite its unfamiliarity. 'Peaceful', that was it.

"Is it a lark, do you think?" Dexter asked.

"Hmm," Dave suggested.

Dave checked his phone and found he'd thumbed up Matchbox, the dating app. Talk about wishful thinking.

They had no female housemates – and no other housemates at all since Vince and Clarkie had gone to find an intact off-licence.

There were women on his phone's screen, distraught from losing partners, but wanting to move on. It was all good and fine to have an online relationship, but sooner or later they always wanted to meet. And then it was all screaming and shouting and arguing, and that was just the travelling to the restaurant. Going on a date should not be a life-or-death decision.

Dave swiped left.

He wasn't serious about getting a girlfriend. Who would be? This wasn't a world in which to build anything. There was no future and–

Ooh, she looked nice: Dawn_372, likes cats, blah-blah... looking for blah-blah.

"Dave!"

Dave jerked around in surprise, trying to see the attacking zombie. "What? What?"

There was nothing he could see and the fences that he, Dexter, Vince and Clarkie had reinforced, looked secure.

"Maybe it's a nightingale," Dexter said.

"Nightingales come out at night." Dave glanced back at his phone to find that he'd swiped right. Maybe it was fate. Maybe not. Nothing would happen.

"What is it then?"

"Pigeon," Dave said.

"Seriously?"

"Well, it's not cawing from over-eating carrion."

"You are so negative."

"Am not."

Dave's mobile pinged!

Perhaps this Dawn_372 was interested in him, and they'd have a virtual one-night stand that led to a kinky sexting relationship, but no, it was a text, short, terse and deadly.

Dave expected to join his work colleagues on Monday morning for their virtual start-of-the-week briefing. He didn't mind Microsoft Teams as it tended to crash and give him a series of breaks during the day. However, this text was about some important meeting.

Hang on!

It said 'in to work' as in 'in to work' – in person, in reality, in the office.

He'd have to – Dave swallowed – commute.

"Holy shit!"

"What is it?" Dexter asked.

Surely, the start of the beginning of the end of the end.

"Well, what is it?" Dexter repeated.

"I have to go into the office."

"Shit... sorry, mate."

Truly, the end was nigh.

2

Keep Calm and Carry On.

WWII slogan (unused)

Dawn checked her reflection in the mirror and adjusted her glasses. Not bad, she thought, given she was the last woman on Earth. She looked her twenty-something, haggard around the eyes and yet about to get on in the world. Sadly, there was no world left to get onto.

Her phone pinged.

She ferreted it out of her bag from amongst the packet of tissues, compact, lipstick, mask, sunglasses, bottle of hand sanitiser, attack alarm and ticket. She checked the notification, but it was only some stupid alert on Matchbox. For a giggle, no doubt, some bloke on the dating app had swiped right. It was probably some zombie acting on a buried impulse – apparently, they could do that, so it was much like a pocket dial.

Some loser – she shouldn't think ill of the undead – called Dave Knight, who was into–

"Dawn, Dawn!" Mr Anderson banged on the door.

Dawn had reflexively reached for the alarm cord, but, instead, she wondered if she could pretend not to be in. However, he had no doubt seen her enter and, worse, he might come in to check on her.

Instead, she said, "Mr Anderson, I'm in the Ladies."

"I need the figures for the meeting."

"Yes. I. Er... oh!"

She'd swiped right.

When everything had gone 'tits up and pear-shaped' as Councillor Grant had put it, the men on the Emergency List had all rushed to Anchor, the nuclear bomb-proof telephone exchange. In the confusion, some had rushed to *The Anchor* across in Digbeth. As their last stand in the snug had been relayed in a series of desperate phone messages and texts, they'd blamed Barry in Logistics for the missing attachment with the map.

The women on the Emergency List had paused to help others and, well, that had been that.

Dawn had only survived because Councillor Grant had needed someone to carry his Emergency Case. She'd struggled with this large, awkward object with a dodgy wheel all the way from the council chambers to Newhall Street.

She'd asked him, "What's all this about?"

"Hurry," he'd said, "I'll explain later."

He had not explained on their rush across to Telephone House and he'd been tight-lipped in the peculiar lift that went down only.

Once they were in the underground in the maze of tunnels, he'd finally explained the situation.

"We're safe."

"From what?"

"Here in these tunnels, we're safe."

"I see."

She was not, however, safe.

There was Mr Anderson for a start.

The complex of tunnels had been constructed in the 1950s for the Cold War, and secretly added to whenever someone, somewhere, had threatened a Conservative government. So, in fits and starts, miles of tunnels crisscrossed under Birmingham beneath the declassified upper level that everyone knew about.

So, she was safe.

The only dangers came from Mr 'Randy' Anderson from Accounts, the asbestos, the out-of-date emergency rations, and – *scream, help, run!* – the zombies that had got into the Smallbrook Exchange tunnel. The latter opening had been boarded up when all the filing cabinets with the Cuban Missile Crisis documentation had been pushed against the OSB sheets.

It had been a close call.

"Dawn." Mr Anderson was back.

"Yes, Mr Anderson."

"Hugh, please."

"What is it you want?"

"You know what I want... I wondered if you'd done the figures for the meeting."

"They're on your desk."

"Yes, but I wondered if you'd go through them with me."

"I'm powdering my nose."

"Look, Dawn," Mr Anderson whined, "stop fighting it. You know you're going to give in, eventually. Might as well enjoy yourself. Have fun. While you're still young."

"Will you..." – She didn't want another disciplinary case, so she bit her tongue. After all, how could he be sent on gardening leave pending an investigation? – "...ask Councillor Grant."

"Oh... you tease."

She heard him walk away and she let go of the alarm cord. If she actually pulled it every time she panicked, it would have long ago broken.

Anderson's attempts had been subtle at first and then desperately relentless, but over the last eighteen months, they had become somewhat lacklustre. His unwanted attention versus her steely disdain had worn them both down.

The Ladies was her refuge. The room had been built to accommodate 50 telephone operators, so it was spacious for the one occupant. It wasn't that the analogue switchboards had given way to digital boxes, it was because she was the only female survivor. She kept her bag with her phone there, rather than carry it around or leave it in the office zone. As there were more people than desks – desks in one piece – she felt it wasn't safe by the ergonomic, kicked and broken foot rest.

There had been a suggestion that all the toilets should be unisex, but Dawn had seen that one off.

So, gradually, she had moved in a comfy chair, coffee table, lamp, bottle of gin, glossy magazines and all the comforts that an executive washroom built in the 1950s, and never redecorated since, could afford. Whatever else, no matter how awful the world had become, she could retreat to the Ladies and her safe, women-only, solitary sanctuary within the last refuge.

Except that Dawn was not, technically, the last woman on Earth. There were many others and you'd need the fingers on both hands, and then some, to count them all. There was Mrs Rogers in Manchester's nuclear bunker, Annette and Jasmine in London, Lt Smyth-Anders on HMS Vigilant (submerged) and the girl who kept crying over the emergency channel.

Everything was 'emergency' down here.

Dawn's initial panic had subsided into dull, repetitive anxiety. They'd decided to do a full lockdown and only access the official government channels to avoid fake news. London gave them regular updates, emergency (that word again) briefings and well-meant thoughts for the day.

She missed chatting with her friends, white wine, those girls' nights out and days in the sunshine on a package holiday. Her memories of that time faded like the intermittent lighting in Tube 2. These days, if it was daytime, she hardly remembered her friends, Snookums her cat, girls' nights out or daylight.

But, as the slogan put it, *keep up appearances and act like everything's fine.*

The trick was to maintain standards. The ethics of civilisation were a series of policy documents worded to prevent grievance procedures. Whereas, once upon a time, regulations and procedures had been the bread and butter of her working life, now they were her starters, main course and dessert. Manners, like using the right knife and fork, kept the descent into barbarism at bay. If you allowed people to spread butter with a fish knife, who knew where it would end. Not that they had any bread or butter to spread.

But she, at least, would start on the outside and work inwards with a napkin on her lap and white wine with fish. She had enough spoons for that, though perhaps not enough cutlery for anything else.

Not that they had any white wine. Or fish.

So, she would follow the good practice and more: use titles and surnames (calling Mr Anderson 'Hugh' – yuck), quote paragraph and sub-section, and keep everything going.

With that in mind, Dawn popped her compact back in her bag with the packet of tissues and all the rest of her paraphernalia, used her black scrunchie to tie her hair back in a business-like pony tail, straightened her smart jacket and stepped out into the concrete underground tunnels.

She was the last woman on Earth (West Midlands Emergency Area) and that counted for something, surely.

A journey of a thousand miles starts with
putting it off.

Pub beermat, 2003

It was always 'Us and Them', Dave thought, one rule for
managers and another for the wage slaves. Go into the
office, for... honestly. Dave had always dreaded Mondays,
but this was off the scale.

In the days of Black Death (1346-1353), it was thought
that licking rats would ward off the bubonic plague.
During the Spanish 'flu epidemic (1918-1920) many
refused to wear masks to prevent the spread of the disease.
These selfish idiots had been called 'slackers'. During the
Thirty Years of Shame (1966-2022) fans still dreamed.

But no-one would be that foolish these days, you'd
have thought. However, during the early days of the
zombie apocalypse, modern slackers thought it was a
research disaster, secret experiments, fake news, UFOs or
arcane sorcery. Cures ranged from green tea to rubbing
the pus from zombies on exposed skin as if it was
sunscreen. Many people had dangerously watered down
existing homoeopathic cures.

Nothing worked.

Except running.

And even that had its limits.

So, Dave went to the armoury to select his weapon of
choice. His favoured option would have been an Uzi 9mm
or a phased plasma pulse rifle in the 40-watt range, but he

had neither. The armoury consisted of a broken mop, bottles of extra-strong bleach, an umbrella, a baseball bat, spare light bulbs and a ball of string. To call it an armoury was overstating it somewhat: it was the broom cupboard. He could use the broken mop's sharp point as a stabbing weapon, but what would he use to clean the kitchen floor? Or, rather, if he ever got around to cleaning the kitchen floor.

So, he selected the baseball bat.

He hefted it and practised a swing, nearly taking out the hall's table lamp.

In the little cupboard under the stairs, he found a box of leftover nails. So, with the aid of a hammer, Savlon and some plasters, he constructed *Brainbiter* – a most fearsome and devastating bludgeon. It looked mightily dangerous.

Upstairs was the place to observe zombies. If anyone curtain twitched downstairs, then all too soon one of the undead would be leaving a bloody handprint on the double glazing and moaning about brains. The front bedroom, Clarkie's, was somehow out of range so long as you didn't shout and scream.

His walls were covered in heavy metal posters, monsters and demons rising from hell or the grave. One was on jet-powered motorcycle. Clarkie must have known what was coming. A bat out of hell, indeed.

Dave turned on the radio before twitching the curtain aside.

"...and that was Coldplay on the cheery hour. Now it's time for the traffic news where you are."

"Thank you, Eamon, and there's little news to tell. The A38 northbound is still congested due to abandoned cars – some people are so thoughtless – and the clean air zone has been barricaded on the north and east sides with the underpasses unpassable. Buses are running again today, but there is a replacement armoured vehicle convoy on the 12A and 87 routes to Dudley. And now over to the weather, Shirley?"

"Thank you, Vinod, and it's going to be a lovely day, sunshine and top temperatures, although it's due to turn chilly by the end of the week with storms due."

"Oh dear, Shirley, that is bad news."

"Yes, it is, Eamon, so I say get out and enjoy it while it lasts."

"Depending on which zone you are in, of course."

"Of course, Eamon, that goes without saying."

"Best say it though, Shirley."

"Yes, Eamon."

"And now the zombie roundup. Edward?"

"Thank you, Eamon, and we have a red alert for Edgbaston and Moseley, but Kings Heath has dropped to orange. Selly Park, Selly Oak and Stirchley are all orange still, Bournville and Cotteridge, orange, as are Northfield, although Longbridge is now officially purple. The city centre has eased up, which is good news for those shoppers trapped in Selfridges – they may have a chance at last – and Digbeth is still a no-go area. Of course, as always, this station accepts no liability for these reports and the drop in Tag-and-Track take-up has made forecasting difficult."

"Thank you, Edward, good news about the city centre."

"It is indeed, Eamon, and–"

Dave turned it off.

He'd counted to ten.

Then counted nine zombies.

They were moving away down the road.

The reason became obvious when Mr and Mrs Penrose from No. 204 came around the corner. They'd been on a shopping trip and their heavily laden bags-for-life swung crazily as they ran for their lives. Mr Penrose swerved around a few zombies in the middle of the road, tripped and oranges tumbled from his bag.

He paused to pick them up.

"Leave them! Leave them!" Mrs Penrose screeched.

But Mr Penrose was made of sterner stuff, buoyed up by the promise of vitamin-C and he swept up most of them.

"GO ON, GO ON," Dave yelled, getting caught up in the excitement. When a few zombies paused and turned, he whispered, "Go on, go on..."

Mr Penrose rescued his other bag just as the walking dead reached him.

"Yes..." Dave announced as Mr Penrose dashed after his wife. "...and he's into the final straight. Mrs Penrose is at the gate, up to the– Oh no! She's fumbled her keys. This is a disaster. Mr Penrose is there, it's a photo finish with the zombies and... they're in, door closed, what a result!"

Five minutes later, the street had settled down and the zombies had returned to their mindless shambling.

He recounted them twice.

"Nine, shit."

Dexter joined him. "You really going?" he asked between mouthfuls of cabbage toast.

"Yes." Dave needed the job... needed the money – things were getting expensive, especially deliveries. Ten quid for a pizza, £5.45 delivery and £39.99 danger money surcharge – it all added up.

"It's fake, of course," Dexter said.

"Eh?"

"There's no apocalypse."

"Eh?"

"Most of the zombies are crisis actors. See that one by the lamppost in the yellow jersey. He was on *Doctors* and *Casualty*."

"You going to nip over and ask him for his autograph?"

Dexter considered this. "Nah, I wouldn't want to disturb him while he's working."

"Why would anyone fake this?"

"Why indeed."

The next task on Dave's agenda was to check his emails. Perhaps the meeting had been cancelled.

It hadn't – bugger – but at least it wasn't until 11am.

After that, he looked at the weather, which was cloudy, sunny intervals, top temperature 17°, wind from the SW, 5 gusting 13, humidity 45%, UV 3, visibility G, with light throngs turning crowded towards the afternoon, solitary intervals later in the week.

What were they talking about?

In no way could nine zombies be classed as a 'light' throng.

He clicked 'refresh' in the hope of improvement.

Imagine, he thought, a circle appearing, going round, disappearing and reappearing, going round, disappearing and reappearing, going round... he didn't have to. It was on the screen in the centre... nope... yes, round and round. The website was never, ever, ever going to load.

No, wait, something new, something fabulous, something... oh, timed out.

At least his computer hadn't crashed this time.

Oh, it had.

He checked his watch – 7am... he'd have to set off soon. The meeting was at 11am and, now there was an apocalypse on, the journey was bound to take longer.

Dave cleared the kitchen table and opened the package. He'd not taken a test in ages and he was worried he'd forgotten how to do it. He needn't have been concerned, because the new tests were completely different anyway. It was the same blue and white box full of bits and pieces in sealed packs with desiccant silica bags and instructions.

"Is it a knee one?" Dexter shouted.

"No," Dave said, checking, "it's... left elbow."

He washed his hands and blew his nose, but the instructions were quite clear, so he blew his nose *and then* washed his hands.

The silver seal on the little plastic tube wouldn't come off. He tried again, pulled, wiped the slippery water off his fingers, and then it stretched becoming longer, but also narrower. It slipped between his fingers.

"Oh for..."

Third time unlucky, but the fourth time was a charm.

Except he spilt some of the precious clear liquid.

Sod it, it would have to do.

He took out the swab and jabbed it up his nose like some sophisticated zombie searching for white matter with a chopstick. It needed to be rotated in his right nostril six times, then his left nostril ten times. Finally, he took his shirt off with the swab held in his teeth, and rubbed up and down on his left elbow.

It made no sense.

After 30 seconds in the little tube of clear liquid, he had to squeeze it out and then drip four drops into the opening on the plastic tester.

The instructions said it was 'C for 'Control' and 'Z for Zombie'. The letters on the tester were 'H' and 'Ψ'.

He set the kitchen timer for the requisite 15 minutes.

"Don't forget your mask," Dexter shouted.

"I've got my.... oh shit, yes, yes, thanks."

He'd also forgotten where he'd left *Brainbiter* and so he had to search the armoury and then retrace his steps. It was in the hall.

The kitchen timer went off like a warning alarm.

The tester had an obvious 'H' line, but the Greek whatever was clear. He was not a zombie and therefore he had to go to the office – worse luck.

He scanned the QR-code and clicked through to the government website. After filling in his details, his name, address, gender, age and date-of-birth (why both?), the site informed him that it was receiving a high level of internet traffic and he should try again later.

"Oh for..."

You had to go through this purgatory just to face the hell that was the outside. Limbo was also on the way to hell and limbering up was one of the seven circles.

Dexter insisted.

So Dave stretched, yawned and then did it properly.

"After all," Dexter said, "it's not like standing in goal. It's more like being a centre forward."

Dexter stood with his belly button sticking out. His stomach had pushed his tracksuit bottoms away from his football t-shirt. Even looking like this, he acted like a Peloton bicycle.

"...and again."

"Dexter, piss off."

"Look, mate, you've done sod all for months. You're going to be a little stiff."

"You don't say," Dave said, stretching his calf muscles. "I feel silly."

"You'll thank me."

"Will I?"

Dave finished, did a little run on the spot and then felt as ready as he'd ever be, i.e., not at all.

Going to the office was insane.

Maybe all right for those people with SUVs covered in armour with one of those snowplough things on the front, but Dave had to use the train. The station was like half a mile away through Cotteridge, which was like a ten-minute walk – *ten minutes!*

The app requested Dave turn on his location services and presently a blue triangle appeared. He was facing north, the front door, and the Jones family next door were clustered as always by their French windows at the back and Mrs Hoskins was in her garden. A few other red dots moved slowly towards the information about the café, newsagent and fish'n'chip shop. The shops were all closed for the apocalypse. The red dots disappeared one by one under the café as if tracking zombies was less important than knowing that it would have been serving coffees and cakes from 7:30 to 7:30.

The area became a green zone, briefly flickering orange when a red dot came from under the café before stepping off the screen completely. There were only a few red dots left in the street and he knew how to deal with those. After all, he'd once been to the pub – which had also been closed – so he was well versed in the tactics of screaming and running.

"Looks safe," Dave said to Dexter.

"Really..."

"I think so."

"You know the vaccine."

"The anti-zombie vaccine?"

"Yeah, well, you know," Dexter said, "it's not a vaccine, it's a chip inserted subcutaneously and used to track people."

"When they're undead, yes."

"And when they're *un*-undead?"

"Yes."

"It's an invasion of privacy."

"Yes, but I'd rather know where all the people and zombies are."

"Not everyone had it."

"Enough did," Dave replied, hoping it was true. Tag-and-Track wasn't perfect as the small print pointed out, but it was a useful guide.

Dave was a green dot in their house. On the phone screen, Dexter wasn't there, but then he did have a lot of strange ideas about everything.

"Why did they call it a vaccine?" Dexter said.

"I suppose because it sounds better than tracking chip," Dave replied, "After all, no-one could object to a vaccine."

"Me and Vince do."

"Vince did."

"It was all pingageddon and beepocalypse... Dave."

"Yes?"

"Good luck."

"Thanks," Dave replied, genuinely touched by his house mate's concern. "What are you going to do?"

"Watch some daytime telly I recorded yesterday."

"Yesterday's?"

"Yeah, they say you should live in the moment, but it means you have to watch the adverts."

"Right. Well. Enjoy that."

"Will do."

"Any advice for me on my journey?"

Dexter gave this some thought. "Yeah, get some crisps on your way back."

So, armed with his deadly baseball bat, his reusable coffee cup-for-life brimming with milk no sugar and his quarter 2 report, Dave was ready.

"Lock me out," he said.

"No fear," Dexter replied. "If you don't come back, can I have your Xbox?"

"It's a PlayStation."

"Is it the up-to-date one?"

"No."

"That's disappointing."

Dave checked his phone: one red dot in the front garden, a few down the end of the road, but otherwise, it seemed clear.

So why was he hesitating?

He had to set off in the next few minutes if he was going to make it in for 8:30.

He took a deep breath... and then another.

"You armed?" Dexter asked.

Dave showed Dexter the fearsome *Brainbiter.*

"So, you're going for 'smash their brains in', rather than 'severe the spine'."

"I thought it best."

"Have you got your key?" Dexter asked.

"Yes."

"Have you got your mask?"

"Yes."

"Don't just wear it around your chin, remember your mouth and nose."

"Yes, mother."

"Remember *Stayin' Alive*," Dexter said.

"Yes, mother."

So, finally, Dave pulled on his mask, readied his bat, opened the door, dodged past the shambler trapped in the front garden by the wheelie bin – "Bye, Clarkie" – and then he was away.

– FLASHBACK –

The 'paradox' is only a conflict between
reality and your feeling of what reality 'ought
to be'.

Richard Feynman

If you take a piece of cardboard and cut two slits in it, four
centimetres or so apart, and then shine a light through one
slit, you get a diffusion pattern. The light cast upon a
screen or the wall of a laboratory is brighter in the centre
and fades further away. Shine it through the other slit and
the same diffusion pattern appears, only shifted to one
side.

However, shine the light through *both* slits at the same
time and, instead of the two diffusion patterns combining,
you get a series of light and dark bands – an interference
pattern.

Doctor Theodore Farley grinned rather fatuously.

It didn't bring Linda... no, best think of her as Miss
Hargreaves.

It didn't bring Miss Hargreaves back. She was dead.
There she lay on the floor, staring up rather accusingly and
unfairly.

I mean, seriously, he thought, he was not debasing
science. Cambridge Actuatica paid well and had the best
interests of their users in mind.

Oh to hell with it, they paid well, very, very, *very well.*

And why shouldn't he enjoy some success?

He turned away from Miss Hargreaves and her beautiful, seductive brown eyes, and back to his joy.

Out of sight, out of mind.

The machine sat there, all expensive, shining, new and paid for by commercial funding. It had lasers, bright red lines that suddenly appeared when the device activated.

It was not activated.

The laser did not shine and the rotating mirrors did not spin and the central chamber did not glow with an ethereal light.

A bit of soldering, that's all it needed.

It looked to the trained eye like a normal laser-based Mach–Zehnder interferometer, which was the expensive, in this case bloody expensive, version of the cardboard and torch double-slit experiment.

To the trained eye.

To a genius, however, it might be clear that it had been turned inside out, upside down and backwards.

His theory would erase the Copenhagen interpretation from the textbooks. It would be the Cardiff interpretation.

No, the Farley Theory of Observer Duality.

If you look at a wave as it washes through a double-slit experiment, then it *becomes* a particle. The act of observing it changes the behaviour of this tiny speck. If you observed the experiment looking for a particle, then lo! It was a particle. The interference pattern became a diffusion pattern. Look away, by removing the detector, and the bands of light and dark reappeared.

Doctor Farley knew this.

Everyone knew this.

Interns knew this, even the attractive ones.

He'd been to lectures, read books, skimmed scientific papers and had long, tedious arguments with students. They paid his salary, they said, so he had to explain why the electron did whatever it did and his lunch break decayed away like a lump of plutonium in a box with a cat.

But quantum mechanics was that rabbit hole down which the seemingly impossible became commonplace. This made the explanations go on and on, the mathematics use more than the entire Greek alphabet, and for Doctor Farley's patience to run out.

Stupid faculty.

Stupid disciplinary panel.

Stupid Miss Hargreaves.

Doctor Farley dabbed the soldering iron on the circuit and the metal moved like quicksilver. The blob formed, reflecting his gigantic-looking eyes, magnified as they were by the looking glass.

It was done.

Now all he had to do was test it.

He would uncollapse the eigenstate in the Hilbert space and entangle the observational matrix. And not, as Miss Hargreaves had put it, fiddle with reality with his evil mind controller.

There was some uncertainty about it, of course.

Hence this test.

He reached for the 'on' switch, but it was irritatingly just out of reach. 'FFS' as they said in textspeak.

"Miss Hargreaves, could you..."

Oh, she was dead.

He'd killed her.

And after all her waffle about ethics and morals and telling his wife about their affair. Dear me, interns were more trouble than they were worth, not that they were worth much.

He shifted over, glanced at the control panel, and hit the activate button. The machine hummed as the coils warmed up, the laser flickered across the apparatus and the phase inducer spun up to speed.

Wait, his head wasn't fully in the observation frame.

It wouldn't work without an observer, obviously.

Stupid Miss Hargreaves and her jiggling bosom, happy smile and arrant nonsense. He shouldn't have hit her with the safety equipment box, he knew that, but her holier-than-thou drivel had really got his goat. If only she'd kept her pretty mouth shut until after he'd completed the experiment. Disposing of the body and coping with the inevitable questions was going to be awkward. Getting another intern would be easy, they were ten a penny or rather an infinite number for no pennies.

Even so, and proving that he did indeed have scruples, he wished she was still alive.

He felt his mind tingle.

Or one side of his head as he was only partly in the machine's scanning range.

An odd feeling.

The display on the laptop changed and he knew that it had worked.

"It worked!"

He felt like Colin Clive as Dr Frankenstein when he'd yelled, "It's alive!" It must have deafened Boris Karloff.

Doctor Farley checked the results again.

Yes, there it was – observation could change the behaviour of fundamental particles and now, he had just demonstrated the reverse. Adjusting the wave/particle duality modified *observation*. Just as thought changed wave into particle, so changing particle into wave changed thought.

And what did it matter if those right-wingers were going to use it to alter people's minds for them? They needed changing. Free will? Nothing worth anything was free, everyone knew that. Interns, love and – what was it she'd said? – virtue.

Honestly.

Instead, he'd get the second cheque from Cambridge Actuatica and he'd be able to buy anything and anybody. He'd also get the Nobel prize for physics and that would show them.

And the Nobel prize for peace for there'd be no war, after all, as everyone would toe the line. If not, then clickety-click, fundamental particle jiggery-pokery and everyone would change their minds.

And it would be far easier than all those interns posting propaganda on Facebook, WhatsApp, Instagram, Twitter, TikTok, Snapchat, Pinterest, Reddit, LinkedIn and Friends Reunited. The list went on and on, so much work. Although, apparently, Friends Reunited wasn't a thing anymore. Shame as it would be nice to bring Friends back again.

He had solved it all and he would be the father of a new utopia: one machine, one message, one world.

Which made him a veritable genius, his brain better than all those other ordinary, second rate, play-it-safe scientists.

"Brains... brains..."

"I'm sorry, Linda," Doctor Farley replied, "what was that?"

No, wait, she was dead, wasn't she?

She gave him a little nibble on his earlobe and a tiny, playful love bite on his neck, before tucking in properly.

"Miss Har*greaves!!!*"

The greatest, most sustainable happiness
comes from making others happy. It is our
privilege to deliver you happiness every single
day.

Zoom's Mission Statement

Dawn sat in the waiting room. The meeting host would
let her in soon, it said. She looked around for a moment at
the peeling walls with its cracks and powdery concrete.
And this was supposed to withstand an atom bomb.

She was late, as usual, as she'd waited to see which PC
Mr Anderson would choose, so she could pick the other
computer room.

Mr Aspin-Arbuthnot finally let her in.

She joined with sound and video. Mr Franklyn was
droning on about cuts in this and that, and the need to
streamline operations now that they were short of staff.
This seemed to involve cutting more staff.

Already present were the usual middle managers of the
Supplies and Acquisitions Committee: Mr Anderson held
his figures ready, Mr Drake had his camera off, Mr... *oh
no,* Dawn's hair was sticking up.

Could she just wiggle it off camera and flatten it?

She tried, quickly and urgently, and her action made it
worse and wafted one of the post-it notes off her screen. It
fell like a dejected autumn leaf.

"...so, let's see," Mr Franklyn said, using his summing up voice, "that'll be a ten per cent cut in both catering and security—"

"Not security," Aspin-Arbuthnot interjected.

"No, of course, but we all have to make sacrifices for the good of the government," Franklyn said. "We can't cut anyone from management."

"Obviously," Aspin-Arbuthnot agreed, "but surely not security? We've cut ours to the very bone."

"Security doesn't need to cover quite so many facilities now with the loss of HMS Belfast and the issues with the Westminster bunker and station. Manchester must make some concessions. Birmingham?"

"Yes," Anderson said.

"Can you cut security by ten per cent?"

"Well... no."

"Surely, if you try."

"Well, there's Ahmed, Pete and Rob, so it would have to be a thirty-three per cent cut."

"There, see, Manchester," Franklyn said. "Birmingham has the right attitude."

"But..." Aspin-Arbuthnot waved his arms such that the shadow on the bookcase behind him rippled as his green screen moved.

"Unless you've any other ideas, which frankly—"

"Ah! Wait! What about cutting Project Eve?"

"Shhh, shhh..." Mr Franklyn motioned with his head towards the edge of the screen ducking behind Dawn's surviving post-it note. That one was about loo paper, so the other one on the floor would be what exactly?

Aspin-Arbuthnot had looked the other way and realised something. "Ah, yes, of course."

"Excuse me," Dawn found herself saying, suddenly talking over Mr Franklyn. "Sorry. Sorry again. What's... sorry, but what's Project Eve?"

"Oh. Ah. Erm. Stands for... oh, er... Emergency, erm, Viability Expansion or something. Anyway, it's cancelled and a replacement will be needed."

"Yes, but what—"

"And the minister will explain, I'm sure."

"...is it?"

"Excellent, moving on... acquisitions?"

"None," Mr Drake said from behind his yellow-framed darkness.

"I'm sorry," Dawn said, "is the minister going to join our Zoom?"

"Oh no," Franklyn said – Dawn felt a wave of relief – "he's coming in person."

"In person!"

"Yes."

"He's leaving London?"

"That's what I said."

But... but... Dawn saw the crumbling concrete, the yellow litter on the floor, her hideous hairstyle, and the dire loo roll situation.

"He's announcing a new phase of government policy," Franklyn informed everyone.

Government policy had changed as the emergency progressed and it had gone through three distinct phases.

Phase #1 – We don't give a fuck.

It was really a Wuhan problem, maybe the whole of China, and that wasn't going to affect the UK. Perhaps an issue for those wanting to visit India on business and then, later, probably not a good idea to choose Greece for a holiday. Damn good job we had Brexit, really, otherwise we might have ended up like Italy. However, just to be on the safe side, best to put off that weekend break in Paris. But there's no need to panic as Calais is the other side of the channel.

Phase #2 – Oh fuck!

OK, some cases in A&E in London led to a few deaths and there was that unfortunate outbreak in Oxford and some problems 'up North', but once the nature of the outbreak had been assessed, it was found that most patients were 'undead', so a simple redefinition meant that actual deaths in the national statistics dropped radically. And, by back-dating this change, previous deaths were also removed, which is practically bringing people back from the dead (no pun intended). This redefinition of 'dead' to 'actually dead' saved more lives than the NHS had, so, obviously, it was a triumph of government policy.

Phase #3 – Clusterfuck.

Look, swearing is not big or clever. It doesn't help when we should be having a reasonable and rational debate about a serious issue. Screaming and running about and biting each other is not following government advice. People should just grow up and stop complaining when the government is doing its best in these difficult times. We are here to listen.

Dawn could rarely get a word in edgeways.

"Can he bring supplies?" she blurted.

"I suppose."

"Toilet paper and..." – she glanced down but the other square of information had landed sticky side up – "...other things."

"I'm sure, if we can spare them," Mr Franklyn said. "Now, moving on to–"

But Mr Aspin-Arbuthnot screamed!

Everyone else looked startled.

Mr Aspin-Arbuthnot's office in Manchester shook, the green screen suddenly visible and his collection of fine, hardbound books vanished before reappearing as solid as ever. A zombie burst through the cloth, but struggled in the folds as if it was tearing indestructible shelving apart.

Mr Aspin-Arbuthnot fought bravely and briefly, but his staple gun did not have enough range or firepower. The image became so jittered and bouncy that his virtual background broke up. The ordered shelves of books split and numerous zombies appeared, briefly, a flash in the top right, a smudge by his shoulder, a blurt everywhere and each appearance made more and more sense of his panic and desperation.

He keeled over backwards and the lovely old books reappeared, except where the cloth was torn or splattered with blood.

"I think we better adjourn and restart the meeting," Mr Franklyn suggested.

"We can't," said the mysterious Mr Drake, "Aspin-Arbuthnot's the host."

"Ah."

Mr Aspin-Arbuthnot's microphone picked up sounds of munching and slobbering. A zombie reappeared, lurched through the last of the bookshelves and the virtual background gave up. Mr Aspin-Arbuthnot's office had white tiles, Dawn realised... *had* white tiles.

"I think that means Manchester has made the required cuts," Mr Franklyn said. "Hugh?"

"I'll have to get the figures redone," Anderson said.

"Right. Good," Mr Franklyn said. "Well, we best... er, leave. Out of respect for our recently... well, he was a good man and he'll be sadly missed."

Mr Aspin-Arbuthnot himself reappeared, bleeding profusely from his neck wounds.

"Bye," Mr Franklyn said as he and the others vanished.

The screen jumped as the software displayed Dawn and the late Mr Aspin-Arbuthnot side-by-side.

"Mr Aspin–"

The late Mr Aspin-Arbuthnot, seeing the screen with his already sunken eyes, pounced to attack Dawn.

She jerked backwards, rolling on her office chair into the back wall. She was safe, but the horror of the new world order seemed ever closer. She reached for her mouse and, trying not to look, she guided the little arrow to the 'leave' button.

"Brains, brains..." Mr Aspin-Arbuthnot said.

Dawn left the meeting.

STAY HOME
DON'T GO OUT
SAVE LIVES

Government advice

Dave mumbled under his breath, "You can tell by the way I use my walk, I'm a woman's man."

He had his deadly weapon ready. It felt good, solid in his hands. He'd seen a YouTube video that proved that an axe was more effective than a shotgun against people pretending to be zombies. A baseball bat with nails was like an axe.

He had a good view up and down the street.

Nice and clear, apart from that one and those two over there, and five back there.

Still, no point in *Stayin' Alive* just yet.

He pulled his mask aside and took a sip of his coffee.

The rules had recently changed again. You were now allowed to go out in groups of six. They kept bringing it down. How were you supposed to be able to protect yourself if there were only six of you?

Even for supplies, you were supposed to use click-and-collect, wait three weeks for a slot and try not to eat too much in the meantime.

Dave remembered the Penroses running down the street. He was glad they'd made it, but, honestly, going out just the two of them was far too risky.

And he was in a group of one.

There were two exceptions that allowed this.

One – Commuting.

Public transport was fine as there were likely to be six or more passengers onboard, and you had to get from your front door to the station or bus stop.

Two – Exercise.

Government advice recommended getting out of the house for at least an hour's exercise a day. This usually involved vigorous running.

Being alone, without the armour of the house's brick walls, made Dave feel big and small at the same time. It was the first time he'd been outside, not counting the patio, for months. He found the pleasant streets of these fashionable suburbs with their lovely gardens, hedges, lawns, red brick buildings and old-fashioned chimney stacks, terrifying.

What the f-ing hell was he doing outside!?

I'm stayin' alive, stayin' alive, ah, ha, ha, ha, gettin' a stitch, gettin' a stitch, oh! Ah, ah, ah.

Each beat gave him the extra impetus for each step, and each step took him further away from his front door and further towards the unknown with all its red dots.

Don't look at the phone!

Not all zombies were red dots, some had been turned before Tag-and-Track was rolled out and others refused the vaccine chip injection. Red dots were a guide only.

He looked up – shambler, shambler, *ah, ha, ha, ha...*

Always check your six.

That bloke who may, or may not have been in *Doctors* and *Casualty,* certainly looked like he needed A&E.

Always look where you are going.

Shambler, shambler, orange...

There was an orange lying on the road. It had rolled to the kerb, but looked bright and inviting. Dave picked it up.

Mr Penrose from 204 had dropped it.

I should take it back, Dave thought as he pocketed it.

Vitamin-C was important for staying alive, *stayin' alive.*

A delivery van barrelled down the road behind him, roared past and then met another going the other way. Sainsbury's faced off against Ocado, bumper to bumper, machine gun port to shotgun nest, their zombie grills almost locked together like stags on heat.

As the Sainsbury's SWAT team jumped out, the shotgun riders yelled at each other

"Oi, right of way."

"We've gone further."

"Highway code."

"Common sense."

"Just shift it."

"You shift it."

There was no room to manoeuvre due to all the parked cards and an old barricade.

Dave sprinted past, dodging a few shamblers as he did so and spilling most of his coffee.

The zombies reached both vehicles at the same time. Both drivers shoved their vehicles into reverse and sped off, their thick tyres scrunching obstacles as the vans careened backwards.

"Hey, wait for us?"

The Sainsbury's delivery guy had appeared from a nearby house along with his black-clad security. He dumped the food tray and started sprinting. The heavily protected security guys tried to keep up, but their body armour slowed them down.

The zombies, always slow on the uptake, spotted the fresh food as it ran away.

"Brains, brains..."

The creatures shambled and rambled in pursuit.

The slower of the two security guards was set upon.

"Brains, brains, brains..." mumbled the zombies as they struggled to open the packaging, but eventually they found a way through the steel helmet, bullet proof vest, elbow and knee pads. The Sainsburys van reappeared, ramming into the crowd. Blood splattered over the 'Live well for less' slogan. It read 'Live... for less' and then 'Live'.

Good advice.

Dave kept going and arrived at that part of Cotteridge with the shops and wide pavements. He needed to reach the end, negotiate Cotteridge island, which was really a pair of roundabouts, one mini and one small, and then Kings Norton station lay a short distance beyond. The shops curved slightly making it tricky to see all the way. This wasn't helped by the trees, bus stops and crashed vehicles. One shambling zombie lurched down the road, startled each time it saw itself reflected in the shop windows that weren't broken.

A van hugged a lamppost with its shattered radiator. The rear doors were open and black office chairs with tilt and lumbar support lay about, abandoned.

Further on, an attempt had been made to fortify the Kings Norton post office delivery depot with temporary metal fencing. This had proved to be too temporary. The unfinished graffiti suggested everyone should 'Abandon hop'.

Dave used both legs to walk further.

The full stop at the end of 'hop' was splodged.

Now, Dave thought, sneak along the shop fronts to avoid being seen and risk being surprised, or go down the centre of the road where the visibility was better?

He compromised and moved from tree to tree, and to a burned-out car parked on the pavement without a thought for pedestrians.

About half a dozen people sat on top of the bus stop.

Dave panicked.

Where were the zombies?

Could he jump up fast enough?

"Wha... I mean, what?"

A bored woman pointed over the road to where a man in a trench coat and leather hat sat on top of the other stop.

Crouching, Dave crossed the road.

"Wha' yow got tha' for?" drawled the man. He took a drag on a thin roll-up. Odd to see smoke coming from someone's mouth and nose that wasn't vape based.

"What?" Dave said, shouting through his mask.

"Tha' rounders bat."

Dave looked at the object gripped in his hands. "It's a baseball bat."

"Useless."

"It's got nails."

"That's why it's useless. Yow wanna cricket bat or an axe, or better still, a gardenin' tool like an 'hoe."

"Gardening–"

"Edgin' tool is best."

Dave straightened up as if he was trying face-off with this man sitting high on the bus stop.

"Who are you?" Dave asked.

"Speak up."

"Who are you!"

The man cupped his ear.

"WHO ARE YOU!" Dave repeated much louder.

"Take yow mask off."

Dave realised and lowered his mask. The shambler by the shop window paused, almost sniffing the air before it moved on.

"Who are you?" Dave repeated.

"Yam the Conductor."

Dave glanced up and down the road. There were no buses except for the one burnt-out on its side in front of the curry house at the junction. Given that his mask was down, he took a sip of his coffee.

"There aren't any conductors on buses," Dave said.

"Yow saft? Bay a buzz conductor, numpty. Arm The Conductor."

"The conductor?"

"Arr. I conduct people on their journeys. I tek 'em where it's safe. I can smell zombies. It's a sixth sense."

"Smell is, you know, the second sense."

"It ay my smell."

"Rubbish."

"Tha's one," he said, nodding towards the shambler as it reached Gregg's and the card shop.

"Right."

"Yow want in on the 7:40."

"You're sitting on a number 11 stop. That goes round Birmingham, not into town."

"We're tekin' the train."

"So am I."

"Bournville."

"Kings Norton is closer."

"Only one way in."

"I only need one way."

"Ay Kings Norton, mate," the Conductor said, his finger sliding on the edge of his nose, "Bournville."

"That's much further," Dave protested.

"Arr, but there am two ways onto the platform at Bournville, both sides, so if summat were to 'appen, ay saying it will mind, but if it did, then there's them two exits."

"Ah."

"And the fare might be cheaper."

"I've got a pass," Dave said and as he said it, he realised it had lapsed.

The Conductor shrugged.

Dave checked his watch: fifteen minutes to the... 7:40, did he say?

"The next train is the 7:32," Dave said.

"From Bournville."

"That would be around 7:38."

"Autumn timetable."

"It's not autumn."

"No bugger changed it back," the Conductor said, "and it ay on British Summer Time neither."

"Oh great."

The Conductor leaned closer. "Mate, yow want some advice."

"Yes."

"Ditch yow rounders bat, yow numpty, and come with us to Bournville."

"What's in it for you?"

"Twenty quid."

"On top of the train fare?"

"Arr."

"Get lost."

"Suit yourself."

Dave pulled his mask back on, left the cowboy at the bus stop, recrossed the road and went around the chemist at the end. He crossed by the double roundabout of Cotteridge island. Cotteridge was odd, lying between Kings Norton Post Office and Kings Norton station.

Or was it that Kings Norton was a funny shape?

Anyway, if nothing else, with that lot going to Bournville, he'd be more likely to get a seat.

Kings Norton station beckoned.

6

BARRICADE YOURSELF INDOORS
TURN OUT THE LIGHTS
KEEP QUIET

Government advice

"Dawn, might I have a word?"

It was surreal to stand in the underground corridor outside the second computer room. Dawn listened with her eyes closed and her back against the curved concrete. The place hummed with a heartbeat of generators.

Fuel!

That was the other item she'd needed to bring up in Any Other Business.

"Dawn?"

Dawn had been surprised to discover that her duties included Emergency Protocol Liaison. Lockdown for her had been a literal lockdown. Birmingham, she discovered to her astonishment, had a large, secret nuclear bunker for council staff. Not all of them, of course. Refuse collectors, park attendants, swimming pool lifeguards and many others were deemed low priority, but Human Resources it turned out was vital.

Not that Human Resources was considered onerous as it had been thought that there would be fewer humans to resource once the bomb had gone off, but there would be some, and it was important, Councillor Grant had informed her, that there would be someone with whom they could discuss their holidays, pensions and life assurance terms.

"Dawn?"

Dawn was secretly pleased with the extra responsibility, even though it meant she'd been in lockdown in a secret nuclear bunker for months... nearly – good heavens – three years!

Her main function was to arbitrate disputes. After all this time, these were becoming more common and more repetitive. For example...

"Dawn?"

Dawn jerked out of her reverie. "Mr Matt?"

"It's George."

"If we're going to talk about work, then I'd prefer us to be professional, Mr Matt."

"Miss Dey, I want a word about holiday allowances."

"Again?"

"Please don't take that negative tone with me," Matt said. He had a sallow complexion, his eyes sunken and dark and his hair thinned on his right side where he tugged at his stray hair. He was desperate. They were all desperate. When was the last time he had taken a zombie test?

"I'm sorry, Mr Matt, but... you first."

"I have been forced to take my holidays."

"Yes."

"In here and that's hardly two weeks in Tenerife."

"Yes, but it is an emergency situation."

"I'm still making payments on the villa, which you are not allowing me to use."

"It's not me, it's–"

"I want to go outside!"

"Well, you can't, Mr Matt," Dawn said, reasonably. "We've been over this quite a number–"

"My opinion hasn't changed."

"Nor has your contract."

"This zombie apocalypse isn't as bad as they are making out."

"I think it's far worse than they are making out."

"Not the public news feed," Matt said. "The memos from the ministry."

Dawn sighed. She did not have clearance to see the memos from the Ministry of Resilience, Calmness and Fortitude. Councillor Grant had pointed out that her role involved any other duties commensurate with her new post. But how could she do that if she wasn't cleared to see the memos from the ministry?

"Well... Miss Dey?"

She thought for something that might fob him off, but nothing came, except a wave of desperation – perhaps she looked like a pre-zombie to Mr Matt – and then the lightbulb moment!

"Might I suggest, Mr Matt," she said, "that you take it up with the minister."

"I'm not on the Zoom list."

"He's coming here."

"Here!"

"In person."

Mr Matt blanched, his skin whitening even further and he tugged at his hair. How could she suggest a zombie test without the man flying off the handle?

"So, obviously," she continued, "everyone will have to take a zombie test."

"Another one... but no-one's been outside in months."

"Good job too. If you'd have it witnessed, please, and spread the word."

Dawn turned and sauntered off to find one of the tests that swabbed the back of the knee rather than the left armpit. That way, she'd not have to take her blouse off in front of one of the men. The right to be witnessed by a female member of staff was fair and reasonable, a good policy, but there wasn't another female member of staff.

In Stores 3, she grabbed a test kit and then reached behind the cupboard for one of the last few of the old tests. She found Ahmed eating stale crackers in Security.

"Ahmed, sorry," she said, dropping the kit the table.

"Again... but I don't look pale." He laughed.

Ahmed was jolly and there were laughter lines around his eyes, though they were red from staring at screens all day. Behind him were the security lockers with their nasty collection of items and to one side was a small sink and kettle. Contraband pot noodle cartons lay in the bin. Dawn stayed by the door and studiously did not look at the wall Ahmed usually faced.

"The minister is coming," she said, "so..."

He sighed and expertly ripped the packet open, wiped the crumbs off his hands, and then went through the motions. Dawn did the same, although she was less practised. Ahmed had been outside, so he'd had tests pre-quarantine and post-isolation.

"You'll be going up top when the minister gets here," Ahmed said as he reached into his shirt with his swab.

"Me?"

"We got to meet the minister on the helipad in person," Ahmed said with a chuckle. "We got to show 'em Birmingham's under control."

"But it isn't."

Ahmed laughed again, deep and full of hard echoes from the close confines of the tiny security room. He laughed a lot now, sometimes inappropriately, because of what he'd seen.

What he saw every day.

What he could see now.

But he didn't talk about that.

No-one talked about that.

Whatever *that* was.

"Excuse me," Dawn said.

"I got to witness."

"Yes, but..."

Ahmed turned away to let Dawn pull her tights down with some privacy. Perhaps these old tests weren't more dignified, after all.

"We'll get to use the gun," Ahmed said.

"Oh... do we have to?" Dawn said as she gently rubbed the cotton end of the stick against the back of her right knee – three times while turning it. "You know what happened to America?"

Ahmed shrugged. "If you want to make it there and back."

He pointed at the monitors.

Automatically, Dawn looked.

The bank of CCTV images clearly showed members of staff lurching around in the foyer, their arms out in front as they searched for the living. They shambled off one monitor to appear on another. Dawn knew they were there, but she tried her hardest to forget. Their smell, armpits and backs of knees included, sometimes wafted down through the air-conditioning.

The idea of fighting their way up there terrified her more than running out of fuel, loo paper or back-of-the-knee tests.

"We'll be fine," Ahmed said. He laughed making a hollow sound in his throat. "We're prepared."

The United States of America had been prepared, well prepared, with its citizens already armed with guns, guns, guns and more guns. The zombie apocalypse was exactly what they had been preparing for since the signing of the Second Amendment. Indeed, such was their enthusiasm that they started well before the virus reached their shores. And when the dead began to rise, their joy was unparalleled as they got to kill everyone again – once through friendly fire and then again for real.

Eventually, everyone was safe in their survivalist bunkers and underground weapons stores and the rednecks declared their freedom, liberty and democratic rights upheld.

Good old US of A.

There were feudal battles for control of the southern states now, but accurate news was slight on the evangelist TV channels. For them, it was the End of Days, *yee ha!*

It was three storeys up to ground level, six storeys up Telephone House and then three more to the Helipad on the Fleet Street side of the building.

"Are there any of the fast ones?" Dawn asked.

The World Health Organisation recognized five types of zombie: Type 1, Type 2, Type 2b, Type 3 and Type 4. The EU had gone for Variante Un, Variante Deux, Variante Deux-B, Variante Trois and Variante Quatre. The UK, given that it had voted for Brexit and, therefore, it didn't have to abide by any of this foreign nonsense, had a different system. They had six variants: Variant A, Variant B, Variant B2, Variant C and Variant E. There was no Variant D nor were there actually six variants and it all seemed very similar to the EU system, but that was just nonsense and we all needed to move on.

Later on, to avoid confusion the British Government adopted names based upon the NATO callsigns: Alpha, Bravo, Bravo-B, Charlie and Delta. After the Charlie-Yankee incident, when a special forces unit identified themselves as fourth-level zombies and were wiped out by a drone attack, the government tried Egyptian hieroglyphs: Two Reeds, Lion, Twisted Flax, Horned Viper, Wavy Lines and the Eye of Horus.

There had been research done in Cambridge to come up with a more definitive, scientific taxonomy. These were Seems OK, Oh Dear, Let Me Out and then, unfortunately, the research had ended.

People themselves needed something that made more sense in their everyday lives. The question "Is that a 2B or not a 2B?" is no good when it's critical to decide whether to run or to run very fast. It was literally a matter of life and undeath.

So, eventually, all the survivors settled on three types: shamblers, ramblers and joggers. These became associated with the appropriate three responses: walk away quickly, run away, and run away very fast while praying.

"Yeah," Ahmed said, "it's full of the bastards."

Dawn swallowed.

"Twenty-seven," Ahmed added.

Dawn didn't want to go outside.

Why did Mr Matt?

Why would anyone?

It would be madness to be outside.

7

You only need to remember the Rule of Six.
Don't leave home in groups of less than six
and watch each other's backs.

Government advice

Meanwhile, outside, Dave crossed the road before trotting past a line of shops.

Stayin' alive, he thought, ah, ha, ha, ha, stayin' alive, stayin' alive, oh! Ah, something, something, stayin' alive.

Stayin' Alive gave the beat you are supposed to use when doing CPR. (Not that anyone gave the kiss of life anymore – imagine if they died while you were giving two quick breaths blown into their lungs, then you'd be in trouble.) The Bee Gees' song also turned out to be the ideal rhythm to run away from shamblers. You needed to keep away from them, sure, but you also didn't want to tire too quickly or run round a corner so fast you couldn't stop.

Dave rounded the telephone box and paused.

Two shamblers gathered at the single entrance to the station as if drawn there by some vague memory of commuting.

There was no way to go around them.

One froze, turned and then took a few clumsy steps towards Dave.

Dave was panting from the jog, not much but enough for his breath to escape his mask and so the thing had detected him.

"Brains," it mumbled.

He couldn't go around it, so he hefted *Brainbiter* one-handed as he still had his coffee in the other, and waited. In football, it wasn't how hard you booted the ball, but how precisely you kicked it.

At the perfect moment, one-handed, Dave swung the bat. It connected with a skull-crunching, brain smashing crack and the zombie went down.

Back of the net!

Finally, he'd found something else he was good at – watching football *and killing zombies.*

The nails in the bat stuck in the zombie's head.

Dave pulled, but it wouldn't come out. Instead, it lifted the thing's head which was still connected to the body.

Euwww, gross.

The second shambler said, "Brains, brains..."

Shit, it was close.

Not close! On top of him!

Dave lobbed his cup-for-life at it – direct hit – but all this did was splash coffee dregs all over the place.

So, with a desperate effort as if it was injury time and you were one down, Dave jerked the baseball bat free. With a savage uppercut, he caught the second shambler as it reached down with its broken, yellowed nails.

Up it went, its neck breaking backwards and yanking the bat from Dave's grip.

It sailed over to splat on the forecourt's fancy brickwork.

Absolute legend.

Another shambler came out of the station, which was lucky because it held up the rambler behind it.

Dave grabbed the handle of his bat and pulled, but it held fast, the nails firmly driven into the zombie's head. Its decaying flesh held on like the suckers of calamari. Pus went everywhere like spicy mayonnaise sauce flavoured with coffee.

More zombies came out of the station, which was unfair because this was the morning and commuters were supposed to go into the station.

"Brains," said one.

"Brains," said another.

"Shit," said Dave. He let go of the baseball bat and it slid out of the zombie to tumble onto the floor.

"Brains, brains..." The refrain was picked up by the other, their song being slow, steady and inexorable.

Dave grabbed *Brainbiter*.

When facing a shambler, it was *Stayin' Alive*, ah, ha, ha, ha, stayin' alive, stayin' alive, oh!

Dave turned from the ramblers and – what was it? – you win some, lose some, all the same to me, the only card I need is the ace of spades, *the ace of spades...*

He got the lyrics wrong, but he got the pace right as he bolted over the road at the pedestrian lights without pausing to press the button, or look left and right.

I don't wanna live forever, the only card for me, the ace of spades, ah, ha, ha, ha... *arrrrgh. Oh! Oh!*

Dave doubled over with a stitch.

He glanced behind.

The ramblers had his scent now. They'd follow him to hell. One of them picked up its knees – shit, a jogger!

What song had a faster beat than Motörhead's *The Ace of Spades?*

The Birdie Song?

Crazy Frog?

Shit – *Flight of the Bumblebee* didn't have lyrics!!!

Running was hard with a mask on, his breath caused the cloth to balloon and then stick to his mouth like a gag.

There were ramblers at the end of the road, half a dozen strung out forming a barrier. Dave decided to go straight through, dodge and hope they couldn't turn fast enough to grab him.

He swung his bat, and again it connected, but he overbalanced as it stuck fast. Stupid nails.

He went down, not like a footballer tackled and acting, but like a rugby player – hard,

The slavering zombie bent over him, its slobbering mouth showing blood-soaked teeth opened wide to chomp on Dave's neck.

But it stopped.

The bat's handle, which stuck out like a Dalek's eyestalk, had hit the ground.

The thing stood, confused as the thought tried to navigate through the eaten brains in its stomach.

Dave slithered out from under it, got to his feet and ran over the mini-roundabout.

Monsters moaned behind him.

The bus stop appeared in view.

The other commuters perched on top waved and shook their heads like VIPs in the hospitality suite at Aston Villa.

"No room," one yelled.

"But–"

There was no time for debate, so Dave sprinted across the road towards the Conductor.

"Please, please," Dave begged, jumping up and down.

The man rolled paper on his thigh. "Thirty quid."

"You said twenty."

He licked his lips. "Yow price has gone up."

"What?"

He licked the paper. "Danger money."

"All right."

"Cash–"

"I don't have thirty quid in cash."

"Or card?"

"Card! Yes, card."

"Right ho."

The Conductor reached down and Dave grabbed his surprisingly strong, gnarled hands to be hoisted up onto the bus stop's roof.

That had been close.

The seething mass of undead battered against the broken windows and the bus stop pitched as if at sea. Dave felt a wave of panic and nausea as he held on to the smooth curved plastic.

The Conductor calmly stored the roll-up between his lips and fiddled in his leather satchel for his credit card machine.

"Thirty quid."

Dave swallowed. "Can we do it when they're not rocking the bus stop?"

"Ah, doe be saft."

"I'm not..."

Dave realised he wasn't going to win the argument, so he fished in his jacket pocket for his phone. He used his nose to swipe open and thumbed his code one handed as he wasn't going to let go with both hands.

Thankfully, the card reader was contactless.

Beep.

He was thirty quid down and he was still in Cotteridge.

There were a lot of zombies now, milling about under the bus stop and the stop opposite with the other commuters. It didn't look like he'd get to the office or even return to home working.

But at least Dave was fine: his suit was covered in specks of blood and goo, but he was fine. His quarter 2 report was crumpled, but it was still safe in his inside jacket pocket. His ultimate weapon on zombie destruction currently stuck in the head of the approaching rambler was fine. He wouldn't make it in for 8:30, more like 9:00, but that was also fine.

And he was part of a group now.

It reminded him of 'Clap for Zombies'. It had brought whole communities together. Neighbours would come out on their porches or front steps to clap hands, drum drums, rattle rattles, whistle whistles and make noise. This would attract zombies and thus move them up the street, then the low numbers would move them back again.

And so on.

It was an attempt to exhaust the zombies and render them harmless.

It had a couple of drawbacks. It didn't exhaust the zombies and it didn't render them harmless. And the number of neighbours taking part dropped until one household would make a noise, attract zombies and then everyone else would remember them on the WhatsApp group.

"Do I get a refund if we don't make it?"

The Conductor chuckled, lit his cigarette from a cheap zippo. "A refund, ha."

– NEWSFLASH –

You can fool some of the people all the time,
and all of the people some of the time, and if
you fool enough of the people enough of the
time, then those you don't fool, don't count.

Handbook of Political Campaigning
(Random Harper-Hatchette and Simon Macmillan)
3rd Ed

It was a meme.

Peter Maguire took a drag on his cigarette, enjoying the ashen taste and letting the smoke billow up towards the skylight.

The office was quiet.

It was something to look out of the seventh-floor window and watch the fools believing it all.

They'd started with stories about the EU banning good old British bent bananas, continued with 'the economy is safe in Conservative hands', moved on to 'immigrants are claiming benefits paid by your taxes *and stealing your jobs'* and, finally, do as you are told in these times of apocalypse.

Maguire laughed, coughing as he did so.

Honestly, it was like gullible wasn't in the dictionary.

Crazes came and went.

Deeley boppers, skiffle groups, yo-yos, Rubik's cubes, trousers below your backside, fidget spinners, floss dancing, cryptocurrency, non-fungible tokens–

He coughed again, laughing up the phlegm.

They'd made people pay money, thousands and even millions, for something that didn't exist. Not even for the emperor's new clothes, but for the right to say you'd seen the emperor's new clothes.

There were jokes and then there was beyond the joke.

Money talked.

Facebook let them run targeted campaigns for political parties, manifesto promises that pledged this to the right and the opposite to the left.

Make 'em believe this, make 'em trust that and make 'em swallow the other.

They even had psychologists using taxpayers' money to find out how to make taxpayers pay more.

Down in the street, people ran past.

The panic was so funny.

They actually believed there was a virus, rather than something on the internet that had gone viral. They'd believed it, even though Wikipedia listed it as a hoax.

Oh, *ha-ha*, there were three people down there now pretending to be zombies. He watched as they shambled along, arms outstretched and mumbling, "Brains... brains..."

God, maybe they even believed they were zombies.

They'd believed everything else.

Maguire had done his job for his boss. Not Jack, the independent, advocate of press freedom, champion of investigative journalism and social rights campaigner, the senior editor – no, not for him. Maguire knew he worked for the man who owned the holding company that owned the media empire that owned the paper – the boss.

The boss kept on printing the newspaper to stay in the newspaper business. Being somewhat fluid about the actual news, the physical paper had become more important. They also needed it so that the TV news could quote the papers without that awkward need to be accurate. Not us, they'd tell Ofcom, it's in the newspaper, so it must be true.

The three messing about in the street staggered across the road. They were still keeping up the act.

If Ofcom or anyone had a go at the newspaper, it was 'freedom of the press'.

Or fact-checkers.

Maguire had thought the party over when they had appeared but then fact-checkers could include any sort of fact.

And influencers? What was that all about? So-and-so with 8 million followers, so it can't be wrong.

Thousands of lemmings threw themselves off cliffs.

Hmm, he'd have to check that one. Hadn't Disney thrown lemmings off cliffs to get the footage?

Ah, it didn't matter, lemmings jumped off cliffs now.

He lit another cigarette, chain-smoking again to get as close to his 20-a-day given that there was no-one else in the office today.

Briefly, he wondered where they all were.

Rushing to some story, no doubt, when they could just sit at home in their pyjamas and copy-and-paste from Twitter.

He continued to watch the girl on the street stumble about until an ersatz zombie jumped out at her. She screeched and yelled.

Honestly, talk about over-acting.

The zombie ripped the girl's throat out with his teeth.

Actually, that was quite realistic, except that the blood spray was wrong. In proper modern, CGI-laden films, the blood came out as if it was fired from a top-of-the-range super soaker. She dropped to the floor and the fake zombie moved on to her screaming boyfriend. There was a brief tussle and then he too 'died'.

Oh, and now the girl was jerking her limbs and 'coming back to life'.

You had to giggle.

By the time Maguire had finished his second cigarette, the three of them had stumbled further down the street, the original and the two he had tagged as 'it', closing on other gullibles.

Gullible's Travels – that was a good title for a book on the subject. He could write all about his personal and uplifting journey away from the truth.

The three 'infected' a few more unwary suckers.

We make our gods in our own image, Maguire thought. He'd read that somewhere in a Sunday supplement opinion piece. Or was it a book review?

If people believe the Earth is flat, that the Sun circulates daily for no reason, that the journalism in the Telegraph and Daily Mail is true and that the lies of politicians are trustworthy, then they'll swallow anything. They believe, really believe, and they'll ignore everything to the contrary, because the alternative is to realise that they've been had, that they are gullible and stupid. No-one wants that.

So, little by little, bent bananas to saving our fishing fleets, renaming chocolate to immigrant invasions, £350 million to the NHS to anti-mask movements in a zombie apocalypse, Brexit is a good idea to... whatever they liked.

No, he wouldn't spill the beans with a tell-all exposé about unprofessional journalism and their too-good-to-check culture. He was onto a good thing, after all, and there was no money in books.

And he still had some pride – he was a journalist, not an advertiser. He wasn't about to bite the hand of the multi-billionaire media magnate.

The 'zombies' moved away around the corner of the building opposite.

Out of sight, out of mind, Maguire thought.

He took another drag of 'quitting will improve your health' gold blend.

Perhaps next year, he thought, they might persuade the public that people were developing superpowers.

That was a two-cigarette idea.

Or aliens walk amongst us?

That wouldn't require anything other than fuzzy photographs and there was an obvious celebrity angle. Someone from, say, *Strictly* could tearfully go on about how they had been abducted and anally probed.

Would they do that?

Of course, they would. Anything for their 15-minutes plus repeats on Dave.

Yes, aliens next.

God, people were such fools.

8

As well as your thoughts and prayers, try
telling one another a joke. A little light levity
can go a long way to raising people's spirits –
that's raising their spirits, not their dead
bodies. See what I did there?

The BBC's replacement for
Mock the Week *and* The Mash Report,
pilot episode – cancelled

Dawn repaired the bunting by cutting out triangles of
coloured paper and sellotaping them onto a length of
electrical cord. It looked pretty, festive even, although
there were gaps as she'd had to remove the snowmen and
reindeer. She hoped the minister would appreciate the
gesture.

He was due any moment.

They'd had two Christmases, two Easters, two
birthdays – she wasn't getting any younger as Mr Anderson
had told her a number of times – and two Valentine's
Days.

Dawn shuddered.

She found another Santa and began replacing him.

How did it all start?

Some said a virus, others talked of lights in the sky
complete with fuzzy photographs, and more talked about a
CIA plot, the Illuminati, terrorists, and still more thought
it was unreal, faked, a conspiracy. Apparently, the CIA
had done it deliberately *and faked it.* A case of the right

hand not knowing what the far-right hand was doing. Precisely why they'd do this, none of the pundits could completely explain.

Mr Matt had his theories. Mr Anderson talked about a Bacchanalian party as if there was no hope. Councillor Grant worried.

And if it was extra-terrestrials turning the dead into their soldiers, then she for one would welcome the alien overlords, if it meant getting out of this concrete mausoleum.

Not that she wanted to just at the moment.

She'd heard about how it had all started in the UK on the news. An 'incident', they'd called it, at Waterloo had been reported as 'troubling' with 17 dead and 28 undead. That was the first time Dawn had heard the term used outside of a horror film.

'Undead' – the word had a temporary feeling as if the victim was undecided. Soon they'd be declared 'alive' thanks to the NHS, or, as it turned out, 'dead'. Everyone's thoughts and prayers would go to their grieving families, and the world would be able to carry on with the business of carrying on.

The Prime Minister had appointed a special Zombie Minster, pointing out that he was still on the ball even from his villa during his much-needed holiday in Malaga. The opposition parties sympathised with the families of the victims and those who found themselves undead, calling upon the government to do all it could and pointing out that the new post should be the Minister for Zombies.

"Does the Right Honourable Gentleman not agree that he is not a zombie minister, but that he is very much a living minister."

The Right Honourable Gentleman had agreed that he was for the meantime.

The backbenches guffawed.

It had been a good joke.

Dawn reached the end of the bunting. She'd simply given herself something to do to stop worrying about going outside. By now, everyone would know that they were about to brave the upstairs.

They may not know how the apocalypse started, but they all knew only too well how it had spread. It had been funny when the reports had started coming in, a great flood of them arriving in the communications room. But this deluge had slowly petered to a trickle.

Not funny ha-ha, but funny horrible.

Jokes travelled along the grapevine. If one person tells two people about the dog with no nose, and those people tell two more people, then soon enough, doubling every hour, it's not long – 33 hours – until everyone in the world has heard it.

This rate of expansion was the joke's R-number, although it was unlikely that 'my dog's got no nose' would have an R-number as high as 2. It would be a lot less. Probably higher around Christmas if the gag got into a cracker.

However, if the R-number is above 1, then the joke spreads; if it's less than 1, then the joke gradually fizzles out – or becomes cryogenically frozen in a joke book ready for another outbreak.

An R-number of 1 means that one person tells another who in turn tells just one more person. The joke's influence neither increases nor decreases, but remains static until whoever heard the joke last gets hit by a bus.

Dawn fetched the ladder from Stores 3 and hung her decorations across the concrete beam. It would be the first thing the minister would see when he came through the blast doors.

"Lovely view."

Dawn turned round as best she could on the ladder.

"Thank you," she said and then saw Anderson staring up at her legs and tight-skirted behind. "Mr Anderson!"

"Pleasure."

Dawn made her way – "No, I do not need you to hold the ladder!" – down.

They faced each other.

"You can't fight it forever," Anderson said.

Dawn had heard this before many times, too many times.

"Mr Anderson," she said, "I didn't choose to work with you."

"You did choose me."

"I did not."

"You were on the recruitment panel when I was interviewed," Anderson retorted.

"Only in an advisory capacity!"

"And what did you advise?"

"That's confidential!"

"You can tell me."

"No, I can't," Dawn snapped. "It's against policy."

"No need to be so sharp."

"I'm sorry, I'm sorry, I'm just a little tense."

"Official visits can do that."

"Yes."

"And we do need to get our shit together down here."

"Oh, please."

"Get our poo together?"

"Mr Anderson."

"Get our number two's together?"

"Have you organised the buffet?" Dawn asked.

"George's doing it."

"What is it?"

"It's Spam."

"Is there a vegetarian option?"

"Vegetarian Spam?"

"No... something other than Spam."

"That's all there is," Anderson admitted. "When this place was built and stocked in the 1970s, there was no such thing as a vegetarian option."

"So, it's either fifty-year-old reconstituted meat or nothing?"

"That's it. Spam... the '71 or '72?"

When Anderson stood back, he did pause to appreciate the bunting. He nodded to himself, approving.

Perhaps he was all right really despite his crumpled suit and his sexism. Being cooped up in this concrete tomb had got on everyone's nerves. That, and the screaming terror of the zombie apocalypse.

She should make allowances.

"That bit's crooked," Anderson said.

"Would you mind putting away the ladder," Dawn replied, "please?"

"I didn't get it out."

"I'm a weak and feeble woman and you're a brave, strong man."

Anderson laughed, but he picked up the ladder and carried it off towards Stores 2.

"It goes... never mind."

She was fed up with Anderson, the bunker, the end of the world, everything – why should she be the one to make allowances? – but what could she do?

So, instead of screaming, she calmly admired her work, but she'd seen it before each Christmas. She had looked forward to the festive season, but Santa had not come down the triple filter locked air pipe chimney.

Other things spread like jokes: fashions, computer viruses, internet memes, cat pictures, social media fads, infectious diseases, Mexican waves and zombies.

When everyone is on the bandwagon, this is called 'herd mentality'.

Once everyone is thoroughly fed up with a joke and no longer cares about the noseless dog, then the joke just stops. This is called the 'heard it' effect.

They were going through the motions of civilised life, discussing policy documents, putting up decorations, wrapping Spam tins for presents and avoiding being caught under the mistletoe by slimy middle managers.

She needed some trail, a scent to escape from this horror, but there was no way out, nowhere to escape to and no hope. She needed Father Christmas to visit with freedom and escape wrapped up in tinsel or a knight in shining armour to ride up on a white charger – not that there were any of those.

She was a dog with no nose as if it had fallen off like the rotting flesh of a zombie.

9

A pint and a half in every limb.

Unknown

"So," Dave said, "how are you going to earn your danger money?"

"Wi' knowledge, numpty."

"Go on."

The bus stop rattled. Dave realised that his mask had slipped, so every word he spoke attracted more zombies.

The Conductor glanced surreptitiously at his watch.

"Thing is, mate," the man said in a long-drawn-out drawl as he savoured every one of the three syllables. Nothing happened, so he carried on lugubriously. "Knowledge is power. I know... things, tha' I do."

"Like what?"

Zombies surrounded them. There was no escape. He was going to become a mindless, slavering beast, but even so, the thirty quid rankled.

"Like buzzes come in threes," the Conductor said.

"Everyone knows that," Dave piped up. He didn't care now. He was going to give this jerk a good piece of his mind. He took a deep breath – to hell with attracting zombies, might as well go down to a crowd as to a slight throng.

Even the zombies seemed to pause for his tirade.

"Number 11," the Conductor said, "am right on time."

Incredibly, as if on cue, a bus came around the corner. The zombies moved towards it and the double-decker slammed into them, clearing a path. There was 'severe the spine', 'smash their brains in' and there was 'mash them to a pulp'.

Another bus followed and a third brought up the rear.

"Thay trained for years," the Conductor said. "Dates back to the first world war. It am a secret pact between drivers and conductors."

"There are no conductors–"

"Thay tried to stop it, efficiency and such, but thay kept the tactic. We travel in threes."

The first bus, bright in its blood-splattered livery of red and white, went straight through, but the second stopped at the bus stop opposite. A hatch welded over an angle-grinded hole opened into the top deck. Hands reached out and plucked those cowering on the bus stop roof up into safety.

A hundred zombies massed around the corner.

They chanted, "Brains, brains..." and, "Bus, bus..."

The third bus reversed, smashing into the mob – back and forth – as the swarm came around the battered vehicle. They reached up, trying to grasp at the passengers within through the steel bars welded over the windows.

Just as it was about to be overwhelmed, it set off, overtaking the bus collecting passengers and pulled in behind the lead bus. All three vehicles then set off down Linden Road, smashing an abandoned car aside at the zebra crossing and careening on towards the Bournville Bastille.

"Holy cow," Dave said, "but we're still..."

The mass of slavering brutes ran on behind the fleeing public transport and the last few stragglers staggered to keep up.

A great calm settled upon Cotteridge.

"Buses seem safe," Dave said.

"Aye."

"But we're going by train."

"Aye."

"Great."

"We best be goin'," the Conductor said. He slid off the roof and landed with practised ease.

Dave wasn't sure how he'd managed the athletic prowess required to get onto the roof in the first place. Adrenalin, he suspected. He crawled around on his belly and then lowered himself as far as he could before dropping down.

The few others, who had stayed on the bus stop opposite, crossed the road to join them.

"Them're my passengers," the Conductor explained.

Twenty quid times lots plus his thirty was a tidy profit.

Dave checked his phone: a tight cluster of green dots over the other side of the road and a mass of red dots hurtling down the map.

"Tag-and-Track ain't perfect," the Conductor said.

"No," Dave admitted, "but it's a guide."

The green dots reached their side of the road.

"This am Frank," the Conductor said.

"Hi," Frank said. He held out his hand and Dave shook it. "I was in the army."

Frank had all the appearance of someone who was in the army, all rugby player, and at some point, he'd broken his nose.

"And this am Denzel the surgeon."

Denzel the surgeon nodded to Dave.

The Conductor finished the introductions. "And this am Bex and so on."

"Hi," Bex said, "I'm in trains."

The others took it in turns to nod, shake hands or look away. They introduced themselves, articulating carefully to overcome the muffle of their masks.

"Guy, fitness instructor."

"Lucy, psychologist."

"Axel, I find things."

"Thief, more like," the Conductor said.

"I prefer freelance in acquisitions," Axel said.

"Give 'im his watch back."

Axel did so.

"And this am Dave," the Conductor said. "He'll be useful, no doubt."

"I'm in advertising," Dave added as he put his watch back on.

Dave felt relieved at last.

This was great, because this mysterious Conductor knew all the tricks to get them there, and they had a soldier, a doctor (a surgeon no less), a train expert – fitness and psychology weren't that useful as they'd all been practising running recently and none of them were screaming externally, but even so they might be handy in a pinch – and Dave was an advertising copywriter, so he could update their vital social media, Twitter, TikTok and Instagram accounts.

What a team!

The surgeon even had a heavy bag of equipment, probably full of defibrillators, painkillers, anti-virus drugs, bandages, CPRs and MRI scanners.

Yes, this was the best choice. It was good to be in the first squad.

"Remember," the Conductor said. "Keep two metres away from a zombie."

"Why two metres?" Dave asked.

"'Cos them are bloody dangerous."

The Conductor adjusted his wide-brimmed leather hat and set off. He just assumed everyone would follow him.

They did.

Frank in army fatigues, Denzel in jeans and a camping coat, Bex in a stylish outfit that sparkled, Guy in a red and blue tracksuit, Lucy with a long scarf and Axel with a fisherman's waistcoat full of bulging pockets.

Dave turned to Bex. "Are we going all the way down Linden?"

She shook her head, a quick motion so as not to disturb her constant scanning of their surroundings.

"When the zombies reach the Bournville barricade," she said, "they get repelled and come back this way."

"Oh... ah." Dave squinted down Linden Road, but it had hills, so it was impossible to see even as far as the Tesco Express and Esso garage.

"We take Franklin," the Conductor said.

"Sir, doesn't that go past Cotteridge Park?" Guy asked.

"Aye."

"Park..." Dave realised. "Oh shit."

Franklin Road was a long terrace of Edwardian houses built of solid red brick with low defensive walls and small gardens of no-man's land. The other side opened out on the park.

Like pigeons and foxes, there were town zombies and country zombies. Being undead amongst the trees and open green spaces had made these park zombies feral. They moved quicker, and they often ambushed the unwary and the wary. Ramblers, rather than shamblers with more than their share of joggers.

There were a lot of parks around Bournville. What had George Cadbury been thinking when he designed his model village? It should have been fortified walls, not pleasant open spaces with lots of trees for the undead to loiter behind.

The last few houses had 'For Sale' signs up as if anyone would buy a house with a magnificent view of a park in this day and age. Indeed, when the apocalypse started house prices plummeted, the first sign of civilisation collapsing.

The park did look peaceful. Its wide-open grass was punctuated with big, solid trees, divided by lazy tarmac paths and in pride of place stood a kiddies' play area. Here and there, like scarecrows, members of the undead shambled and–

Three dark figures came from the trees, running straight towards them.

"Joggers!" Frank yelled.

Dave raised his hands and realised he didn't have his baseball bat anymore.

"Cars!" The Conductor bounded up onto the bonnet of a Ford Fiesta, stepped up onto its roof and then jumped the gap to a BMW. The others realised and did the same.

Dave was in the middle of the pack.

They were safe on the top of the cars, but not on the bonnets and boots.

A Volvo had an open roof.

Frank's foot disappeared into the interior.

"Come on," Dave yelled, grabbing his hand. He pulled, nearly toppled over backwards when Frank came free and then they carried on – Mercedes, large gap to a Vauxhall, two Hondas and then a skip!

Dave bounced across the discarded mattresses and trampolined out onto the roof of a white van.

They reached the top of the hill, where the start of Beaumont Road went off to the left.

They all needed their breaths back.

Their masks puffed out and sucked back.

Behind them, the zombies fell upon a victim like a rugby scrum. They feasted, red entrails hanging from their vicious teeth. Dave checked their party, counting... he couldn't remember how many had started out. And he couldn't recall the name of the missing.

Frank was limping, the bloke with the big bag, Bex, red and blue tracksuit... and... scarf girl, the Conductor and himself. There were only seven of them left.

"Shit," he said.

"Thay doe," the Conductor said. "We best be moving before tha' want seconds."

However, the team didn't make their way straight along Franklin Road, but instead stopped at the edge of the park by a small fenced-off substation. The Conductor made his way there, paused to check everything was clear and then went to the latch. The padlock was secure, but the clasp had been ripped from the wood and replaced to make it look like it was locked.

Inside, the Conductor recovered a variety of gardening implements: spade, fork, rake, hoe, edging tool, long-handled pruners and a brush. He handed them out.

"Good spade," the surgeon remarked.

Bex got the fork as Dave checked over the brush. The Conductor kept an edging tool for himself.

"Yow am on point, Dave," the Conductor said putting the brush in Dave's hands.

"Me!"

It was a short walk along the rest of Franklin Road until they reached the small garage and Bournville Social Club.

Dave stopped before the road widened for the junction with Mary Vale Road. He could hear the zombie horde chanting "Brains, brains..." – a guttural sound that seemed to emanate from some vast and hellish choir.

"This am where it gets hairy," the Conductor said.

Dave didn't like the sound of that. "Gets?"

"We're about to enter the Bournville Exclusion Zone."

"Oh."

"Yow know what Bournville residents am like."

"No."

"Let's just say, tha' don't share tha' Dairy Milk."

Bournville had been one of the most picturesque parts of Birmingham boasting Selly Oak manor, a village green, a carillon, alms houses and a chocolate factory. These days, it also had the Linden Road barricade, the Sycamore entrenchments, the Oak Tree Lane embankments and the Bourn River moat.

When the disaster had happened, the Bournvillians had walled themselves into the model village with the horrors on the outside and the chocolate factory on the inside. They had a motto: Stay at Work, Protect the Factory, Save the Chocolate.

And they did.

The Bournville Bastille was a massive fortification, a wall on the far side of Bournville Lane sealed the chocolate factory from Linden Road to the railway line. This was the southern barricade. It crossed the line, blocking the tunnel underneath and used the canal as a long straight moat covering the western approaches from Stirchley before turning across Laburnum Road and Sycamore Road. The shops that faced the green had been boarded up. Finally, with St Francis's church acting as the cornerstone, the wall travelled back along Linden Road. It didn't surround all of Bournville – the school, Quaker House, Rest House, Selly Manor and the station had all been abandoned, but the Bastille did contain two swimming pools, a cricket ground that had been converted into allotments, the Cadbury Experience and, of course, more chocolate than could be conceivably consumed in a sensible time.

Surrounding this bastion, a horde of enraged zombies beat at the ramparts in a maddened frenzy.

"Brains... brains..." they mumbled or, "Fruit... nut..."

Inside, the residents worked the allotments, played on the African Adventure, visited Aztec World and ate their dwindling supplies with a queasy feeling. For them, survival was a race between running out of Double Deckers, Crunchies and Cream Eggs versus the slow growth of onions, parsnips and King Edwards.

"Wim along Mary Vale," the Conductor said, "and use the walkway from the bridge to the station."

Looking right, Dave checked that the way was clear along Mary Vale Road. He could see the hump of the bridge, perhaps 200m away, before the road curved. The bridge went over the railway and the canal. He knew there were walkways down to the station platforms; thankfully, the city-bound platform was the nearest.

Keeping low, Dave led the way.

He kicked something on the floor!

A can that rattled across the pavement.

The low moan of zombies panicked everyone.

Where?

There!

Three shambling forms appeared from behind the abandoned cars, their arms reaching up stiffly as they turned to stalk towards them.

Getting to the office was going to be delayed again.

The team backtracked, silently trying not to breathe. The Conductor led them to the newsagent's shop. Four steps took them to the red-edged, glass door. He held the door open and they slipped inside.

The shelves had been stripped bare. Stationery lay on the floor amongst broken glass and the fridge for soft drinks had lost its door.

"Ahh," said Bex.

"Shhh..." the Conductor ordered.

"It's just–"

"Shhh..."

Bex pointed at the ceiling.

A body hung from the light fitting... no, a puppet dangling by its strings. A sign hung from its neck that read, 'Looter's will be shot'.

"It's a guy," Lucy said.

"I'm Guy," Guy said.

"I meant a guy to scare away thieves."

"Tha' only thief be... where's Axel?"

They all looked away: Axel hadn't made it.

Staring upwards, Dave examined the guy. It was the sort kids used to take around saying 'Penny for the Guy' – a macabre touch, somehow more disturbing than the walking corpses moving past outside and the barricade of shopping trolleys.

"It's creepy," Lucy said, and she was a psychologist, so she'd know.

Dave shivered – that apostrophe in 'Looter's' – *urrrgh*.

"Tha' am going," the Conductor said.

Dave made his way back and peered between the posters and adverts plastered on the windows.

The three shamblers had turned down that little road that went down to the chocolate factory. These zombies went to rejoin the multitude that surrounded the great fortification that Cadbury's had become.

"Let's give 'em ten minutes," the Conductor said. He hadn't looked round, but simply assumed everyone hung on his every word.

"What have we got to look forward to?" Dave asked him.

"The end of the world."

"I meant, what dangers?"

"It all be dangerous."

"More dangerous than going to Bournville station?"

"Five Ways station."

"Oh."

"New Street is worse."

"Er..."

"Doe worry, we're bay goin' to New Street," the Conductor said. "I doe have a death wish. Terminates at Five Ways."

"Ah." Dave didn't like the sound of 'terminates'.

"Let's go."

It hadn't been ten minutes, but the Conductor clearly lived dangerously.

They slipped out and along the pavement towards the station leaving it to the last minute to cross the road. The other side was more open and exposed due to the large car park.

On the other side of the tracks lay Stirchley with all its trendy cafés and tap rooms – the Attic Brewery, the Cork and Cage, Wildcat, Artefact, Stir, Couch, Anjuna Lounge, the Birmingham Brewing Co., balti houses, Eat Vietnam... all just out of reach. The Attic was just there... Dave could see it, almost taste the hops and barley.

"Oh lord," Bex said.

A zombie paused, turning slowly to contemplate the rise to the bridge with its sunken, bloodshot eyes.

Dave grabbed Bex and pulled her towards the gap in the bridge wall. Beneath an ironwork gateway, a ramp led down to the platform below.

A group of business types stood at intervals, all armed with clubs and poles.

The Conductor's group hurried down to join them.

The tannoy crackled into action: *"...and the 7:50 is delayed in the Bromsgrove direction by the wrong sort of bodies on the line."*

Many on the opposite platform shrugged and tutted.

Dave, Frank and Bex needed tickets. Denzel, Guy and Lucy had season tickets or had bought theirs online.

So, Dave joined the queue.

"Five Ways," the Conductor said.

"I need to go into the city centre," Frank said. Dave did too as his office was just off the top end of New Street.

"Like I said, not via New Street station, unless you've a death wish. Five Ways and then we take the tram."

"Trams not working,"

The Conductor tapped his nose knowingly.

Bex faffed with the controls and had to do it again, and then made the same mistake. Dave, looking over her shoulder, could see what Bex was doing wrong, which made him seethe silently.

A return to Five Ways seemed optimistic.

Frank was next. He knew what to do.

Dave glanced at the overhead display.

1st 08:10 Erdington via B'ham New St   On time
Calling at: versity, Five Ways, NOT B'ham New S
08:18:52

Could he get a ticket in one minute, eight... now one minute, five seconds?

Erdington? It terminated at Five Ways, didn't it? The timetable can't have been updated, although the scrolling 'NOT B'ham New St, University, Five W' sounded like a partial change. Or a warning.

Frank finished.

Dave pressed the screen quickly, too quickly, and needed to press harder.

"Come on, come on," he said under his breath and into his mask.

Five Ways, day return, card... it said to follow the instructions – what instructions? On the card reader. He held his card against the scanning area, turned it around, tried again.

"Come on! Come on!" Dave yelled at the machine. All this time, the far entrance disgorged zombies onto the platform. The other commuters fought back.

It accepted it.

Finally.

The printer began to screech as the train screeched and the zombies screeched and the dying commuters screeched as the train's brakes screeched – all sound and fury.

The clatter of the approaching train grew louder and the stupid machine chunnered away printing as slowly as was mechanically possible.

The first ticket, outbound, dropped out of the chute.

Dave grabbed it.

"Leave the rest," the Conductor commanded. "We need yow."

"But I paid–"

Like a string of buses, the train pulled in.

"It's only got four carriages," Guy declared. "Typical."

"Not that many commuters, these days," Lucy replied.

The second ticket dropped down.

The Conductor grabbed Dave by his jacket and yanked him towards the train. The second ticket, the return, suddenly became everything to Dave. He had to have it. If he didn't then he knew, just knew, that he wouldn't make it back. It wasn't superstition so much as a divine understanding of the universe.

The fallen zombies on the line squelched as the train's brakes whined.

Dave pulled out of the Conductor's grip, jumped to the machine and put his hand into the drawer. The ticket fluttered away like a wounded moth, but Dave caught it and snatched it out.

A zombie caught his hand!

The ticket machine whirred to produce Dave's receipt.

The train doors opened.

Dave brushed the zombie back with his broom.

The slavering beast staggered back.

But the zombie recovered and raised it arms ready to attack again.

Dave's weapon was useless. The bristles couldn't severe a spine, smash in brains or mash to a pulp. All he could do was push the undead away to gain a few more, pointless seconds.

And more zombies tumbled out of the train filling the platform with the undead.

"Last carriage!" the Conductor instructed.

They all ran along the platform dodging the undead and piled into the final carriage just as the doors hissed shut.

Dave found himself safely on the train.

He still held the crumpled and precious return ticket in his hand – *phew*. Saved.

The last carriage's other commuters, those from Kings Norton, Northfield, Longbridge and beyond, welcomed them – "Brains, brains..."

10

Stay home, stay indoors, stay still, stay put,
don't go anywhere. Which part of 'don't go
anywhere' do you not understand? Stay
where you are.

Government spokesman

Dawn had imagined that there would be time to sort out a
proper reception for the minister, say, nibbles (if Stores
had any) with wine. It would be a chance to build team
morale with an event. But no, not even a set of
interminable sub-committee meetings – he was arriving
today.

They gathered in the canteen for a coffee: Councillor
Grant, Mr Anderson and Mr Matt.

"Right," Dawn began, "put your hands up if you took a
zombie test."

Everyone put their hands up.

"Put your hands up if you passed the test."

Everyone did.

"Put your hands up if you like putting your hands up."

Everyone did, so that was everyone not paying
attention.

Dawn raised her voice. "LISTEN, does anyone need a
fresh mask?"

"You don't need a mask," Anderson said. "And why
would you want to hide such a pretty face?"

"It is government policy," Dawn replied, holding up
her FFP3. None of the others had a mask.

"Government policy." – Anderson snorted. – "And what's wrong with looking attractive."

"We are the government."

"Local government."

"Emergency government."

"Please," Councillor Grant interjected. "Mask wearing is voluntary."

"Councillor," Dawn said, "if one person in the group doesn't wear a mask, then everyone will be attacked."

"It's a matter of individual conscience."

"But, Councillor–"

"And you'll have to wear heels."

"Heels!"

"You're meeting the minister."

"But we have to get through a lot of zombies."

"No reason to lower standards."

"I might need to run."

"Fine," Councillor Grant said. "You can take them in your bag and change on the roof."

"Thank you."

"So, it's Hugh and Dawn to meet the minister."

"Me?" Anderson said. "Why aren't... surely the Councillor ought to be part of the welcoming group."

"Oh no, I'm needed down here."

"But–"

"There are only two or three zombies there."

"Twenty-seven," Dawn said, remembering what Ahmed had said.

"Nonsense," Councillor Grant said.

"On the CCTV – maybe more."

"No... well, that's not my responsibility," Councillor Grant informed them. "And that number is well within government guidelines for an office of our size. As the acting Health and Safety expert on site, Dawn, you are responsible for keeping the numbers down."

"But we might die."

"Well, if you have a grievance, we have procedures as you are well aware."

"Not much use when we're shamblers."

"If you do become zombies," Anderson said, enjoying the situation, "then we will have to suspend you while we have an investigation and, I warn you, we may have to take disciplinary action."

"I might become a jogger then you'd be sorry."

"You? A jogger? In heels?"

"Mr Anderson, I've a good mind to give you a piece of my mind."

"I'm not a zombie," Anderson quipped, "So there's no need to feed me any brains."

"I should go," Mr Matt said, interrupting. "After all, I'm Head of Logistics. I insist."

"I'll stand down," Anderson said.

"That's settled then," Councillor Grant replied. "So, the two of you meet at Blast Door Three."

"Just the two of us?" Dawn asked.

"Three's a crowd," Anderson added.

"With security," said the Councillor.

"Have we reduced security yet," Anderson asked.

"Hmm... probably best not tell them until after the minister's stay."

"He's staying?" Dawn said.

"Oh yes, project... never mind."

"Project Never Mind?"

"Miss Dey... heels."

Dawn rolled her eyes and then nipped off to her bunk to collect her posh shoes.

She had her belongings in the women's dormitory. It was smaller than the men's, but there was only her. She found her shoe collection – not all fit – and selected a pair with heels. She went to the Ladies – her sanctuary – and checked herself in the mirror. All this time underground had made her look pale and wan.

She tied her hair back to look professional.

This whole exercise was insane.

She should pull the panic cord, endlessly until they locked her up, but instead she pocketed her phone, left her bag and walked to the main exit.

Mr Matt, Mr Anderson and the security guards, Ahmed, Pete and Rob, waited at the blast door.

"Do we all have to go?" Dawn asked.

"Yes," Mr Matt replied. "Of course."

"But won't we get in each other's way on the staircases and–"

"We all go," Matt said.

"She has a point," Ahmed said.

"We all go," Matt repeated. "Although, shouldn't we take some preventative medicine?"

"You mean like cod liver oil?" Anderson said.

"Check the medical kit," Matt insisted. "Anything else?"

Anderson took the medical kit down off the wall and ferreted through its contents.

"There are place bows," Anderson said.

"Do they work?"

"Guaranteed."

"I'll have a place bow then."

"It's placebo... plac-*e*-bo," Dawn said.

"All right, plac-*eee*-bo. What do they do anyway?" Matt said.

"Nothing," Dawn said.

"What!"

"Nothing. They're used as controls during medical experiments."

"What?" Matt said. He tugged at his hair again.

"One group takes the tablets and the other, unknown to them of course, takes pills made of sugar, placebos. It's so that positive expectations don't have an adverse effect on the experiment."

"And we have them for what reason?"

"Well, there's no cure for zombie infection, so they are included to make us feel better."

"But you said they have no effect."

"Yes, but if you didn't know that and thought they had an effect, then you'd feel much better."

"But you've just told us!" Matt said.

"Yes," Dawn admitted. "They're no use at all now."

"Oh God."

"You'd better take two then," Anderson said. "And you don't need masks."

"But surely in the circumstances?" Dawn said.

"In the circumstances, we are meeting the minister," Anderson said. "What's he going to think if we turn up wearing masks."

"But–"

"No masks."

Reluctantly, they all put away their FFP3s. As they did so, the Councillor's reassuring voice boomed over the tannoy from the safety of the Control Room.

"GOOD LUCK."

So, they opened the big blast door and Rob took out a waiting zombie with the shotgun – **BOOM, BOOM.**

Dawn jumped at each appalling detonation.

"Got 'im," Rob said. "Straight to the head."

"Save the ammunition," Pete said.

"What and not kill the zombies?" Rob said.

"Just saying. One shot per zombie. What if there had been two zombies?"

"I'd have used one shot per zombie."

"What if there had been three zombies?" Dawn asked.

"They're not buses," Rob replied as he reloaded.

"How many cartridges left?" Pete asked.

"Three."

"Well, don't waste them."

"They were evil buggers."

"Mister... Rob!" Dawn shouted. This was all getting on her nerves. "They are not 'evil b...', they are... were people and I trust you'll use the proper nomenclature."

"Which is?"

Dawn tried to remember.

The zombies came in various variants and there was talk about what to name them. Variant US/8/TN1 was not helpful and 'American zombies' was felt to be misleading, and the President objected.

So, a committee was formed at the World Health Organisation and a variety of executives turned up to debate the matter. There were Greek letters, Viking runes and even a man who favoured the alphabet of the Aztecs. This latter one was rejected as there wasn't a Unicode symbol for each character.

The dispute had gone on and it was clearly going to be a long day, so the various dignitaries wondered about lunch and where they might get a drink. One delegate complained of stomach cramps and made his excuses. Luckily, a buffet had been laid on, but this hadn't been labelled either. Two of the delegates were lactose intolerant, another had an aunt who was allergic to peanuts, three were Muslims fearful of pork, another was a lapsed Hindu, who still didn't want beef, and so the discussion moved to whether that was cheese or egg, and what was in the pie.

So heated was the argument that no-one noticed when the ill delegate returned and soon everyone was fighting over the rapidly diminishing supply of fresh brains.

So, the media had named the semi-stationary ones 'shamblers', the slow ones 'ramblers' and the quicker ones, 'joggers'. The latter name came about due to that viral video, which was funny. A group of lads tormented some poor zombie in Lycra forcing him to trot this way and that way. It was funny in that 'Would you like to see a jogger running about?' kind of way.

The next week, after the success of the video clip, the lads had gone back to make another, but that one remained forever on the phone dropped in the gutter when a rush of joggers had cornered the film crew.

"Which is?" Rob repeated.

"Not buggers."

"Why not?"

Why could they not understand that sticking to policy, following procedure and keeping everything woke all that kept the wolf from the door, the vandals from sacking Rome and her mind from going completely doolally.

She took a deep breath, "These terms are offensive and lead people to devalue those who have passed away. We prefer the term 'recently returned' or 'life challenged'. This is a disability issue."

"You can't libel the dead."

"Mister..." – Dawn forced herself to look – "...Jackson is not dead... technically."

"Is now."

"Oh for Pete's sake."

"I didn't do anything," Pete said.

"It's dead," Rob insisted.

"You should not have fired on him without due and proper process."

"It's a zombie!"

"It's! Really? Honestly, Rob? Is that Mr Jackson's preferred choice of pronoun?" Dawn gave him a withering smile. "I think not."

Rob had nothing to say to that.

So, having won the argument, Dawn stomped away along the passage. She tried not to see the bloody corpse as she stepped through the steel door frame and left the safety of the bunker. She also tried not to curse the day she'd come into this concrete tomb.

Pete sealed the door behind them. It clanged with heavy finality.

Oh bother, Dawn realised, she was wearing her heels and she'd left her bag in the Ladies.

"Rob, take point," Ahmed said.

So, Rob went ahead, posing with the shotgun, with Pete, Dawn was next, and Ahmed and Matt took up the rear.

The passage led to the stairs, which in turn went up to who knew what.

11

"People who help run food banks are wonderful. When I was running London, I help set up loads of food banks and they're fantastic things."

Boris Johnson

"The typical user of a food bank is not someone that's languishing in poverty: it's someone who has a cash flow problem."

Dominic Raab

"To have charitable support given by people voluntarily to support their fellow citizens I think is rather uplifting and shows what a good, compassionate country we are and, as I say, inevitably, the state can't do everything, so I think that there is good within food banks."

Jacob Rees-Mogg

Will work for food.

Homeless man's sign

The Conductor used a garden edging tool, its half-circle blade ideal for hacking into the necks of the zombies. Their heads came off, and their bodies fell to become obstacles that even joggers had problems with. The surgeon made use of his spade, the army guy hacked and stabbed with his rake, Bex used her fork to devastating effect, Guy kept them at bay with his hoe, Lucy picked off a few with her long-handled pruners and Dave did his best with his brush.

"The door," the Conductor ordered.

Dave asked for clarification. "Eh?"

"The door, numpty."

Dave realised and when the Conductor shoved a zombie into that awkward air-lock between carriages, Dave got the door closed... except the zombie's hand caught hold and prevented the seal. Lucy stepped in and *snip,* the limb fell away. It spasmed on the floor as if it was trying to decide between finding its body or attacking.

The door sealed.

The Conductor had a piece of metal shaped to hold the handle in place.

They were safe in the carriage and pulling out of Bournville station.

Phew.

He checked, saw Guy's red and blue tracksuit, Lucy's long scarf, Frank's camouflage, Denzel's outdoor coat and Bex's sparkling outfit. There were others too in this middle carriage who had already been on the train. Dave sat down next to two of them. It didn't seem to matter which seat he took. He patted his jacket and felt the reassurance of the dreadful sales figures.

He'd felt the same motion sickness queasiness once before when he'd played a first-person shooter wearing a VR headset. If this was a video game, he realised, he'd be holding his brush out in front of him and his itinerary would be phone x 1, mask x1, report (quarter 2) x 1, train tickets x 2, orange x 1... he had an orange!

He took out Mr Penrose's orange and tried to tear the skin off, but his hands shook. His fingers vibrated all on their own and Dave found it strangely fascinating. They seemed to belong to someone else as if they had a life that was theirs alone like a severed limb that was still attached.

He glanced at the display board.

Welcome aboard this service to Five Ways
Next stop: Selly Oak...

There were two stops before Five Ways, plenty of time, so Dave bit into the orange, tore the hunks off and slurped up the juice and bit the flesh from the skin.

"I'd rather you didn't do that," Bex said. She was sitting opposite.

"Eh?"

"Eat that like a zombie, it makes me think about what's going to happen to you... *urgh*, please."

Dave realised that he was being savage, and the juice dribbled down his chin.

"It's not blood," he said. "Orange, not red."

"Even so." She looked away. There was something there, a trauma, that spoke of an experience far away from sitting on a patio drinking faux Pimm's.

Dave turned away too and ate the rest of the orange. It tasted good, sweet, and not like blood, not that he knew what blood tasted like.

The train lurched and slowed down.

"Selly Oak next," said the man opposite.

Dave swallowed.

"You'll be fine," the bloke said. "I'm Bob."

"Dave."

"Je suis... I am, comment dit on, Monique," a pretty brunette opposite said.

"Hello," Bob said.

"Hi," said Dave.

"Bonjour."

"I was in the volunteer response."

93

"Useful," Dave said. "I'm in advertising."

"Je suis le coordinateur principal de l'unité de'intervention tactique contre les morts-vivants," Monique said.

"Right," Bob said.

"Eh?" Dave said.

"Comment dit on... *FENNEL.*"

"Right, fennel?"

"Eh?"

"La Ligue Fédérale des Catastrophes Nationales de l'Europe du Nord."

"Right..."

"Eh?"

"Oui."

"I wouldn't want to be volunteering now."

"No."

"Non."

"They're facing zombie dogs – severe."

"Ah!"

"Oui."

"Like they defended us, right, and–"

"Yes."

"J'en ai déjà entendu parler."

"Attacked the zombies."

"Right."

"Merde, il peut parler."

"But they bite 'em and, like, bites transmit."

"Yes."

"Et alors tous les chiens sont des chiens zombis."

"And then every dog's a zombie."

"Ah."

"Tue moi maintenant."

"Worse in Dudley."

"Eh?"

"Pourquoi?"

"Zombie elephant."

"No shit?"

"Non! Merde!"

"They had a zoo, so zombie lions, zombie tigers, zombie penguins."

"No."

"Mon dieu."

"And an elephant."

"Really?"

"C'est incroyable."

"Could be, I don't know its name."

"Thank God, we're... er, in Selly Oak," Dave said, checking out of the window.

Frank and Bex joined them, sitting either side of Dave.

"We'll be fine," Frank said, "so long as we don't stop."

"And if we stop?" Dave said.

"Zombies'll surround the train, we'll be trapped and eventually they'll get in."

"Let's not stop," Dave said.

They didn't.

Instead, the train went straight through at Selly Oak – not good.

"Something's happened," Bex said.

"Nah," Bob said. "Students live at Selly Oak."

"So?" Dave said.

Bob's brow furrowed. "Students."

"Eh?"

"Parties, raves, student halls... perfect environment for the undead to spread," Bob explained. "And with them all looking hung-over and shattered normally, pale with lack of sunlight, well, no-one noticed... until it was too late."

Welcome aboard this service to Five Ways
Next stop: University...

The train was already whining down its gears and then it pulled slowly into University station.

"N'y aurait-il pas des étudiants de plus à l'université?" Monique asked.

Dave asked for a translation. "Eh?"

"If you wish to alight now," the driver said over the tannoy, *"remember that the station only exists for the back of the train. Disembark here for the University and for the MHZ."*

Dave wiped the window with his sleeve.

The razor wire on top of the steel barriers of the Militarised Hospital Zone glinted in the morning light. Faceless men in gas masks patrolled, their SA-80s slung loosely across their bulletproof Kevlar.

"Jam guns," Frank said.

"Uh?"

"Jam guns – British rifle, always jamming, useless. That's why there are so many up there. Got to have squaddies firing while some poor sod unjams his rifle."

"Oh."

"The new ones are OK, but they all went to the units abroad."

"Ah."

"And we know what happened to them."

"Hmm."

"They're wearing Osprey body armour as if being bulletproof will stop a zombie biting your neck."

The doors opened.

Everyone tensed.

Feral nurses sprang on board.

"We've vaccines," one shouted, "vaccines."

But anti-vaxxers were already hustling them off with promises of food. A nurse paused, torn between saving lives and a can of tomato soup. She opted for the soup.

"It's all lies," an anti-vaxxer yelled. "There aren't zombies. They're all actors. You look round here, they've all been on *Doctors* and *Holby City.*"

This again, Dave thought, but he had to agree. He'd seen quite a few he'd almost recognized. Theatres and cinemas had seen the worst outbreaks at the start of the apocalypse. He realised that this bloke and his housemate, Dexter, must be on the same Discord channel.

"Merde," Monique said.

"It is the elephant in the room," Bob agreed.

"We're actors," a passenger replied. He sat in the seats over the aisle.

"See, they admit it," the anti-vaxxer yelled.

"I'm Jason. I'm on *The Archers*, I play–"

"*The Archers* is still on?" Dave asked.

"Oh yes," Jason said, "it's very calming for people in this time of need. Our listeners like something familiar."

Dave could hear the theme tune in his head and it made him smile.

"I'm in it too," said Jason's seatmate. "I play a zombie. Brains, brains... ha, ha. It's a proper speaking part."

"See," the anti-vaxxer shouted, "he's an actor who plays a zombie."

"*The Archers* is very cutting edge," Jason's zombie-playing friend continued, "and deals with real-world events that affect country folk."

The doors hissed shut.

The electrics whined and squealed as the train picked up speed. They slid out of the MHZ clattering onwards towards Birmingham.

Welcome aboard this service to Five Ways
Next stop: Five Ways...

The train slowed, probably due to the wrong sort of bodies on the line. The gap between University and their destination was the longest stretch between stations. At this rate it would take forever.

The tannoy crackled. *"Next stop– help, get out... No!"* Everyone froze.

"The train'll stop!" Frank said.

The train didn't stop.

"If it doesn't stop at Five Ways..." Frank continued, "we end up in New Street."

"No, no, no, not New Street!" Bob said.

"Non, non, non pas La Nouvelle Rue!" Monique said.

"If something went wrong with the driver, the train would stop," Frank said. "Dead man's pedal."

"Not if he be undead," the Conductor said, his edging tool at the ready.

"Oh... oh!" Dave said.

The tannoy crackled once more. *"Brains, brains..."* the driver announced.

Everyone glanced towards the front of the train. In their imaginations, the train hurtled on forever or crashed into another, the 7:32.

"We have to..." Frank said.

"It's three carriages!" Bob said.

"C'est trois voitures!" Monique added.

Dave nodded. He didn't want to, three carriages sounded impossible, but they had to. Otherwise, eventually the train would stop, suddenly and brutally, and any survivors would have to deal with those who hadn't.

But the Conductor had his edging tool.

Frank the army man had his rake.

Denzel the surgeon had his spade and his medical bag.

Bex had her fork.

Guy had his hoe.

Lucy had her long-handled pruners.

Bob and Monique had a cricket bat and a tennis racket.

The actors had their stage fighting training.

The anti-vaxxers had their leaflets.

So, Dave hefted his brush.

12

If you need to meet someone, do so in an
outdoor space like a local park. This affords
good sightlines and multiple exits. These
escape routes will also offer an opportunity
for exercise. Do not meet indoors and do
not go up in tower blocks as you may
become trapped and thus become part of the
problem.

Government advice

The ground floor was all quiet and art deco, lovely cream
walls with the decoration picked out in pastel blue. The
barricades at the front entrance seemed secure, the pile of
filing cabinets looked solid and dependable. If they ever
needed to look anything up, it would be a nightmare.

Daylight, actual daylight, shone through the partially
obscured fancy window above the double doors. Mr Matt
stopped to stare up at it and his hand hesitated by his hair.
The beauty of it held Dawn's gaze too. She licked her lips
as if she could taste the beams of yellow within which
danced motes of dust like sprites.

She looked at the others to see them entranced.

"Er..." she said, "shouldn't someone be watching out
for zombies?"

"Yeah," Ahmed agreed and then, "Oh shit. Rob, Pete."

They went back to their positions surrounding Mr
Matt and Dawn.

Then they moved towards the stairs.

Ahmed had counted twenty-seven on the CCTV, but the cameras didn't cover everywhere. If the barricade had held, and the other entrances were similarly secure, it meant that the only zombies in the building came from the office staff – a hundred and sixty-seven minus nineteen made a hundred and forty-eight... minus two more. She tried not to think about who they had been, but she'd seen and recognized a tie and a woolly jumper.

Should she organise a big card and a leaving do?

Telephone House was a large building, so the one hundred and forty-six zombies might be anywhere, spread out or bunched up. No one knew, unless some semblance of coherent thought still existed in the decaying brains of the research team.

"Ugh," Matt said, stepping over a corpse that lay across the floor by the lifts.

Dawn felt the same.

Next to the lift doors by a break-glass-fronted fire point complete with hose and fire axe, was a sight even more remarkable than the angelic stream of daylight: a chocolate dispensing machine. There was... oh... and... oh.

The others went past.

She could just... but she had no change. She'd left her purse in her bag in the Ladies in the bunker!

"Does anyone have any money?" she asked.

Matt glanced back, "Wouldn't help," he said. "No power."

"Can you open this?"

He shook his head.

"Yes," Dawn insisted, "you can."

"I don't have a key."

"Then you could prise it open."

"I can't."

"Of course, you can."

"It's not ours," Matt explained. "It's leased."

"But..."

"Come on."

Dawn took one last, longing look at the chocolate bars, Mars, Snickers, Twix and Dairy Milk. She pressed a few buttons, but B7, C3 and D2 all remained behind the toughened glass.

There was a sign by the buttons to call the lift that said, 'In the case of an emergency, use the stairs.'

Everything was an emergency now.

It was all climbing stairs.

They went up as quietly as Dawn's heels allowed on the marble staircase.

A moan issued from above.

Rob raised the shotgun, but Pete touched his arm.

"Just a shambler," Pete said. "Save the ammo."

They waited.

A shadow appeared.

Everyone took a deep breath.

Keith from Accounts came around the corner.

No, not Keith, who had been friendly and had meant well when he'd groped Fiona at the Christmas party – they'd all had too much fizz. No, not Keith, but some broken shambling semblance that lurched down the stairs.

They stood aside to give it space as the shotgun cartridge was more precious than their safety.

It paused by Dawn, its blank, depressed and dark eyes trying to focus. Perhaps it remembered when she'd supported Fiona at the disciplinary.

It moved on, dragging its left foot, slowing it down.

Dawn felt her face turning red, her vision swimming and her cheeks expanding with the pressure of needing to exhale. She was going to faint and it was a long way down off these heels and the stairs.

But it worked.

The zombie simply shambled past.

Just another few steps and maybe she could open her mouth – not to take a breath because that would draw attention to herself fatally – but perhaps to let the oxygen diffuse gradually into her aching lungs.

She could feel her blood turning to sludge.

Ping-ping-ping-ping...

Her phone overrode the volume control with the vital and urgent news that a zombie was nearby.

...ping-ping-ping...

She struggled with it, clutched the stupid thing and breathed out explosively.

...ping-ping-ping...

Low oxygen meant that her fingers and thumbs were all fingers and thumbs.

...ping-ping-ping...

She got to the app, fumbled to acknowledge it.

...ping-ping- "*proximity alert... proximity alert...*"

Silence.

Finally.

"Brains," said the zombie pausing on the staircase.

Dawn clamped her mouth shut.

The zombie tried to locate the source of the breath.

Dawn closed her eyes. She wanted to be back in the bunker, she wanted to live, really live, but she also wanted to wet herself as she smelt the putrefaction close by.

Her face felt flushed, reddening as the oxygen ran out and tiny sparks appeared in her peripheral vision. She was thingy and her wotnot flashed before her eyes. In an emergency, the brain thinks, let's shut down all non-essential functions... like language, for example. Hers had decided she didn't need doobrie whatsit either.

Thingy doodad tugged at her arm.

Pete!

He pulled on her jacket sleeve to lead her upwards into the encroaching darkness.

She walked without any feeling in her legs as if she was a zombie already. She needed to run, but none of her muscles had any oxygen. Her legs stumbled, her knees crumpled, but Pete got her around the corner.

Dawn doubled over onto her hands and knees, forcing herself to breathe deeply and slowly. Stars buzzed around her in her vision.

"Ahhhhhh!!!"

"Brains," said Keith the zombie. She could hear him limping towards them.

Still on all fours, Dawn crawled upwards with the others, their baby motion slightly faster than the zombie. Thank God, it was a shambler.

At the next landing, Dawn pulled herself up using the banister for support.

When her wotnot had flashed before her eyes, it had all been meetings and evenings alone with Chardonnay and her cat with something weepy on Netflix. She needed to get a wotnot... a life!

"I wish to register a grievance," Matt said.

"Sorry," Dawn replied.

"Anderson insisted we don't wear masks and this contravenes health and safety."

"Can we... oh... handle this when we get back to my office, please?"

"No, I want it dealt with now."

"I don't have the right forms."

Matt dithered and then realised he wasn't going to win the argument. He tugged another few strands of hair away. "Well, just so long as it's done."

Dawn nodded.

They'd waited on the landing too long and the zombie staggered up suddenly.

Rob was ready for him.

B-BOM-OM.

The gunshot was savage, tearing the creature's shirt and tie to shreds, and splattering decaying flesh across the wall. It took both barrels and the thing dropped.

"Got it," Rob announced.

Dawn breathed again.

And then her gasps became rapid and uncontrolled.

Pete yelled, "What did you do that for?"

"Zomb–"

"Rob," Dawn shouted, "you cannot – and I cannot stress this enough – you cannot, absolutely cannot shoot members of staff without following proper procedure."

"Prop–"

"This is... was Mr Carlton, Keith," Dawn explained in tones reserved for three-year-olds and new staff.

They all looked down at Keith Carlton's quivering corpse.

"Did you give Mr Carlton a written warning?" Dawn demanded to know.

"Not as such, I–"

"Did you even give him a verbal warning?"

"I could have shouted 'die zombie scum', I suppose."

"Die... zombie... scum, really. I am going to mention your language in a report, Rob."

"But–"

"Rob, you are not, that's NOT, to kill anyone else without them being allowed a union representative."

"Union... where is the union rep?"

"I think," Ahmed said, "he's decapitated on floor three."

"I'm sure the union will appoint another one," Dawn said. "There does seem to be no end of them."

"Always another zombie."

"No, I meant union reps."

Rob went back on point with a single cartridge in the shotgun. The others brought up the rear.

They came out through the roof access door and then they were outside!

Actually outside in the outside world!

The light dazzled, its colour so warm and orange after the blue hues of the LED lighting in the bunker.

Dawn blinked, trying to take it in, and the ceiling seemed so high and far away. The fresh air, devoid of any car fumes, filled her lungs and she felt giddy with the rush of all these long-forgotten sensations.

"We're outside," Dawn said. "Outside!"

"Yeah," Matt said, "pity it's such a crap day."

Now Dawn's eyes were used to the change, she did see that it was overcast with rain gathering on the far horizon for later.

And it was windy this high up.

Dawn shivered.

She had a feeling of vertigo, agoraphobia and a chill. She hadn't seen even this overcast sky in many, many months. She wished she'd bought her sunglasses as it was so bright. Weather always made the days different from one another. In the bunker, it was just one cross on the calendar after another. She missed the seasons too. Was it spring, summer, autumn or winter?

This wasn't the very top. They needed to clamber up a ladder from this lower level.

It was even windier higher up, but the black scrunchie holding Dawn's ponytail was made of stern stuff.

"How long?" Dawn asked.

"Not long," Ahmed said, checking his watch.

Pete and Rob scanned the perimeter as everyone gazed into the grey clouds. No zombie could get up here, Dawn thought, so they were safe... weren't they?

The Birmingham skyline appeared familiar, although she'd never seen it from the top of Telephone House before. Some of the buildings were burnt-out shells. A tower block had toppled like a domino. Somewhere off to the Jewellery Quarter smoke billowed towards the heavens. She pitied anyone who might have survived this long – perhaps a few people holed up where there was food.

Reflexively, Dawn checked her phone – perhaps she could call someone, though there was no-one left alive that she had known. But wait, the Tag-and-Track app showed little green dots.

People alive!

So the reports she'd received were exaggerated. They weren't the last people in the West Midlands Emergency Area, although as she watched, one dot was surrounded by little red dots until it too went red.

She was about to put her phone away when she noticed a notification.

It was the dating app.

She checked, turned on location services, and there was a little flashing tick signifying that someone had swiped her right and she had swiped him right.

The someone was a 'Dave' – disappointingly friendly. What was wrong with 'David', she wondered.

Should she?

He looked out of focus, which made him oddly mysterious.

Maybe he was alive.

No, of course not.

No point getting her hopes up and she was busy saving the world. And that was job satisfaction, surely? Except it never felt like it stuck in the bunker.

But it did give her a strange feeling... hope.

What was the point of that?

Indeed, what was the point of anything?

She went to check his location, but Mr Matt interrupted her.

"There," Matt said.

Where he pointed, a tiny black shape like an angry mosquito descended from the clouds. It seemed to take forever to become a hornet and then a whining crow before the mechanical marvel...

"Heels," Matt reminded her.

"I am wearing heels," Dawn said.

"Not stilettos," Matt said, disappointed.

Dawn turned on him to give him a piece of her mind, but her words and hairdo were whipped away by the downdraft of the rotor blades.

The helicopter couldn't land, but the pilot bravely placed one strut down on the flat roof and hovered.

Three men got out, two wearing gas masks and carrying submachine guns, and another in a dark overcoat. Bags were dragged out too and a suitcase.

"Thank God, we're saved," Matt said. "The minister's here."

13

BE VERY CAREFUL
DO NOT BECOME INFECTED
SAVE EVERYONE'S LIFE

Government advice

"Should we say something encouraging?" Dave asked. "Like be very careful, do not blah-blah... or whatever the advice is this week. Or maybe something that's not government advice."

The Conductor agreed. "Everyone, tha' shouldn't get jedded."

"I've played a colonel," Jason said.

"Go on then," Dave said.

"Er... it wasn't me who murdered the butler... it's all I can remember."

"Jeez," the Conductor said and he led them to the connecting door. He grabbed the piece of metal and nodded to the others. "Yow know what ter do," he said.

"Actually–" Dave said.

The metal pinged away, the door opened and two zombies fell through. The Conductor edged one, Bex forked the other and Dave brushed up.

And then they were through, running and screaming, slicing, digging, forking, hitting and sweeping. Blood splattered on the windows, doors, emergency alarm, sticky floor, posters for long finished pantomimes and the scrolling display.

They reached the far door.

"This isn't real," the anti-vaxxer shouted and then, for him, it was all too real. He joined the true believers in the apocalypse and quoted their mantra, "Brains, brains..."

Guy hacked into the zombies trapped between carriages with his hoe, stabbing, shoving and occasionally getting a good strike to the neck. Once the walking corpses were lying down corpses, they heaved themselves over, stepping on the rubbery flesh.

This middle carriage was designated the quiet zone.

"For f–"

"Run!"

"Sauve qui peut!"

"There!"

"Watch out!"

Bob fell, his scream louder than any train engine.

"Nonnnnnnnn..." Monique shouted.

Bex froze.

Dave threw his brush aside, grabbed Bex and Bob, and yanked them free.

A chaotic struggle followed.

Dave and Bex pulled Bob along the carriage and plonked him onto a set of three seats. He could lie down there.

"He's..." Bex said.

"Yes," Dave agreed.

"And..."

"Yes." What else was there to say?

"Oh god," Bob cried out, "don't let me turn."

He was bleeding, difficult to know whether the blood was his or a zombie's.

"Of course not," Dave said.

"There, there," Bex added.

The others clustered around their fallen comrade.

"We need... what's the surgeon's name," Dave said.

"Dunno," Bex admitted.

Dave yelled – "Medic! Medic!"

"Make way, make way," Jason shouted as he battled his way over. "I've played a doctor!"

"Can you help him?"

"God, no!"

Dave changed tack. "Surgeon! Surgeon!"

Denzel shouldered his way through.

"Help him," Dave said to the surgeon, indicating Bob.

"Me?" Denzel said.

"Yes, you're a surgeon."

"I'm a tree surgeon."

"Tree... what?"

"You know, elms, oaks... I do bushes too."

"Of for... where's Frank?"

"Here," said Frank.

"Help Bob."

"Me?" Frank replied.

"Yes," Dave said. This was getting surreal. "You're in the army, you know all about field dressings."

"Salad dressings."

"What?"

"I'm a chef."

"Chef?"

"An army chef. I specialise in catering for large groups. You know, beef casserole and–"

"Never mind... perhaps," Dave said, thinking aloud, "you and Denzel could carry Bob, while the rest of us hold off the zombies."

"Oh, great plan, Dave," Bex yelled.

"I'm trying my best, you–"

"Look," said Bex, but she got no further.

Bob coughed, gargled his last, unheard words and died.

They looked at their fallen comrade like relations around a grave.

And then Bob coughed again.

"He's alive," Bex exclaimed.

"Brains," Bob mumbled.

"Oh shit," said Dave. "Run."

Bex didn't move!

And some of the zombies they'd knocked over were back on their unsteady feet, their heads still connected, their brains intact and their bodies unpulped.

Dave readied his brush, except he didn't have it. He couldn't brush them aside as he'd thrown his brush aside. He could see it, leaning against the seating further up.

"Er..." Dave said.

"Retraite stratégique!" Monique shouted.

"Never mind that," Frank shouted back. "Run!"

Frank was nimble for such a big framed man.

Dave grabbed Bex by the arm, shook her and then yanked her towards the driver's door. She seemed to reappear behind her dead eyes as if she had teleported back into her head.

The next door led to the front carriage.

Guy thrust with his hoe to push the pursuit away.

A zombie fell.

Monique rushed to safety.

The others followed.

The Conductor grabbed the brush as he went past.

Dave took the hoe off Guy as he went past.

Monique shouted, "Vite! Vite!"

Dave went through the first door to enter the tunnel between the carriages.

Something moaned by his shoulder.

Dave twisted round to defend himself.

The door into the next carriage slammed behind him.

Trapped!

"Nooo...."

He turned back, hammered on the door not caring if this would attract more zombies, because they were already after him. Through the window, he could see Bex shouting at the Conductor.

"We need him," she mouthed.

"Come on," Dave shouted.

"Brains," said Bob behind Dave, "brains..."

Dave spun round to face his fellow teammate.

Bob was right there!

Dave stabbed with the hoe and the monster deflected it to one side and it jammed in the narrow tunnel.

The door opened behind him and he fell backwards.

The hoe pinned Bob in place as he stretched his arms out to grab the living.

The Conductor slammed the door on Dave's legs.

"Owww!" Dave pointed out.

Bex snatched at Dave's jacket and pulled him over the threshold

The door slammed and the Conductor secured it.

"Thank you," Dave said to an upside-down Bex. He rolled over to his hands and knees to stand.

"You're welcome."

"Yow two can get a room later," the Conductor said. "We've bay much time."

The display in this carriage confirmed it.

Welcome aboard this service to Five Ways
Next stop: Five Ways...

The train was slow, but not that slow.

After the quiet zone, this carriage was the moaning, wailing and screaming zone.

The Conductor led the way.

Two zombies squinted up from a bloody brunch, glowered and then staggered towards them.

112

Dave was defenceless.

'The Conductor handed Dave his brush.

"Thank you," Dave said.

Dave readied his weapon, experimentally flipping it over to see which end would be the deadliest, the bristles or the rounded top. Neither struck him as being particularly effective.

The door back to the quiet carriage didn't hold and disgorged more zombies, Bob included.

They understood doors.

The first zombie reached him, thank goodness trains were narrow and acting like the pass at Thermopylae. Except that they were only nine... eight of them and the zombies seemed countless... plus one.

Dave brushed.

The zombie seemed confused.

Dave poked.

The zombie seemed enraged.

Dave... ran away.

The Conductor blocked the escape route. The man took a drag of his roll-up, puffed an almighty cloud to obscure the no-smoking sign and then jabbed with his edging tool. The blade hit the zombie's windpipe and partially severed its head.

It dropped.

The Conductor used both hands on the end for the next one and dispatched it with two thrusts.

The edging tool was the weapon of choice, Dave could see that.

"We won't have long," the Conductor said. "Guy and I will 'old 'em off."

"I gave Dave the hoe," Guy said.

"Frank and I then. Yow stop the train."

True enough, more zombies struggled into the front carriage.

"Come on," Dave said to Monique.

"Oui, allons-y."

The others followed Dave's heroic lead of following the Conductor's instructions.

They reached the front of the train to find the heavy, locked and impregnable door to the driver's cab.

Frank tried the handle, but despite his strong arms the door didn't budge. "Where's the control to open the door?"

"It's locked from the other side," Bex said.

"Why?"

"In case someone tries to highjack the train."

"But it only goes to New Street and back."

They had to get through the door, but Axel – if he could pick the lock – was dead back in Bournville.

"Anyone know how to pick a lock?" Dave asked.

"I've played a thief," Jason said.

"And?"

"It was in a short film and it was one of those turning dial safes."

"And this door?"

"Sorry, no, beyond my range."

"Oh for–"

"Here," the surgeon said, "let me try."

"What," Dave snapped, "is the use of a *tree surgeon?*"

But the surgeon ignored him, stepped up to the door and took a chainsaw – an *f-ing chainsaw* – from his bag! He pulled the starter cord once, twice, and the thing growled into action. **Vrroo***OOOOOM* like a motorcycle engine revving up. The motor's roar filled the cramped space and any pretence of hiding evaporated.

The chainsaw made short work of the laminated heavy duty chipboard and the lock fell away.

"Why didn't you use that on zombies!" Dave shouted.

"And ruin the teeth!" the surgeon replied.

"What?"

"This is a precision instrument, designed for green wood, not for use on flesh and bone. And cleaning it afterwards will be a nightmare."

"And this isn't a nightmare?"

"No need to be so—"

"Just do it."

"You'll pay for new teeth?"

"Do it or we die!"

The zombie horde had pushed the Conductor and Frank backwards. There was little room left.

It went dark, suddenly and ominously, just as the cab door sprang open. The driver, red-eyed and crazed, lurched into the carriage.

"Brains, brains..."

Zombies on both sides!

"Brains, brains," muttered Bob.

"Merde, merde!" Monique yelled.

The train lurched to a halt throwing everyone forward. Of course, the undead had stepped off the dead man's pedal.

There was a struggle, spades and pruners and edging tools all clanging together. Dave grabbed the surgeon's arm and propelled him into the way. The chainsaw *vrroooOOOOOMM*ed and blood and tissue splattered everywhere.

"Fair enough," said the surgeon. He tested the weight of his superweapon and then expertly stepped into the approaching forest of zombies sawing left and right. Blood went everywhere like a ketchup bottle shaken without its lid. He severed spines, he smashed brains, he pulped bodies and he hacked them into tiny pieces. Zombies lost limbs, heads and entire torsos were chopped in half. They dropped like felled trees.

"Holy cow!" Dave said.

The lighting flickered reminding them of the darkness outside.

"We're in the tunnel," Frank said. "It's too late."

"Perhaps the carriages at the back aren't," Dave said.

So, they all went back through the train and the second carriage, the quiet zone, was brightly lit. After a moment, they whooped with delight.

They'd made it.

Five Ways was one stop short of New Street station and Birmingham's central district. All that remained was a short walk along Broad Street.

"What's the plan?" Dave asked.

"We get to the fortifications at Edgbaston village, then take the tram," the Conductor explained. "It smashes through owt."

"It goes all the way to New Street station."

"And beyond, but we get off long before New Street. Doe want to risk goin' anywhere near that station."

"No, I suppose not."

"First things first mind," said the Conductor. "Dave."

The Conductor led the way and Dave joined him at the door. The mechanism whined as the hydraulics hissed it open. Dave stuck his head out, and glanced right and left. There were a couple of shamblers way off – nothing the team couldn't manage. The stairs to his right led upwards towards street level.

"Do we–"

A hand nestled into the small of his back and pushed.

Dave stumbled out, minding the gap by falling onto the hard floor of the platform.

"What the–"

The Conductor loomed in the doorway. "We 'ave to clear the walkway, lad."

Dave saw the walkway now, a glass-walled metal bridge that led from Platform 1 to the exit above Platform 2. Within the blue-tinted safety glass, zombies massed and shifted, a horde moving his way.

"Yow clear the walkway," the Conductor said.

"How am I supposed to do that?"

"Run that way." The Conductor pointed back along the platform. "Yow might make it back to University.

116

Yow might not. Either way, they'll be chasing yow and our way'll be clear."

"You complete–"

"Tha's a good lad. We're a team, last in, first out."

"Now–"

"We always sacrifice someone to the zombies. It's spiritual. See, there's Tyrone and Mel and... there's little Nathan."

Dave saw Tyrone, Mel and little Nathan and dozens of others besides. So, he leapt to his feet and jumped towards the door.

But it hissed and slammed shut, leaving Dave standing on the platform alone.

"But we have a chainsaw!"

Behind the smeared windows, the Conductor shook his head slowly. He was right, Dave realised, even a chainsaw wouldn't be enough against the advancing tide.

"Oh for f–"

"Brains, brains..."

The zombies had come over the bridge and turned to shamble down the steps. The first few fell, other tumbling over them and the whole stinking, rotting mass rolled into a heap at the foot of the stairs. The lump writhed and twisted, its damaged limbs flailing and then the pile began to disentangle. Zombies gathered themselves up, heaved their broken bodies to their feet and their sunken eye sockets zeroed in on the living bait before them.

"Brains, brains..."

"Oh shit."

– INCIDENT –

←→↑→↕↗↖↔↜⊤↦↻ ∩↯↕↘ ↓↔
↖↟↘↕↩⅂, ↗←. ↕↕↕ ←↓↓ – ↑Ɫ↯
↗↙→↓↓←→↖, ↕↑↓↯↩↘ →Γ ↳ ↻↻
↓↑↕↕ ↓↕↓.

↻↘Ϛ↕↑←→↖↻

T'hayt-oo nodded to himself, an odd movement that always felt unnatural, but he'd picked it up in the years he'd been here. The reactivated natives shuffled along the tarmac line, hunting and slobbering.

T'hat-oo's head felt loose.

He should have it fixed, but they weren't going to be on Earth for much longer. It was an awkward disguise. He had originally thought these creatures were outstanding marvels of evolution. They had, after all, shins and calves of the right length and joints that bent to right angles, which meant they could sit for long periods at their computers. However, upon reflection, they needed two hands to operate a keyboard and another for their mouse, so they were an upper limb short.

Some of these pests screamed and ran past him using their 'designed for sitting' legs. They had no chance as, at long last, the plan – the latest plan – was working.

This was excellent as the first eight had been hopeless.

They had unleashed the three B'toothant of the V'K'ag. These were K'pak, K'panoth and K'poot.

The very names caused a shiver of fear, except that, in the local language, they translated as War, Pestilence and Cost of Living.

T'hayt-oo shook his head – it wobbled.

War and Pestilence were decent translations, but 'Cost of Living' or, possibly, 'Economic Collapse' was just awful. It was a sign that these creatures weren't that intelligent. With all that sitting down, you'd have thought they'd have done some thinking.

Plan 1 had been War, a global conflict, and the creatures had thrown themselves into it with gusto, cleverness and remarkable stupidity. Millions of the things wiped out trying to wipe the other lot out. Marvellous, until they'd just stopped. Weird.

Plan 2 had been Pestilence, a nasty influenza strain, genetically manipulated, that these creatures had called 'Spanish'. They had released it after the war and it had killed far more than the conflict had. It had looked promising, but the creatures had worn masks and been careful.

Plan 3 had been the evil of Cost of Living – it was embarrassing – with a stock market collapse, but the effects of this had merely lasted the decade of what the creatures had called the 1930s.

So, the three B'toothant were unleashed again.

Plan 4 had been a second War, worse than before, and this had even reached the crescendo of nuclear fission and fusion explosions, but then it had just stopped. Irritating.

Plan 5 had been Pestilence again, which had been named locally as 'Asian 'flu'.

Plan 6 was to have been another War. Yes, they were repeating themselves, but this one would have included total nuclear Armageddon. However – and T'hayt-oo felt like using the b-word – the creatures had talked to each other with their floppy mouths and their pointy fingers.

Plan 7 had been Famine, thwarted by pop songs and concerts. This hadn't even been a traditional B'toothant of the V'K'ag, but such had been Commander Q't'yan's desperation to get something, anything, to work.

Eighth was Climate Change, which was going to make such a mess of the place and there'd be a lot of cleaning up to do post-invasion – needs must. Luckily, the creatures had dutifully pumped carbon dioxide and worse into their atmosphere to turn off its life support capabilities. They'd done this for... what was it again? Oh yes, currency, lying and cheating each other to be rich at the cost of their own survival.

And it had worked!

But so slowly and there were even signs that the creatures were realising. They were – he nearly used the b-word again – recycling... hateful.

So, finally, Plan 9 – they'd used the Reanimator Ray.

The creatures he was watching were running the other way now. It was funny to see them trying to increase their velocity on those two legs, the top-heavy p'zootons.

"Ha-ha, run, run," T'hayt-oo shouted, and then, he added in his own tongue, "K'laatu b'arada ni k'to!"

He looked forward to writing his final report describing these daft beings and their final demise. He had a particularly pithy closing sentence in mind, poetic with all the final arrows pointing downwards.

"Brains... brains..." said a nearby creature.

Ha, stupid p'zooton, and it did need brains as it was its own stupid fault – and the Reanimator Ray, of course, that had led to its b'hoo-vo k'spoot and...

"No, no..." T'hayt-oo shouted as the undead p'zooton bit into his neck and his head fell off. Dying, he screamed at the top of his acoustic range, "B'rex-*it!!!*"

– 14 –

What I'm really looking for is a bit of
forgiveness.

Statement from an ex-minister, now celebrity

The very important person strode over the roof as the
helicopter rose into the sky. The downdraft caught his
heavy, woollen coat and flapped it about like the wings of a
dark angel. His head shone, his bald pate at once glowing
and recognizable.

"I am the Right Honourable Fenton-Briggs," he said,
"and I have arrived."

"Sir, I... er..." Matt said as he tugged at his hair.

"Yes, thank you. My case."

"Er... yes." Matt scurried off to collect the suitcase.
The two gasmask-wearing soldiers ignored him.

"Mr Fenton-Briggs," Dawn said.

"That's me," he saw her for the first time, looked her
up and down, lingering as he savoured her hips, waist and
chest. "Please, you can call me Neil."

"I'm Dawn... er, Miss Dey."

"Ah, Miss Day."

"Dey with an 'E'," Dawn replied, pleased that she was
known in such high circles.

"Day Withany."

"That's it."

Matt returned, struggling with the suitcase.

"Mister Fenton-Briggs," Matt said. "I'm George Matt
and I have a grievance."

Dawn's heart sank. "Perhaps not on the roof."

"I couldn't see my wife when she went into hospital," Matt continued.

"I understand and empathise with your situation," Fenton-Briggs replied.

"Or my brother when he was turned."

"We've all made sacrifices."

"And you seem to think it's fine to stand around drinking champagne."

"Since Brexit, it's Prosecco."

"Ah-ha."

"Like I said, we've all made sacrifices."

One of the faceless soldiers returned.

"Perimeter secure, sir."

Dawn glanced around the top of the roof. She could clearly see in those few moments that there were only eight of them on the roof.

"Let's go downstairs," Fenton-Briggs said.

"Sir." The man was a man of action and so he immediately discovered that he didn't know how to go downstairs. "Sir?"

"It's this way," Dawn said and she led them to the ladder. It looked a long way down, far scarier than when she'd climbed up. Going down involved both looking down and going towards the zombies.

"You! Case," Fenton-Briggs said.

"It's George, not Hugh."

"Pardon."

"Mister Anderson is Hugh, I'm George, George Matt."

"Really."

The two faceless soldiers went first, followed by Ahmed, Rob and Pete, all wanting to show how efficient they were.

Dawn realised that she was still holding her phone. On the dating app, a dot dithered on the map – Five Ways station. She looked across the buildings south and thought she could see Five Ways. He was there, or more likely, his zombie was there, undead and tethered by a recharging cable to a plug socket.

As she put her phone away, she shook her head. It wasn't like some knight in shining armour was going to come and save her, was it? But she could dream, she supposed.

"After you," Fenton-Briggs said to Dawn.

"Thank you."

Dawn struggled to turn properly to get her heels down onto the rungs of the ladder. She tried one way and then succeeded another. She took each rung one at a time leading with her right leg. Fenton-Briggs's handmade patent leather shoes were only a few rungs higher and, despite the man clearly having enjoyed a few business breakfasts, all-expenses paid lunches and charity dinners, he was spritely.

Dawn had to keep moving to avoid having her finger trodden on.

Once they were on the level down, they joined the others by the door that led into the building.

"Er... excuse me." Matt barely made his voice heard. He was still on the higher roof area.

Dawn mimed an exaggerated shrug at him.

"I can't get the case down," Matt shouted back.

"He could chuck it," Rob suggested.

"I could chuck you," the Minister replied.

"We could lower it with rope," Ahmed said.

"Got any?" Fenton-Briggs asked.

"I think there's some in Stores 3," Dawn said.

"One of you will have to come back for it."

"Well... that might be dangerous."

"Yes," the Minister agreed. "Miss Day-Withany."

"It's—"

"There are two types of people," Fenton-Briggs continued. "This zombie apocalypse is a reckoning. Yes, a reckoning for all of us. Do we live or just exist?"

"Live," Dawn said.

"You are one of us, then, rather than one of them."

"Thank you."

Fenton-Briggs glanced across the Birmingham skyline. "Hard to believe there's an apocalypse on."

With that, he went through the door and down the stairs.

Dawn followed the others.

Matt's plaintive cry was cut short when the door closed.

Speaking softly to Dawn, Ahmed said, "Best not think about it."

Dawn didn't want to.

Quite a few people didn't.

So many didn't believe, or want to believe, that there was a full-scale zombie apocalypse. This refusal wasn't countered by any evidence like the many videos that had appeared online.

In the early days, these had gone viral.

A lot of these clips showed people tormenting some poor zombie, pushing them over with sticks or painting rude words on their backs.

These were early shamblers, of course.

Others jumped on the bandwagon.

Tim_Amazing438 of Exeter famously live-streamed attacking a zombie in the town centre followed by a live-stream of him being attacked by zombies and ending with an 11-hour live-stream of him attacking innocent people.

He had met a party of early ramblers.

This episode proved to be controversial, not least because the camera angle was bad and the lens had blood all over it for most of the time. An American republican, Rev Marcus Zimmaldi, declared it to be fake. He went on to hire a video effects company to fake a similar video, so that he could reveal that it too was fake. To save money, and to meet the tight deadline, the effects company pushed a member of staff out of the fire exit with a camera strapped to his forehead. They then gave the subsequent footage a pass through a filter, so that it looked fake.

The Rev Marcus Zimmaldi presented this indisputable evidence to his congregation, who didn't listen and ripped him to shreds. His position on gun ownership didn't appear to have helped him much either.

He had preached to those converted; unfortunately converted into early joggers.

However, despite this, many continued to believe it was a government conspiracy, something dreamt up by those in the Big Four of the Illuminati with 'cosmic clearance' from their base in Area 51.

In the UK, it was all the work of MI5 and the Milk Marketing Board to secretly import zombies into the country hidden in boatloads of illegal immigrants. It had to be the case, it had to be deliberate, because even the British government couldn't be that incompetent, surely?

Despite being able to see, with their own eyes, the zombies shuffling down the streets, these conspiracy theorists claimed they were affected by contrail chemicals, 5G masts, the MMR jab or that the zombies were actors.

If the truth be told, some of them were actors – quite famous ones too – method acting as slavering monsters, arms out straight and "brains" upon their slavering lips.

As Dawn descended – jumping out of her skin every time the two soldiers fired their guns – she glanced at the various CCTV cameras wondering if the Councillor and Mr Anderson were watching. They'd surely be interested to know that the minister was here.

And Mr Matt wasn't.

– 15 –

TAKE A DEEP BREATH
RETREAT SLOWLY
SAVE YOUR LIFE

Government advice

"Let me in, let me in!"

Dave banged the glass of the door with the palms of his hands.

The Conductor paused in the act of licking his roll-up to shrug back. He tilted his leather hat back and mouthed, 'Best run,' with a nod south.

"For pity's..."

Dave turned away and sprinted down the platform, running between the train and the posters for no longer best-selling novels.

The overhead roof was held up by metal columns and Dave had to dodge around these to avoid the shamblers. It was the ramblers – he risked a glance behind him – and joggers – *shit* – that worried him. The platform stretched ahead curving gently to the right. It was long, he'd never seen one as long, but then, when the raised tarmac and paved edging ran out, what was he supposed to do?

Outpace the joggers?

They didn't tire.

And Dave was already shattered.

He needed his second coffee of the day.

He hadn't even finished his first.

Where was his cup-for-life!?

He'd thrown it at a zombie.

He reached the back of the train.

Barely slowing down, he turned off the platform and jumped down onto the track.

Don't touch the electric rail, don't touch... there wasn't one. It was overhead cables.

He tripped over a non-electric rail, stumbled and bruised his hands, and then he ran back along the train on the outbound track, trying to land on the sleepers. His stride meant he missed every third step and he felt the crunch of the stony ballast.

A plan was forming.

It involved staying at home and never going out again.

He reached the cab end.

The door to the driving compartment was open. He jumped up, slipped, bashed his shin against the protruding metal step, but then paused in his angry panic long enough the get his toe on the plate and haul himself into the driver's compartment.

Ha!

The body of the ex-undead driver, now a headless corpse, lay where it had fallen back into the cab.

In front of him were levers, switches and buttons.

Where was the steering wheel?

Oh, of course.

But which one was the 'go' control?

They were labelled – incredible.

So he turned a lever from 'stop' into the 'slow' area.

Nothing happened.

Oh for... go, go, *go!*

It wouldn't.

Why not?

Stupid, stupid, stupid thing!

Ah, deadman's pedal.

Dave – oh, disgusting – pulled the dead man off the deadman's pedal and put his living foot down hard.

The train whined and complained and lurched forward into the tunnel ahead... and stopped. Dave eyeballed everything at once: there had to be a clutch, gearstick, hyperspace button, something he had missed.

There was a scream, so loud he heard it through the closed window.

Now it was the Conductor's turn to bang on a door.

"Dave, Dave! Yow cor go down the tunnel!" he yelled.

"Watch me," Dave said, turning to face the utter bastard who had tried to kill him. He glared at the closed door so hard and viciously that some of his hatred must have penetrated.

"We'll be trapped between the zombies at Five Ways and... oh God, man, New Street station!"

Dave went back to the controls, figured a few things out and the train jerked ahead – this time it kept going. Clattering further into the dark tunnel.

The door burst open. It had been chainsawed to bits after all.

The Conductor raised his edging tool.

Dave dodged aside. His foot came off the pedal and the train came to a sudden halt. Everyone was thrown forwards. The Conductor fell awkwardly to the floor, so Dave was able to snatch up the edging tool. It felt good, better than *Brainbiter* – *Brainbiter 2.0,* then.

"Mine, I think," Dave said.

"Yow've killed us all," the Conductor said.

"Piss off."

"Merde, merde, vous les anglais êtes si stupides."

"What do we do?" Bex said. She looked to Dave with her big eyes and Dave felt important.

"We can't go back," Dave said, "so we go on."

Dave slammed his foot down on the pedal and turned the speed control. The train lurched forward, its electric gears whining. If he could just get the stupid thing to go faster than five miles an hour, perhaps they could smash the train through to New Street.

But the metal squealed and something struck the front window. A screech nailed across a blackboard, followed by a terrible crunching sound, a juddering and finally a pranging.

It stopped.

He'd crashed the train into some barrier.

"The train's buggered," Frank said.

It seemed to be. They'd hit something.

"We walk," Dave said.

This elicited a variety of opinions: "You have to be kidding!", "Nooooo....." and "Nonnnnn..."

Dave grabbed a kit bag stowed in the driver's cab. As he'd expected and hoped, it had a couple of torches for just such emergencies.

"Come on," he said, decisively.

He'd dropped one torch by the time he'd clambered out and jumped down. He hit the gravel below and pitched forward into the brick wall. He felt the soot and dirt smear across his face and suit.

"Bugger."

In front of the train, mangled by the impact, was a wall of metal sheets, lengths of twisted gantry, iron bars and office chairs, all hurriedly welded together. Dave swept the torch around to find a way around, but the only way to the other side would be to climb it.

"Careful of the electric rail," Frank said.

"Which is the live rail?" Guy asked, looking around as if he was suddenly standing in a minefield.

"There isn't one," Bex said.

Dave relaxed; she knew about trains after all.

He got the torch working and shone the beam about. They were in a brick-built tunnel, a marvel of Victorian engineering, but it seemed dark, dank and claustrophobic.

But Dave was not afraid of the dark – much.

Instead, he suffered from full-blown kinemortophobia, which was a fear of zombies and there were loads of them shuffling towards them at the limit of the torch's light.

129

The barrier extended across both rails, so they clambered up the bits of metal and debris. It would slow the zombies down, but the monsters had their scent and the train had created gaps and damage.

Once they got to the top, Dave checked that his mask was secure.

"This barricade was built to stop zombies using the tunnel," Frank observed. He rubbed his finger along his bent nose.

Dave shook his head. While he had been furloughed, drinking Pimm's on the patio and living off his hoard of panic-bought Brexit supplies, others had been fighting for their lives.

"They didn't want them getting into Birmingham," Bex said.

"Nah," Frank said, "stop 'em getting out. You can see by the way the thing's built."

"Stop them getting out," Guy said, pointing into the gloom, "but that would mean there are more of them this side."

The tunnel led away into a dark unknown.

The others clambered up to join Dave, Frank and Bex on top of the barrier. They moved only when Dave shone his light near them and they could see the handholds and footholds. In the pitch, their clothing became dull. Guy's tracksuit was black and grey, and Bex's outfit lost its sparkle.

Should they go on to New Street or backtrack to Five Ways?

"Yow can't get rid of maey," the Conductor shouted down as he climbed out of the train. "Ye need maey. Ye won't survive without maey."

"I wasn't going to survive with you," Dave shouted back. The others with him looked away.

"T'was only one to save hundreds."

"There are seven of us," Dave said, deliberately not counting the Conductor.

"I've led hundreds into Brum-a-jum."

"And sacrificed how many?"

The Conductor looked up at him. "One a day, sometimes two. Fair trade."

"So," Dave said, summing up, "you sacrificed hundreds to save the same few every time."

"Gotta go to work, gotta keep the wheels of commerce and industry running."

"Piss off."

Bex touched Dave on the arm. "We need him."

"Then he goes centre forward," Dave said.

The Conductor climbed up. "Arl need–"

"Nope."

Dave gave him the brush.

The Conductor set off clambering down into the pool of torchlight. The others followed.

Dave glanced at the shamblers working around the train. Time to be *Stayin' Alive*, he thought.

He checked his phone. Ominous red dots lumbered along in a line quite at odds with the streets and pavements on the map. The zombies from Five Ways were drawing near. Further on, there were no dots, no green pixels fleeing from red blobs.

It was like pacman with the ghosts gobbling up the big mouth to make other ghosts.

He swung the phone around like a tricorder.

"There's nothing ahead," he said, his voice undecided between hope and fear.

"'Course ay," the Conductor said. "Nay 5G signal down 'ere, yow numpty."

"Why would that..." Dave trailed off in his objection. He knew why. None of the microchips injected into people's arms during the Tag-and-Track programme would work outside the safe 5G cell of a phone mast. The heat of a living body powered it transmitting to say 'green dot here'. When a person became undead, the microchip

131

detected the state of decay, the same putrefaction that powered it, and so it became 'red dot' on the display.

Why did all those morons burn down the masts?

"Why now-one risks the tunnels," the Conductor said.

"But it worked on the train," Dave said.

"Train's got free wifi."

"Oh."

"But there were lots of false negatives and true... you know what I mean," Bex said.

"And all those who wouldn't have the jab."

"Just so selfish."

"Bloody anti-vaccers," Dave said under his breath.

Frank appeared at Dave's shoulder. "We should get moving."

"New Street," Dave said glancing into the forbidding darkness of the tunnel, "or Five Ways?"

As he looked back, he saw a few undead passengers stumbling towards them and more zombified commuters spilling out of the front carriage.

"Like yow gave us a choice," the Conductor said.

"But you said New Street was dangerous," Lucy bleated.

"Yeah, I did." The Conductor set off, not looking back. Of course, he didn't have to, Dave realised, as he'd know soon enough if there were any joggers amongst the zombies when the rest of them started screaming for help.

"Come on, it can't be far," Jason said. "I've played a leading man."

The actor set off into the gloom overtaking the Conductor, but then a bright flash illuminated everything with a sharp angry discharge and the tunnel filled with the ethereal perfume of ozone and the earthy reek of burnt pork.

Jason found one of the non-existent live rails.

Dave crept closer, shining his light forward.

Jason jerked, flickers of electricity burning his legs and arms.

Lucy leapt forward.

"No!" Dave caught her just in time. "He's dead."

"But—"

"Touch him and you'll get a shock too."

"There's no live rail," Bex insisted.

Dave shone his torch up and around, showing everyone where the overhead electrical cables had come down. The comforting circle of illumination came back to poor Jason. His body twitched with 750 volts and then with the hideous effect of reanimation.

"Didn't he play a body in *Casualty?*" Denzel said.

"In the limelight now," Frank added.

"That's awful," Bex said.

"One star then."

"Et alors il y en n'avait que sept," Monique said.

"Brains, brai – *bzzzt!* – ains..." Jason mumbled.

"But he wasn't bitten," Bex said, "and he's turned."

Frank started to explain, "The virus–"

"We don't know it's a virus."

"Or whatever, is airborne, so any dead body comes back."

"But the government said..."

"The government say a lot of things," Dave said. He took hold of Bex's hand feeling guilty. He had, after all, actually written a lot of what the government had said in catchy three liners.

"Perhaps it was only the electricity reanimated him?"

"That's Frankenstein," Dave said and he tugged her away from the horror that was Jason, singed and burnt, and staggering to his feet.

They ran away with short awkward strides as they stepped from one railway sleeper to the next, unsure whether to take them two or three at a time. Each step took them deeper into the unknown, a zone so lacking in light that even the Tag-and-Track indicators were absent.

A mere patch of torchlight showed the way, until some took their phones out. They made bright, blazing light as if they were attending a rock concert in a bleak underground music venue.

The moaning for brains echoed behind them as if the zombies were multiplying – they probably were.

Like a rush of wind, a howling sound funnelled through the tunnels.

"That's not a zombie," Dave muttered.

"New variant?" Bex said, a catch in her voice.

"Werewolf," Guy said.

"Doe be a numpty," the Conductor replied. "Tha's ridiculous."

"Why is that ridiculous," Guy replied. "It's no more ridiculous than zombies."

"Maybe our world in the multiverse gets zombies," Lucy said. "And in a parallel world, it's werewolves and in another, vampires."

"Vampires! Honestly," the Conductor said.

"Why not?"

"How would yow get vampires?"

"I don't know," Guy said. "Maybe... ah-ha, a virus. There are bat viruses that start in China. There was SARS-CoV in 2002 and MERS-CoV in 2012, so we were due for another in 2022. It's late... or perhaps it's already with us."

"But instead, we got zombies."

"So, in another universe, there's a pandemic of some CoV and everyone's infected."

"Makes sense."

"Except it's a bat virus," Guy said, "so victims take on bat powers – you know, wings, biting necks for blood, only coming out at night, that sort of thing – and the survivors in that world are fighting vampires."

"There'll be a world infected by mummies, invisible men, giant ants... you know," Bex said. "We're lucky."

"This is lucky?" Denzel said.

Bex nodded, an energetic up-and-down motion like a demented wobble head.

"Can't argue with that," Dave said.

"No," Frank agreed, "'cos it's stupid."

They moved on, content to be fleeing only zombies.

"Look," Bex said. She pointed.

Dave shone the beam ahead.

"No, turn it off," Bex added.

Dave did so.

Ahead, Dave could make out a smudge of ethereal light like a twinkle of fairy light.

"What is it?" Frank asked.

"It's light at the end of the tunnel," Bex said.

"Knowing our luck," Frank said, "it's an oncoming train."

The light turned out to be the light in the middle of the tunnel. They each stepped into the bright patch and gazed upwards in wonder.

Dave did too.

He winced and held up his hand to shield himself from the sunlight. The brick archways opened to the vivid blue sky.

"We could climb out," he said.

"How?" the Conductor said.

Dave continued to check the walls, so high and sheer, and realised that it was impossible. Even so, the opening promised escape. The foliage above, gripping the cracks, made it seem like a bountiful paradise, a Babylon's Garden hanging from above.

A pigeon cooed with that heavy Brummie accent.

At least it wasn't a crow. Crows had done very well out of the walking corpses.

Dave sat down, his limbs buckling before his backside settled on the black-stained stones. It was like when the coffee in his system dropped below the level of buzzing. It had been adrenaline and it had run out.

Automatically, he got out his phone and checked for a signal – no bars. He was in a tunnel, after all. Few places had a good signal after the first days of the apocalypse.

There had been a theory that the 5G towers spread zombie-ism, so mobs had been out burning down the towers. As they'd gathered around the pyres, they'd found they weren't able to post about their valiant efforts to save everyone on social media. Something to do with having no signal. And their noise had attracted zombies and then mobs had turned upon themselves after the first few bites.

Dave grimaced.

In a way, the 5G network had spread the disaster with the conspiracy theory on social media and the believers gathering in such numbers by the towers.

It was late, they'd lost time, and he'd never get into the office for 09:00. More like 9:30, but that was OK. He'd still be able to have a coffee and check his emails before the meeting. That wasn't until 11:00 – plenty of time.

He checked his other apps. So many memorialised on Facebook... and found himself staring at the photo of Dawn_372 – she looked good. Out of his league, certainly, but he could dream. He could also wonder if she was still alive and what her laugh sounded like.

"Who be that?" The Conductor was standing nearby, staring.

"Dunno..."

"Lovely dark 'air. Makes 'er mysterious. Wench'll be jed... walkin' around 'ere somewhere."

"She doesn't move from Newhall Street."

"Jed then."

Dave held his phone against his chest to keep this Dawn safe within the glass, but he knew in his heart that her blob on the screen never moved. It was merely her phone eking out the last of its battery power or it was connected to the mains or a solar panel or she was just a glitch in the system.

"Time to get moving," said Frank.

"Yeah, coming," Dave said.

"Let's get on," Frank said to the others.

"Oui, c'est l'heure de partir," Monique added.

"We could go back," Bex suggested.

"Non, absolument pas. Nous avons déjà dépassé la moitié du chemin."

"Wim in blood, stepped in so far that should we wade no more," the Conductor said. "Returnin' am as tedious as goin' o'er."

Dave felt the hairs on his neck prickle as if a bucket of ice was about to cascade down his shirt collar. "Eh?"

"*Macbeth*, somewhere in the middle."

"I don't care what Macbeth says somewhere in the middle."

"It means we've passed the middle," Bex explained. "To go on is as easy as going back."

"Or as difficult," Dave agreed.

"Look," Frank said, "there's certain death behind us if we try and go back to Five Ways."

"Whereas to go on means we get to New Street station and you know the reputation that has for infections," Bex said.

"Oh great," Dave said. "Let's go. It's... er, more tedious to stand around here arguing."

Dave took a last look at the sky. If he could just take off, then he could fly away from everything. Soar upwards like all those superheroes into the clouds– accepting that he'd somehow get over his fear of heights – and zoom off into the sunset to land on some uninhabited island (which would, therefore, be zombie-free) to settle down with... well, it wouldn't be completely uninhabited. He'd find someone there walking on the sand by the ocean, someone with whom he could be alive.

Dawn_372, perhaps.

But after staring upwards, the tunnel appeared darker, sucking out all hope, foreboding and–

Lucy shrieked.

"What! What?" Dave said, running over with the edging tool at the ready.

"Bloody drip went down the back of my neck."

Dave spent a few moments slowing his breathing down as Lucy adjusted her long scarf to seal the gap.

They moved on silently, each step taking them further from the pursuing shamblers and closer to the horror that was Birmingham's city centre. It had been a nightmare before the apocalypse, crammed full of shoppers, browsers and type 2b variant bargain hunters.

An eerie glow appeared ahead, but this one wasn't bright sunshine of hopeful days, but rather the artificial, flickering illumination designed to create shadows and dark places. Dave turned the torch away and then off. Its comforting beam vanished.

The brick tunnel curved and opened out to reveal the open rails of many converging tracks that led into the forbidding caves of the underground station.

They'd made it.

They'd actually made it.

All the way through the tunnels and now into the light at the end. The last of the darkness hung on as if trying to tug them back, but it was just the open area to cross, a few more steps into the neon and LED light of the vast station auditorium.

The Conductor took a drag on his smoke. "Now yow troubles really start."

16

We're in this together, right up to here.

Prime Minister's Questions

"Sergeant, what you got?" Ahmed asked one of the soldiers. Dawn saw the three stripes on his shoulder epaulette for the first time.

"Heckler and Koch MP5, the Glock 17M and stun grenades," the evil-looking sergeant replied, his voice Vaderesque behind his gas mask.

"Oh cool," Pete said.

"Could we borrow one of yours?" Ahmed asked.

"No," the sergeant replied.

"If we're to help... and we've only got one cartridge for the single shotgun."

"Oh, for... give him your Glock."

The other soldier handed over his sidearm.

"Remember," the soldier said, "there are smart soldiers and casual soldiers. They become smarties or casualties."

"I know, I know," Ahmed said. "Can I borrow your holster?"

If the soldier's eyes rolled behind his gas mask, the anonymous, tinted giant eyes did not reveal it.

Ahmed pranced about in the big equipment belt and practised drawing the black handgun a few times.

Then they continued downstairs, round and round, with the sergeant and the soldier leading. The progress consisted of sudden movements and pauses, which was agony on Dawn's ankles and she so wanted to take off her heels.

Ahmed, Rob and Pete took up the rear after a brief argument about whose turn it was with the shotgun. Rob won.

Rat-a-tat TAT-TAT-TAT.

"Eeek!" Dawn cried out.

Zombies spun from the impacts and dropped on the stairs.

"Good, aren't they?" Fenton-Briggs said.

"Yes," Dawn agreed.

"Pat's a chef and Donnie does origami."

"Oh, really. That's nice."

They reached the ground floor.

A zombie lurched out behind them.

Ahmed expertly drew the Glock like one of the best cowboys ever, fumbled it and then failed to fire it.

"Cock it, you dick," the soldier yelled.

"Oh. Yeah," Ahmed replied. He cocked the gun.

Rob fired the shotgun.

BOOM.

Pete screamed, his shoulder peppered with pellets, and then Ahmed fired the handgun. It took him three shots – **BANG, BANG-BANG** – to get his aim in and then he hit the zombie in the centre of its forehead.

Pete lay on the floor, holding his neck.

"Bad luck," the sergeant said. He aimed with his automatic.

"No, no," Dawn shouted. "We have to save his life."

The sergeant looked at her with those big black eyes.

"Mr Fenton-Briggs," Dawn said. "We have to try."

"Good idea," Fenton-Briggs said. "Someone try."

The sergeant's breath rasped in his gas mask filter, but he did take out a first aid kit. This, he handed to Rob.

"I'm not trained in first aid," Rob said.

"Me neither," Ahmed admitted. "Dawn?"

"The duty first aider is... Pete," Dawn said.

"Oh."

They looked down at Pete.

The man held his neck, keeping pressure on the wound. "I'm... I'm," he sputtered, keeping the patient talking and trying to focus on staying awake. He didn't, his eyes rolled upwards until he looked dead, then he spasmed and died.

The sergeant stepped up with his automatic.

"Please, don't," Dawn said.

Pete's body jerked as he began to turn.

The sergeant took aim.

Dawn looked away, but she jumped when the – **BANG** – detonated.

No-one said anything as they went down through the basement levels leaving Pete without so much as taking a collection for his leaving present.

17

If you stare into the darkness, the darkness
stares back at you. You can't see this, of
course, Frederick, because it's dark.

Nietzsche's friend, Richter

A mess of twisted metal greeted them as they reached the
end of the tunnel. New Street station lay ahead with
numerous tracks converging on the many platforms with
the sky above. They had to cross this well-lit zone. No
problem as such.

A voice called to them, siren-like.

"Please leave the station by the nearest available exit."

Dave led the small band of survivors along the track.
He bent down, his feet scrunching on the black stained
stones between the sleepers as he kept lower than the
platform. They appeared like heads bobbing along.

Did they dare go up onto the platform?

They had to.

Dave chose a spot as good as any other.

"Please leave the station by the nearest available exit."

He put the edging tool on the bumps of the edge
flagstones and hauled himself up. He rolled on the white
letters 'MIND THE GAP' and came up onto his toes.

"What can you see?" Bex whispered.

"Shhh," Dave replied.

He couldn't see any danger as such but he wanted to
listen. The station was eerie, quiet – too quiet? – and the–

"Please leave the station by the nearest available exit."

...the automatic voice wouldn't shut up.

The lighting had failed in places. Within the general gloom, cones of illumination showed him distant parts of the station. The low ceiling made the space claustrophobic and yet the cavernous quality had that agoraphobic stomach lurch.

Platform 12 was the highest number.

"Please leave the station by the nearest available exit."

He would love to leave by the nearest available exit, if only the stupid woman would say which exit was available. Every platform had escalators, stairs and lifts galore, but which were available–

"Please leave the station by the nearest available exit."

...and which were death traps?

Platform 11 and 10 seemed illuminated – that had to be a patch of 8, maybe – and then slices of the rest like some strange Escher print. How could zombies have smashed the lights when they just shambled about and the LEDs were suspended from the ceiling?

"Please leave the station by the nearest available exit."

He tilted his head to one side and closed his eyes.

The others panted for breath below his feet.

An escalator hummed.

Something shuffled.

A moan.

A far-distant refrain for brains.

Or maybe they were saying 'trains', which–

"Please leave the station by the nearest available exit."

Could it be as simple as taking platform 12's exit?

He signalled.

They all clambered up onto the stone paving, crouched over the white 'MIND THE GAP' lettering and then stepped gingerly over the yellow line.

Dave led them to the nearest escalator: a down and they needed to go up, but it wasn't running. The large steel steps were still, frozen in place by a power failure or more likely someone had pressed the emergency stop button.

Dave wished there was an emergency stop button for this whole apocalyptic mess.

Disturbingly–

"Please leave the station by the nearest available exit."

...disturbingly, there was blood smeared on the metal and dragged under the metal floor plate. It was a single escalator built as if the architect had realised that anyone travelling to, say, Bournville would never want to return to Birmingham.

Dave turned to the others and whispered, "Let's–"

"Please leave the station by the nearest available exit."

"...leave by the nearest available exit."

Halfway up, where the step lost its bloody stains and returned to its more natural chewing gum patina, Dave crouched.

"What is it?" Frank whispered.

"Shhh..."

"Please leave the station by the nearest available exit."

Something moved, a shape or shadow at the top of the escalator, an ephemeral spectre of movement interested only in one thing.

"Brains."

"Please leave the station by the nearest available exit."

Dave had the edging tool, his *Brainbiter 2.0.* He had his brothers-and-sisters-in-arms, even if they had used him as bait in a diversion. But, if it went south, he would fall over his backup in his panic to escape.

And yet, would any other way out be any safer?

"Don't bunch up," Dave suggested quietly.

He took another giant step – why were escalator steps so huge? – and then another, slowly rising faster than his survival instinct could hunker him down. He rose high enough for the emergency announcement became confined to the dark depths.

"Please leave... by the... exit."

The voice sounded increasingly ghostly and desperate.

Please... exit.

Grand Central, the name of the shopping centre above the station, promised to be bright and airy, and full of the joys of the buying experience. Pity it was full of corpses, but the stench of death masked out most of the pong from the perfume counters.

He was glad of his mask.

Some of the corpses staggered around Yo! Sushi, Tapas Revolution, Caffè Concerto, Frizzenti and a Pret looking for something to eat.

"Brains, brains, brains..."

"I used to get a latte there," Bex said.

"Let's not," Dave said.

"Que j'envie d'un verre du rouge," Monique added.

There were ticket barriers dividing the station from the shopping experience. They were closed. Sometimes they were all open and no-one checked for tickets, but today some idiot had closed the gates as if having a valid ticket was important in a world gone to shit.

Dave panicked – wait, it was all right; he had his ticket and his return.

Wait! Where the hell was his Q2 report?

To hell with it. He could remember a brief summary of its finding – it was bad, it was all bad.

No, it was there in his inside pocket.

Dave fished out the precious rectangles of card.

His hand shook – he wasn't proud – as he slipped the outward ticket into the slot.

The gate sprang open letting him through and then, with a clunk of finality, it closed like giant jaws behind him.

Grand Central's massive auditorium, a cathedral space consecrated to the worship of avarice, hummed with the murmurs of the undead as if hundreds of worshippers knew the plainsong.

He tried to slow his breathing in his mask.

Dave couldn't help thinking he was on the wrong side.

With a loud, reverberating clunk, Frank came next. Bex, the Conductor, Denzel, Lucy, and finally Monique followed, but Guy stayed on the other side.

That made eight... shit, they'd lost someone!

Oh wait, Dave hadn't counted himself.

"I don't have a ticket," Guy whispered.

"Ssss..." Dave hissed.

"There's never an inspector these days," Bex said.

"These end of days?" Frank said.

"No," Bex corrected, "these days since the cuts."

They helped Guy over the barriers, a surprisingly subversive act.

"What do we do now?" Guy whispered.

Dave over-exaggerated a shrug.

A crowd of zombies stared upwards at the departure board. Despite the lack of scrolling yellow text, it held their fascination. Others stood aside staring at battery-flat phones or at their rotting palms. It looked disturbingly normal.

Could Dave and his team sneak past behind them?

"We could pretend to be zombies," Denzel said.

"Eh?" Dave said, wondering why he was now in charge. He glanced around. The Conductor wasn't with them. He counted... seven, plus himself.

He should have counted them on the train or in the tunnel. He had no idea how many hadn't made it this far. Some leader he was turning out to be.

"We disguise ourselves as zombies and sneak out?" Denzel said.

"What!" Lucy said. "Where would we get the make-up and false blood."

"There are loads of make-up shops here," Guy said.

"That would be upstairs past all the zombies," Bex pointed out.

"Well..."

"And what about fake blood?"

"Ketchup."

"Cover ourselves with tomato sauce," Bex said. "I'd rather die."

"Both of you, listen," Lucy insisted. "We don't need any of that. Just hold your phone thus, take a coffee cup and adopt a vacant expression."

"Faisons quelque chose," Monique added, "plutôt que de rester sur place à bavarder."

"Shh," Dave said. "Look, everyone, let's stop yakking and get on."

"Bien," Monique said, "parce que je dois parler au ministre de la résilience, du calme et du courage. C'est urgent. Sinon, il pourrait faire quelque chose de terrible. Encore une fois."

He checked the concourse again. Most of the shuffling corpses had their phones in one hand and many also had a coffee cup in the other. They all had vacant expressions and blood smeared down their chins.

"Why has no-one done this before?" he asked, suspiciously.

"Because most people scream and run," Frank added.

"Yes," Dave said, remembering all the times today that he'd already screamed and run.

So they all took out their phones, ferreted in the bins for Costa or a Starbucks, and then followed Lucy.

Guy had a question, "Do we say br–"

"No."

So, they shuffled onwards like early morning risers without their slippers on properly.

All around them, the familiar refrain sounded from the walking dead, "Brains, brains..." except, maybe not. Dave listened: the zombies weren't all chanting, "Brains, brains..." Their rotted mouths didn't articulate properly, so it was hard to be certain, but it was more like, 'canes', 'danes', 'gains'... or something.

He passed a fresher-looking corpse. Yes, it was, "Trains, trains."

Why were they saying–

Bing-bing-bing.

Someone's phone had gone off!

They all convulsively checked their phones, and then reached into their coats, bags or tapped their back pockets.

Not me, Dave knew.

He snuck a peek at the others and they were doing the same, and each shook their head in answer.

A zombie not ten metres away, jerked in a spasm of reaction.

Zombies turned towards the culprit.

Someone still had percentage and bars in their phone.

"Shit, shit, shit," the zombie refrained. When he looked about in wild panic, the healthy skin tone on his neck became visible.

Dave took a step towards him, copying the shambling gait of all the walking dead around him.

"Er..."

Then the disguised commuter screamed and ran.

The zombies lurched after him.

Three other 'zombies' screamed and ran.

"Mon Dieu, mon Dieu!" Monique exclaimed, and then she screamed and ran.

The first disguised commuter made it around the corner of the shattered coffee shop and part way up the non-moving escalator. Zombies fell from above; such was their desperation to reach the man's living flesh.

"Brains, brains..."

Good idea, Dave thought, and he mumbled, "Brains, brains..." as if praying for insight. He shuffled after the others, tiny half-steps that accelerated to the maximum walking speed available. Each inch took them further away from the chaos that struck at those who had screamed and run.

But now, zombies approached from outside, drawn by the commotion, so the team skipped sideways and made it to the Moleskine shop on the corner. They went through the shattered glass and hid behind the displays.

All Dave could see was notebook after notebook.

Other zombies returned to the concourse, settling after their feast. The disguised commuters were amongst them, their faces pale beneath their now unnecessary make-up. They were all in the way of the exit.

And there was Monique... Dave looked away and wondered about choosing a notebook.

There were so many options: red, black, lined, feint, blank, ruled, hardcover... and then he realised he was overthinking it. He selected according to the nearest and heaviest, tested the weight and feel in his hand, and then threw it for all he was worth.

It whizzed away like a shotput and connected with one of the walking dead.

It jerked about, confused for a moment.

A few nearby came towards him – it was working! They were moving away.

Except, the first one turned towards him and then approached with a falter and a dodder.

Others joined it.

Shit, it hadn't worked!

In fact, it had made things worse.

Dave backed away, crawling between the special offers. He threw more and more, wasting ammunition – he had to keep moving, a case of more stationery to be less stationary.

The terrain forced him to switch from feint to weekly planner. A box of gel refills fared better, the pen being mightier than the paper.

However, he ran out of aisle.

This was it: years of school, art college, a few years of work, a little furlough and it was all over.

"Go!" Bex yelled.

The others piled out from the other side of the shop.

Again, he was a distraction to save others.

"What about Dave?" Frank yelled. "Leave no man behind."

"He's already undead," Bex screamed.

They were gone, running madly for the exit and the horde of zombies started their inexorable pursuit, shuffle by shuffle.

And Dave was alone lying amongst the calendars as if he had all the time in the world.

– 18 –

Ring-a-ring o' roses, a pocketful of posies, a-
tishoo! A-tichoo! We all fall down and then
rise up again to feast upon the living.

Traditional

The table along the far wall had been laid out with a
buffet. Starting on the left, there were plates riffle shuffled
with sheets of precious kitchen roll standing in for
serviettes. Next was pasta salad, salad and fruit salad
before barbeque Spam, skewered Spam, Spam shaped like
chicken wings and pulled Spam. There was sliced Spam
and the remains of the last tin of reconstituted chicken.
Finally, there were pictures of profiteroles, chocolate cake
and little fancies, next to the tinned fruit. No expense had
been spared.

Dawn moved a fruit salad to the dessert end. Her
fingers hovered over a delicious fancy... or the chocolate
cake. It was hard to decide. She wished they were real.
The pictures were meant to spice up meal times, but she
considered them to be torture.

"Something fruity?"

"Mister Anderson, you turn everything and anything
into a smutty innuendo."

"Ooh er..."

She had a pineapple chunk from under the double
chocolate drizzled Belgian chocolate cake.

"Watch your diet," Anderson said. "We wouldn't want
you getting fat in front of the minister."

There was a cough from the councillor.

"Lady and gentlemen," Councillor Grant began, "please welcome the new Minister of Resilience, Calmness and Fortitude, the Right Honourable MP for Zone Eight, Mr Neil Fenton-Briggs, M. P."

There was a ripple of applause.

"Thank you," Fenton-Briggs said, stepping forward. "It's lovely to be here in Zone Five with all you 'Fivers'... or 'Brummies' as you like to be called."

Dawn couldn't recall a Brummie accent, except for Ahmed, but he was more Dudley.

"Let's not stand on ceremony," Fenton-Briggs continued. "There's a buffet."

This elicited another ripple of applause, tempered by the knowledge that the special buffet was the same as every meal, except for the wanton disregard for the kitchen roll supply. Tomorrow, they'd have to wipe their fingers on their clothes, rather than simply doing that anyway.

"Lady first," Fenton-Briggs said.

Dawn shook her head.

"Watching your figure," Anderson whispered.

Dawn jumped. He was always too close. If he'd been a zombie, she'd be one too by now.

Fenton Briggs went first, accepting the privilege as the guest and as an Eton old boy. He attacked the buffet, selecting more than a fair share of Spam shaped like barbeque chicken wings, but turning his nose up at the unadulterated Spam. He tore at it with his teeth, smearing sauce on his lips and hands. Dawn saw for a fleeting moment a zombie ripping at flesh, but this changed in her mind to an altogether more primal monster. Under Fenton Briggs' cultured exterior was a beast, a wolf in a sheepskin coat.

"Mmm... uh... thing," he said.

Dawn was confused until the minister clicked his fingers and pointed.

"Oh, sorry," she said and she fetched a square of kitchen roll.

He wiped his fingers and mouth before handing the red stained and ripped, artfully printed 2-ply back.

"Don't mind me," he said. "Tuck in."

Dawn felt the urge to gorge on more pineapple.

"As the new Minister of Resilience, Calmness and Fortitude..." Fenton-Briggs began before swallowing.

"Well, we have some problems with–" Councillor Grant began.

"And those, whatever they are, are entirely the fault of my predecessors," Fenton Briggs assured him. "Other ministers cocked things up and their failures became our emergencies."

"Do you mean–"

But Fenton Briggs held his finger aloft for silence, and then used it to count off items as if from a well-memorised list. "You know, Brexit, cost of private health care, climate change, immigration, lack of immigration, the cost of living, that hornet business... and now, zombies."

"Yes, well, we–"

"But all that's changed. Under my leadership, we've redefined an emergency as a crisis."

"Oh, isn't that–"

"It means that they are no longer the remit of the Ministry of Resilience, Calmness and Fortitude and their responsibility has returned to the other ministries."

"But that's–"

"You know, Ministry of Brexit Opportunities, Health and Social Care, Environment, Food and Rural Affairs, Home Office, Work and Pensions, Work and Pensions again, the Treasury, Defence and finally, we couldn't fob zombies off on anyone."

"That's a shame, but–"

"So, under this government, the number of emergencies has been reduced from eight to one. A great success, all round."

"It does seem like rearranging the deckchairs on—"

"Exactly, all small potatoes now that most people are walking about dead."

"But, Minister, what about—"

"Let's not talk shop." Fenton-Briggs helped himself to some more barbeque Spam. "We've a meeting for all that later today. What's this flavour?"

"Er... Hugh?"

"Curry," Anderson said.

"Ah, the infamous Zone Five Triangle."

"We prefer the 'Balti Triangle'," Anderson said.

"Invented here," Councillor Grant added, proudly.

"Still exist?" Fenton-Briggs asked.

"Alas, we don't know, Minister."

"Surely, you've reports?"

"The bunker's communications system only has access to the reserved emergency frequencies," Councillor Grant explained. "Sadly, no-one else uses them, so we're a little in the dark here. In the dark... ha-ha... sorry."

"Shame," Fenton-Briggs said. "I wouldn't mind a good curry." He took two stand-in serviettes and wiped the sauce off on them, chucking both in the bin provided.

Dawn licked the last of the pineapple juice off her fingers.

"Sexy," Anderson whispered to her.

Dawn swallowed back pineapple-flavoured bile.

"Let's get this meeting over with," Fenton-Briggs announced. "I've a dinner date."

A little laughter followed, but most had bemused looks, Dawn included.

As they filed out, Ahmed and Rob descended on the special, ministerial buffet with gusto, salivation and then disappointment.

Dawn rushed away to catch up with Councillor Grant.

"Meeting?" Dawn asked him.

"A few streets away, yes."

"Oh... er... outside!"

"You've just been outside."

"Yes, but only the outside of inside the building, not the outside of the outside."

"Don't worry," he assured her. "It'll be a walk in the park."

"Aren't walks in the park dangerous?"

"I meant it figuratively," he said. "It'll be a walk in the streets of Birmingham."

– DIVIDEND –

A bus with the richest 80 people in the world
could contain more wealth than the collective
assets of half the world's population.

Russel Brand

Dmitry Roubalov sipped his martini and stared across the
lawn, over the fine sand of the beach and out towards the
setting sun. San Marie was on fire again, the distant
smudge of black smoke spoiling his view. A view he had
spent thirty million dollars acquiring. Perhaps he should
have built his villa east facing, but he was an evening
person and liked to watch the sun go down.

"YA zaklyuchennyy," his wife shouted from the en suite
bedroom. "Zaklyuchennyy."

She began throwing things about again, which involved
picking them up from the floor first. Her hobby had been
shopping and he had banned her from going to the
mainland.

Didn't she understand that there was a zombie
outbreak there?

She yelled again – something smashed.

He could afford it.

She was pretty, but perhaps it was time to swap her out
for a newer model. Unlike vintage cars, women didn't
appreciate in value with age. She was a gold digger,
hoping that she'd be the one holding the marriage
certificate when it was time for him to cash in his bonds.

He jiggled his olive.

He liked his name, 'Roubalov'. It sounded like 'Roubles' – money. Like that capitalist cartoon, *Richie Rich*. He liked that. He liked martinis and having a private island.

He liked capitalism.

He'd played the game, throwing the dice and going around the board, buying here, charging there, avoiding Income Tax and Luxury Tax. He'd snapped up properties all over London. No-one lived in them, of course, as he didn't want anyone to scratch the minimalism. Refurbishment would be an expense. Prices had gone up and up, though cheap staff had been hard to find.

He started with nothing, just his father's arms empire, his mother's oil business and a few million roubles. He'd carried on selling substandard equipment to the Russian army at huge markups, pilfering the stock back again and selling it on. Nations at war were so desperate for tanks and missiles that they'd buy anything at any price. In a good war, he'd been able to sell to both sides.

And the world was addicted to oil.

Then property, asset stripping, luxury yachts, drugs and guns in the US,

A long time ago, he'd read that the richest people, those who owned half the world's wealth, would fit in a jumbo jet. That had been 388 in 2010. By 2014, they'd fit on a double-decker bus. Dmitry had had to look up what a double-decker bus was, and apparently, lots of them went past his Mayfair property. Two decks would carry the 80 people.

So, 308 has fallen off in four years.

Two years later, and it was 62 on a single-decker bus.

Each month, another fell off the bus.

A crash here, a takeover there, a drop in shares everywhere.

It was a game. They all knew it. The points earning interest in Panama and Switzerland. Money going out to grease palms and come back tenfold.

Gates had gone from Microsoft.

Bezos sold Amazon.

Elon Musk had frittered it away on Twitter. Dmitry's troll farms had made a fortune from politicians eager for re-election.

And then the zombie apocalypse.

Shares had nosedived, but Dmitry had seen the way the wind was blowing.

He'd bought into medical supplies, diversified from missiles and tanks in urban crowd control, and taken money to spread disinformation.

Zukerberg's FaceBook went overnight in a flurry of sads, angrys and wows. Its reign was over, TikTok's clock ran out and everyone was sharing on something else. They'd all depended on advertising revenue and when the living didn't go shopping, that was that.

His wife stormed across the open-plan living area, stomped around the kitchen island and raided the wine fridge.

"YA zaklyuchennyy," she said. She might well be a prisoner, but it was a fine prison. The wine cost $1,000 and the stainless-steel fridge went for $19,000.

Musk's SpaceX had gone: who'd pay money to escape to another planet when there wasn't a five-star hotel built there yet?

And he'd done it.

When the curtain came down and the whistle blew, when the bell rang to close trading and the barman called time, when Earth, Inc., was wound up and the assets divided, he was the last one still standing.

The planet's first trillionaire!

The richest man in the world.

The last man on the bus.

A single tear ran down his cheek, not of sadness, but of joy. The world was over. The sun had set.

He'd won.

19

The Four Horsemen of the Apocalypse:
Lockdown, Furlough, Eat-Out and Back-to-
the-Office.

Anon

The station concourse was eerily empty.

"De do do do, de do do do, de do do do-do-do-do-do-
do de do," Dave trilled, sub-vocally.

The big clock still worked. He wasn't going to make it
in for 9:30, but 10:00 was possible. That would be fine.
His line manager would understand. There'd been a few
delays that was all.

Dave came out beside 'the ramp' from the station to
the main junction between New Street and Corporation
Street. A crumpled sheet of newspaper wafted down the
street like tumbleweed in a western. It caught against the
barricades before being hurled aloft into the contrail-free
sky above.

The silence settled like the pause before a jump scare.

"Too quiet."

Dave nearly leapt out of his skin.

The Conductor leant against a litter bin, licking a roll-
up. Satisfied, he lit it and took a slow drag.

"Yow be givin' back my edgin' tool," he drawled.

"Piss off," said Dave.

Dave walked off and the Conductor followed. When
they reached the level pavement of New Street, Dave
checked up and down. He could see as far as Waterstones

at one end and, just visible between the trees and the burnt-out military vehicles, the Town Hall at the other. He'd never seen the city centre so empty.

"No pigeons," the Conductor whispered.

"No-one to feed them," Dave said.

Somewhere amongst the shops, turnings and squares, a million zombies stood waiting to pounce. Some slowly, some quickly and some like lightning, and all ready to catch the unwary and foolish.

Dave was wary, but, sadly, he was foolish.

"This is stupid," Dave said under his breath. Was any job worth this? Particularly when he could work from his terraced and fortified urban castle.

"Too right."

"Shall we..."

The Conductor had his brush ready.

In both directions, big yellow steel barriers designed to keep terrorists from driving into the happy shoppers had been reinforced with all sorts of bits and pieces. Shop window mannequins poked out of metal clothes racks like bodies buried in first world war trenches.

Giant interlocking concrete blocks kept it all anchored to the ground. Someone had tried to reinforce these with railings as if protecting the way to Europe's largest Primark was a good idea.

In the other direction, the barriers had trapped a military Humvee. It lay on its side, a black skeleton of twisted and burnt metal. Its crew had no doubt defended themselves well, pock-marking the grey stone of the magnificent edifice that was the Apple store. Bags of money lay abandoned in front of the smashed-in Lloyd's Bank opposite and spilled their contents like leaves.

"We could help ourselves," the Conductor said.

"No-one uses cash nowadays," Dave pointed out. "Not since the emergency."

No-one used cash and, if there was no internet connection, no-one used card either. Except they did, but their cash was jewellery, gold and silver, and vouchers for Starbucks and Costa.

The world had changed – once you'd used a tenner for a coffee, now you used a coffee chain's token as a tenner. *'I promise to pay the bearer on demand one mocaccino.'* Coffee itself didn't exist anymore, not since Brexit and the virus reaching the plantations.

This was the new normal.

"Psst!"

It was Frank coming up behind them with Bex.

"Is it safe?" he whispered.

"Where's Denzel?" Dave asked.

The Conductor shrugged. Bex looked away and Frank spotted something fascinating on his shoes.

"Guy and Lucy?" Dave added.

The Conductor pointed up where the tram lines snaked up the road.

They'd all been diversions.

Further up Corporation Street, Guy and Lucy were running for their lives, his red and blue tracksuit just visible and her long scarf trailing behind her. They had created this emptiness behind them with their passing.

"We better get a move on," the Conductor said, dropping his spent roll-up and extinguishing it underfoot. Where he'd stamped, a fallout of stubs littered the spot.

"Which way?" Dave said.

There was Corporation Street, New Street and perhaps some strange route through Needless Alley.

"I go to the Council House," Bex said, "but, you know, I could kill for a latte."

"Espresso," Frank said.

"Americano," the Conductor said.

"Cup of tea," Dave said.

Everyone stood for a moment, their mouths salivating like a dog in a clarion.

"I could murder a pint," Frank said. "The Wellington does real ale. It's third or fourth on the right, up Bennetts Hill where that Italian place is."

Dave nodded. He knew it.

"Can we just pop into Claire's Accessories?" Bex said. "They have these lovely earrings."

"It's not open," Frank growled.

"The main window is smashed," Bex replied, sweetly. She went over, cautiously, with her fork at the ready.

Dave glanced at his watch, considered the age-old argument of yardarms and realised that they all needed something after their desperate ordeal. But...

"I have to get to the office," he said. "I'm late."

"Give me a call," Frank said, "you know, if you change your mind."

Dave nodded.

Bex had started to cross the road.

"Bex," Dave said, "don't you need to get to the station's offices?"

"What for?"

"For work."

"Nah, I work in the bridal shop," she replied. "I do the trains."

"Oh."

She went off in her sparkly outfit and it made sense.

Frank tapped Dave on his shoulder and showed him his phone. Dave entered the number and texted him. Presently, Frank's phone buzzed.

"Best on silent," Frank said.

Dave nodded.

"This am where we go our separate ways," said the Conductor. He picked up the brush and turned back to the station. "I'm on the 5:35 back."

"Maybe," Dave said. Did he want to be conducted and see some other poor sod pushed out of the train?

The Conductor held out his hand for his edging tool.

Dave grimaced and turned away, the weapon leaning on his shoulder like a rifle.

A scream!

Near Claire's Accessories, a clutch of zombies, sadly with Bex included, stumbled about in the shop. She had set him up, Dave knew, saving him only for the Conductor to use him, but it was a pity. Ah well.

"Shiny, Shiny..." they mumbled.

Odd.

"See you," Frank said.

"Yeah," Dave said.

Then, for Dave, it was *Stayin Alive* up New Street to the office. Frank kept pace until he had to turn off for his destination.

Dave checked his watch. So, he wasn't going to make it in for 10:00, but 10:22 wasn't bad. In fact, it was excellent. He had over half an hour before the meeting.

At the glass doors to his office building, Dave had a short argument over the door intercom.

"Name..."

"Barry, it's Dave."

"Dave who?"

"Dave Knight... David Knight."

"Have you been bitten recently?"

"No."

"Do you show any symptoms?"

"Like what?"

"Feeling dead, gangrene, bad smells, loss of smell, loss of nose, loss of appetite, gain in appetite for gangrene, increased appetite for brains–"

"No, no, none of that."

"When did you last take a zombie test?"

"This morning."

"Was it negative?"

"Yes."

"Was it–"

"Barry, just let me in!"

He glanced behind him – a clutch of shamblers approached – but luckily the door buzzed and he pushed.

It didn't open!

"Pull."

Dave pulled, the door opened and then he had made it.

"Dave! Where the hell have you been?"

He was even pleased to see his line manager, Keith, too.

20

Please note that your call may be recorded for
your safety. We are currently experiencing a
high level of calls, so your wait time may be
longer than normal. To discuss a life
assurance policy and the claimant is alive,
please press 1. If the claimant is deceased,
please press 2 and, finally, if the claimant is
undead, please hang up. Your call is
important to us.

Helpline Recording

So, it was back to the main blast doors and another chance
for everyone to fail to notice Dawn's bunting.

Again, the sergeant and soldier took the lead – **rat-a-tat-tat-tat TAT-TAT** – with the minister, Councillor Grant,
Mr Anderson and Dawn ready in the middle. Dawn still
had her heels on. Stupid, but there it was. Ahmed and
Rob, handgunned – **BANG, BANG** – and shotgunned up
– **BOOM**, "I'm out of ammo!" – took the rear.

It was the same short distance along the passage, up the
stairs to the main entrance, but this time it was a blitzkrieg
of warfare – **rat-a-tat, rat-a-tat, BANG**, "Can I have a go?"
– along a corridor to the non-barricaded side door. This
opened into a square area cut into the corner of the
building by design. Dawn paused by the red post-box,
while the armed personnel checked up Newhall Street and
across Fleet Street.

She was outside again!

Not 'out' of the bunker like before, but 'out-out'. At street level! Near shops and cafés and wine bars, and the impossibly high sky wasn't the grey of concrete, but the wonderful grey of an overcast day.

She had a fluttering feeling of butterflies in her stomach.

Excitement?

Nerves?

Utter terror!

"All right," Ahmed said, "we shoot only if we must to avoid attracting anymore."

Rob nodded in reply.

"GO, GO, GO!" the sergeant instructed.

They went, went, went.

Round the corner, bursts of gunfire – **Tat, tata-tat, BANG, rat-a-tat** – and then up Newhall Street towards the city centre. Dawn ran, paused, took off her heels and sprinted barefoot to keep up. They crossed the big intersection at Great Charles Queensway, and then ignored Cogs, the nice coffee shop that did those delicious biscuits and... oh, that lovely wine bar that did good food had burnt down.

"We'll have to slow down," Fenton-Briggs said. "I need to save some energy for this evening."

They moved more slowly.

Dawn put her shoes back on, but her tights were already ruined.

Another batch of zombies came at them.

"Help us," one of them said. It wore a red and blue tracksuit. The one next to it waved her long scarf.

The sergeant and the soldier fired a few rapid bursts – **rat-a-tatatata** – such that the two people jerked from the impact and went down.

"Stop!" Dawn shouted. "They're alive!"

"Not anymore," Fenton-Briggs replied.

"But they were alive."

"Merely... collateral damage."

"That's monstrous."

"Not any—"

The two corpses twitched and rose up.

"Run, run..." said one.

"Brains, brains..." said the other.

"There are living people out here." The realisation hit Dawn like the sugar rush of chocolate fudge along with the horror of a generous slice of chocolate cake dropped onto the carpet.

"Look, dear, much better that they aren't walking corpses, but are now lying down corpses. Better safe than sorry... hmm, that ought to be a new government slogan."

"You can't just kill people!"

"She's right," the sergeant said. "Just wound 'em and then the zombies'll slow down to eat 'em."

"Sergeant!"

"Kill 'em all and let God sort 'em out."

"Sergeant," Dawn said, "that's no good if they identify as atheists."

The man shrugged and led them away.

"After we've had an internal enquiry," Dawn said, "I'm going to report you to the police."

"They are the police," Councillor Grant informed her.

"What!"

She looked at them and saw for the first time the tiny police insignia on their black, full-combat paramilitary fatigues.

"Happy?" the sergeant said.

"I suppose."

They clattered down an alley between two tall buildings – Birmingham was all tall buildings – making their way through all the office blocks and quiet spaces. The guns flared again – **tat-tat, tata-tat-tat** – short bursts that cut an approaching jogger to pieces. Some of the damaged corpses kept twitching as Dawn hurried past, her feet going as fast as they could in her stupid heels.

"You look good in heels," Anderson said to Dawn when they paused at another intersection.

Dawn glared and wondered if she could punch him. "They're stupid for running in."

"Bryce Dallas Howard, the actress, wore heels throughout *Jurassic World* and she was running from dinosaurs, which are a lot faster."

"That was a movie!"

"Just saying."

They reached an anonymous set of doors to a glass-fronted building.

The sergeant flailed about until his soldier pointed to the intercom. He then struggled with his evil gun before he could press the button.

"Name…"

"Sergeant Doberman with Minister Fenton-Briggs."

"First name?"

"What! Martin."

"Have you been bitten recently?"

"Open the fucking door before I kill you!"

"Do you show any symptoms?"

"Open the–"

"Let me," Fenton-Briggs said, shifting the sergeant aside with a deft flick of his hand. "Look, do you know who I am!"

"Minister Fen–"

"So, be a good chap, and let us in."

The door buzzed and it was all fingers and thumbs to open it, and then it was all 'after you's and 'no, after you's to get through.

21

First impressions are the most important.

Good advice

"Your suit, Dave."

"What about it... oh."

"It looks like you've been gardening in it," Keith, Dave's line manager said.

"Oh, this... yes."

Dave put down his edging tool and went to the gents to clean himself up. Checking himself in the mirror revealed specks of blood splattered across his shirt and smudges of grime smearing his suit.

"Oh for..."

He had been fighting zombies, traipsing through underground tunnels and, well, commuting always took it out of him even before the apocalypse.

He took his jacket and shirt off, washed them in the sink, then he realised and washed his hands first. He mopped down his trousers and succeeded in creating a new fashion statement of grey and black streaks. At least he had a matching jacket. Fairly soon his efforts had created a novel wet look. A ream of paper towels didn't seem to make any difference.

Back at his desk, he stood feeling damp and cold by a radiator that felt hard and cold. The office looked the same, but strangely different. It was as if there was something missing... oh, it was Dave himself.

"Is there any heating," Dave asked Bill.

"'Fraid not," Bill said, adjusting his glasses. Bill looked odd too as it was the first time in years he'd seen him without a surrounding frame and possessing his lower half. He was lacking his bookshelves behind him too. Other than that, he looked the same as he did every day on Teams. "We're trying to save on our energy costs."

"Oh... great."

"You could have a cuppa."

"Is there milk?"

"No," Bill admitted, "so make me a coffee."

"I... OK."

At least the exercise might warm him up.

Dave filled the kettle, popped it on and held his hands to the stainless steel. Eventually, it warmed up, burnt his hands, steamed and clicked off.

He took a cup of black tea and a black coffee back to their desks.

"Thanks," Bill said. "When all this started, there was that petrol shortage, well, an everything shortage."

"I remember."

"These blokes followed a tanker. They were desperate for petrol and whichever petrol station it stops at will have petrol, they thought. Stands to reason. So, they followed it for twenty miles, burning fuel all the time, only to discover that it was a tanker full of milk."

"And you wouldn't want to put milk in your car."

"Or petrol in your tea."

Dave sipped his milk-less, petrol-less tea and found it at least warming. Bill took a sip of coffee and his glasses steamed up.

"So, this meeting?" he asked.

"The minister's coming in person."

The upside-down world flipped again for Dave, but that didn't make it the right way up again.

"Why?"

"Back to work, back to the office, back to the wall."

"Not a haiku."

Mandy arrived with a portable electric heater. Dave immediately bowed to her and stood next to it.

"Great to see you, Mand," Dave said.

She looked at him quizzically. "We were on Teams last Friday."

"Yes, I know, but–"

"Heating charges!" Eddie said, storming over.

"It's gas," Mandy said. "This electricity comes from the office lighting budget."

"Oh. Right."

Satisfied, Eddie the overall manager went back to his office.

Dave moved the heater up and down his body. His suit and shirt puffed up and stopped sticking to his skin.

"Everything ready?" Keith asked Mandy.

"More or less," she said.

"More or... less?"

"No milk, no biscuits, no photocopied agendas..."

"No photocopies!"

"Jill's in the photocopying room."

"The quarter two report?" Keith asked Dave.

Dave tapped his jacket pocket and felt the crumpled paper.

"Is it creased?"

"A bit," Dave admitted. "I had a rough commute."

"Well, hmm, nothing we can do about that now. We'll just have to get by on a wing and a prayer."

Dave and Mandy nodded in reply.

"Admittedly," Keith continued, "the wings are gone."

"Any apologies?" Dave asked.

"I've already sent an apology in advance by email," Mandy said. "And I've done a template for everyone to use after the meeting."

"I meant, anyone not able to make it."

"Oh, well, Jill, obviously, Nancy, Spud... easier to list who's here really."

"That would be!"

"The four of us, and Eddie."

"Five?"

"Yeah."

"More biscuits for the rest of us, I suppose."

"If we had biscuits."

Eddie ran over. "They're here," he announced.

Dave reluctantly stepped away from the heater and looked for somewhere to put down his empty mug. They gathered by the lift, and each smoothed their hair, straightened their clothing and checked their flies. Eddie went up and down the line, clucking to himself.

The lift pinged.

"I thought in emergencies, you weren't supposed to use the lift," Dave whispered.

"It's not an emergency," Eddie snapped. "It's a meeting about the emergency."

The doors opened to reveal a full load. Two security men got out and swept their guns from side to side to make everyone even more nervous.

"Hello, hello," Eddie said, holding out his hand.

A man in a smart woollen coat and an even smarter, tailored suit shook Eddie's hand and then moved down the line. His handshake was dry, strong and masonic, whereas Dave knew his grip was weak and literally damp. So much for first impressions.

"Keith, acting manager of slogans."

"Bill."

"Dave."

"I'm the Right Honourable, Fenton-Briggs, MP," the man said. "And not some oik."

"Oh. Sorry. Er..."

"Pulling your leg." The minister moved on to Mandy. "Well, hello."

"Mandy," Mandy said. "Mandy, sir."

Dave kind of remembered Fenton-Briggs from a recent scandal, possibly from an earlier one or maybe from the scandal before that. Something that we all needed to move on from, apparently.

There were others – the black-clad police stayed on the fringes – and they all looked like local government officials.

The last one out was an attractive brunette in heels, dark tights, a nice skirt and blouse with... Dave recognized her and blurted.

"Dawn!"

"Dave!"

– 22 –

Journeys end in lovers meeting.

William Shakespeare (Twelfth Night)

Meetings are like never ending journeys.

Dave Knight, agenda scribble (Item 12)

"D-d-dave?"

"Er... Dawn?"

"Ah, good, you know each other," Anderson said. "That'll make things so much easier."

Dawn stared at Dave like a deer in headlights.

Dave stared at Dawn like a rabbit in headlights.

"Come along," Anderson added.

Dawn followed Anderson with this strange apparition following behind her. This Dave was real, he was here, he was... what!! What?

The conference room was modern, surrounded on three sides by green-tinted, floor-to-ceiling glass. The other wall consisted of a large TV screen with a lectern on one side and a long, polished beech table filled the space. The chairs were steel.

Dawn was so thrown by the presence of this strange non-virtual being suddenly appearing that she accidentally sat next to Anderson.

A PowerPoint slide announced 'Building a Better Future'.

Any future would be better, Dawn thought.

"Any future would be better," this 'Dave' said.

She was imagining him, that was it. That's why he'd said what she'd thought. He was a figment of her imagination, because she'd finally gone mad.

Except he looked real with a nice smile and he was... looking at her!

"Welcome," Councillor Grant said, beaming to the assembled company. "Let me make some introductions. This is the Right Honourable, Neil Fenton-Briggs, MP."

Everyone nodded towards the minister.

Who was this Dave?

His suit was worse than Mr Anderson's.

"And," Councillor Grant continued, "we have Hugh Anderson and Dawn."

Why was he here?

"Ah, Miss Withany," Fenton-Briggs said.

"No," Dawn said, "it's Dawn Dey with an 'E'."

"My mistake, please forgive me, Miss Day-Withany. I have a double-barrelled name myself."

Everyone chuckled.

Including this Dave, who was sitting opposite as if this was the most normal thing in the world.

"And from the advertising company," Councillor Grant continued, "we have Keith Simpson, Bill Burton and... er... Dave Knight."

"With a 'k'," this Dave added.

"That everyone?" Fenton-Briggs said. "Weren't we supposed to have some tart from FENNEL?"

Councillor Grant checked his notes, "Er... let me see, yes, Mademoiselle Monique Blanchet... not turned up, I'm afraid."

"We'll just have to muddle along without her expertise, not that we need any foreign interference."

What was going on?

"So, let me explain what is going on," Councillor Grant went on. "Minister?"

"Please, carry on," Fenton-Briggs said.

"Government policy for the future is..." Councillor Grant said, and then he went on and on and on.

But all Dawn could think was what, why and what!

"So, let's get on with the agenda," Fenton-Briggs announced.

Everyone looked for the agenda.

"Sorry," said Keith or Bill, Dawn hadn't fathomed which was which yet, "we've had a photocopying issue. Here are the printouts."

Dawn waited for hers and when it arrived, it made no sense. It still made no sense when she turned it the right way up.

What was this Dave doing here?

He was looking at her, and now he was studiously staring at the agenda and going red.

What?

Dawn forced herself to concentrate.

"Item one," Fenton-Briggs said, "minutes of the last meeting."

"Very few of us were at the last meeting," Councillor Grant said. "There's been a lot of changes in personnel."

"Well, let's pass them and move on."

The others nodded their approval.

"Good to make some progress," Fenton-Briggs said. "Moving on, item two, situation report."

"That's you, sir," Councillor Grant said.

"Basically," Fenton Briggs began, "and between you and me, Section D Notice and Official Secrets Act and all that, things are not going well in London. Too many people. I mean, it was a zombie apocalypse and there was no manual for that."

"Well, minister," said Keith or Bill, "we did have a plan for emergencies, pandemics and bioterrorism. That plan would have covered a lot of the eventualities."

"Like I said, no manual."

"Sir, the UK Influenza Preparedness Strategy of 2011 gave provision for a lot of–"

"A bad cold is hardly the same."

"And – I must insist, Minister – Operation Cygnus tested our strategy in 2016."

"Did it cover zombies?"

"Not exactly, but the modelled spread of influenza matched the spread of the undead with a... here it is. 96.4% correlation."

"So, we were prepared for the sniffles and, as I said, we had no manual."

"No... sir."

"It's not all bad. Those of us with shares in axes, chainsaws and running shoes have done rather well."

"Yes."

"What we really need is a good war," Fenton-Briggs said. "Something to distract the population from the clusterfuck of this zombie situation."

"Yes, er... sir."

"Can we arrange that?"

"Not from here."

"Well, item three, zombie tests... we should have done this as item one. Everyone taken them?"

Everyone murmured that they had, some rubbing their noses or their armpits, and Dawn felt an unaccountable need to reach under the table and scratch the back of her knees.

"We've all taken zombie tests," Councillor Grant assured him.

"I can see that," Fenton-Briggs said. "You're all alive."

"But best to be certain."

"Why, may I ask, are they so complicated?" the other Keith or Bill, the one with the glasses, asked. "I mean, why do we need to rotate them six times, then eight times and wait fifteen minutes."

"You are?"

"Bill Burton."

"Well, Bill, it's to test whether you are alive."

"Yes, but how?"

"Zombies lack the motor skills and dead people can't–"

"For goodness' sake, you might as well use a kiddie's toy."

"It is a kiddie's toy... painted white."

"You mean, it's fake."

"Certainly not."

"Well, what's the liquid?"

"Bill, Bill, I'm sure it's highly expensive, biologically prepared special... stuff," Councillor Grant informed him.

"It's water," Fenton-Briggs said.

"Special water with special stuff in it," Councillor Grant assured him.

"It's tap water," Fenton-Briggs said.

"Just tap water," Bill said.

"You misunderstand," Fenton Briggs said. "You see, the reading is always non-zombie, because anyone who can perform the test, all the stages and the randomly assigned variations... well, they have to be alive."

"But you are charging a fortune for water."

"It works on the placebo principle," Fenton-Briggs said. "If you know it's a placebo, then it doesn't work, but dress up in a white coat with a stethoscope around your neck and charge a decent rate, and people believe you. So, it works. The patient is cured, the doctor gets a new BMW and I'm rewarded for my diligence, so win, win, win."

"It's immoral."

"Immoral?" Fenton Briggs shook his head slowly. "I'm sorry, you've lost me there."

Bill made an exasperated sigh and dropped his pen on his notes.

"With these tests, it's better to be safe than sorry," Fenton-Briggs said. "Better safe than sorry. Can we work with that, Burton?"

"I'm sure we can... Dave?"

Dave seemed to jerk awake. He turned to Bill Burton.

"Er..." this Dave person began. He'd been staring at Dawn – not in the creepy way that Hugh Anderson did, but in a... Dawn didn't know. She wasn't used to meeting new people.

Dave looked upwards seemingly to gain inspiration from the ceiling tiles, and then he said, "Sorry you've not been safe with government advice–"

Bill coughed. "I don't think that's quite right."

"Oh... er," Dave replied. "I meant 'Better to be safe, follow government advice, do not be sorry...' something like that?"

"Good message and it'll fit that lectern sign, excellent," Fenton-Briggs said.

Everyone nodded in agreement.

It was a terrible slogan, Dawn thought.

"Item four," Fenton-Briggs said, "naming strategies... not this old chestnut."

"It is important," Bill insisted, picking up his pen and using it as a pointer, "that the government shows some consistency."

"The government has been quite consistent," Fenton-Briggs insisted.

"For the various zones," Councillor Grant said.

"I thought it was tiers," Anderson replied. "Dawn?"

"Tiers are what you do in various *areas,*" Dawn clarified.

"There's a lack of understanding here," Fenton-Briggs said. "The Midlands sector–"

"Sector!" Bill threw his pen down again.

"Yes, and that's a perfect example of the Midlands Sector lagging behind."

"The West Midlands zone... I mean area."

"Has been amalgamated with the East Midlands and other areas to create a larger *sector,*" Fenton-Briggs informed them. "Due to the enforced downsizing of area command centres. Why haven't you incorporated this change?"

"Well," Anderson began. "Dawn?"

"It was being co-ordinated through the Department of Works and Pensions based in Five Ways."

"And Miss Day-Withany?" the minister asked.

"Dey," Dawn said.

"Sorry, Miss Withany-Dey, would you explain."

"Just Dey."

"Miss Withany-Justday?"

"Well," Dawn said, giving ground, "They closed the Department of Works and Pensions in Five Ways."

"Why was that?"

"Because everyone was working from home?"

"No, it wasn't," Anderson corrected. "It's because the general population isn't doing enough actual work to qualify for National Insurance contributions and, also, no-one's likely to live long enough to collect a pension."

"I thought that crisis had been resolved," Councillor Grant said.

"Only on paper," Dawn said. "You see, a zombie is no longer classed as a zombie after 28 days."

"I beg your pardon?"

"Councillor, a zombie is no–"

"But that would mean that all the green zones are really orange and all the orange ones are actually red."

"Yes, except..." Dawn paused. How could she make the Councillor understand?

"Except?"

"We've gone back to the tier system, so tier 1 is likely to be tier 2, and tier 2 is tier 3, and..."

"And?"

"Tier 3 will be some new level called tier 4."

"Ah, marvellous," Councillor Grant said, smiling at everyone in turn around the table.

"Except..." Dawn began again.

"Except?"

"It's more like that tier 1... green zones will be red zones and orange zones will be red zones."

"And red zones will be deeper red zones?" Bill said.

"Yes," Dawn said.

"We're..." Bill paused and scowled.

"Yes?"

"Am I allowed to swear?"

"I'd rather you didn't in front of the minister."

"Wonderful," Bill said. He made to toss his pen down again, but it was already lying on his notes.

"You're quite sarcastic," Dawn said.

"Really."

"Well," Fenton-Briggs said, summing up, "it's *sectors,* not tiers and zones, so something you'll have to bring yourselves up to speed on."

"So it's different sectors in each sector," Bill said.

"Bill!" Keith snapped.

"It's just that we're not getting much direction from Westminster," Bill said.

"I do see that," Fenton-Briggs conceded. "It's all flip-flop, U-turns and changes of policy."

"It doesn't work here at area... sector level," Keith said. "It's try this, try that, do the other, go back to whatever. That's the problem with having a zombie government."

"I think that's a tasteless term to use," Dawn said.

"But it is," Fenton-Briggs said. "You see, we had this party – a lot of parties – and, inevitably, he got bitten. Well, at first, he said he hadn't been bitten and then he said he was fine. Said the bite wasn't a zombie, but a secretary's love bite, which was very believable to be fair. Then he said it wasn't his fault and that he didn't mean to get bitten. And that the person he'd bitten had deserved it, and finally, he said... er... brains, a lot. He's sealed in the cabinet room, but essentially, he's still in charge."

"That's appalling," Dawn said.

"He's doing less damage to the economy and the zombie response," Fenton-Briggs said.

"Should he not be replaced?" Anderson suggested.

"I thought that," Fenton-Briggs said. "Someone with vitality, a clear vision and no recent scandals. However, we've no idea how to get rid of him. It needs a decision from the 1922 committee."

"And they said?"

"Brains, brains."

"That's terrible," Dawn was shocked. She'd assumed that London's preparedness would be better than Birmingham's. It couldn't be worse, surely?

"How's the country being run then?" Bill asked.

"They explain issues through the door and watch on CCTV," Fenton-Briggs said. "If the PM goes to the window, we do it, if he staggers to the fireplace, we do the opposite, and if he eats brains, we do what the experts say."

"Eats brains!"

"Doesn't happen often to be fair. Not many brains in the government."

"But that's an appalling way to run the country."

"Is it?" Fenton Briggs said, his brow furrowed. "They are making better decisions now than when they were alive."

"You didn't make the proper preparations to cope with the disaster," Bill insisted.

"Look, it was an honest mistake. We thought we could get away with it, but that turned out to be wrong."

"And–"

"Shall we move on?" Fenton-Briggs said.

"With all due respect, minister, I–"

"We'll move on," Fenton-Briggs insisted. He looked at each person in turn around the table. Dawn felt his gaze like a warm sunlamp that left her feeling sticky.

"Item five, zombie forecasts."

"Yes," Councillor Grant said, "we would like to know what the experts at CHIVES are saying."

"It's not the Civil and Home Office Intelligence Virology Emergency Sub-committee anymore."

"What is it now?"

"The British Association of Scientific Intelligence Liaison committee."

"That's–"

"Please refer to page 10 of their report... ah, why has no-one got the report?"

"Jill won't let us near the photocopier," Bill said.

"Why not?"

"She's a zombie."

"A particularly bitey zombie," Dave added.

"Well, I'll summarise," Fenton-Briggs said. "Basically, the virus is becoming safer. After all, no virus wants to kill its host. It happened with Spanish 'flu, Asian 'flu and all those other foreign 'flus and this'll be the same."

"So we can look forward to a milder form of death," Bill said.

"Exactly. And the government is going to redefine what a zombie is."

"You mean shambler, rambler, jogger and so forth."

"Potential worker, undead employee, zombie–"

"But that's terrible," Dawn said.

"Yes," Fenton-Briggs agreed, "but pleb, prole and peasant got some very bad press."

"When we had press," Councillor Grant said.

"So, those alive are assigned to fortified offices, those semi-undead can be on zero-hours contracts, the pre-turned–"

"Look, someone is dead or alive – that's it," Bill pronounced.

"Miss Withany-Justday?"

"It's just 'Dey'."

"I said, Withany-Justday."

"Just 'Dey'."

"Miss Justday."

Dawn signed inwardly. "Saying someone is alive or dead is so prejudiced, Mr Burton. It's not binary, dead or alive. There are many shades in between. There's positive alive, depressed alive, hurting inside, quietly screaming, and then dead, really dead, and in between, undead. Even the undead are shamblers, ramblers or joggers."

"Shamblers, Dawn?" Councillor Grant said.

"Sorry, variant A, etcetera."

"There, see?" Fenton-Briggs was triumphant. "It's us and them, once we get the buggers to do some work."

"Is that even possible?" Bill asked.

"Of course," Fenton-Briggs assured him. "We'd just need HR to clear them for employment."

"There's more to it than that," Keith said.

"They'd need a medical check," Dawn added.

"Think of it," Fenton-Briggs said, "if we can re-integrate them into the workforce. All these employees aren't technically alive, so we wouldn't need to pay a *living* wage."

It was Bill's turn to object. "You still need to–"

"They're not living."

"But what about normal people?"

"Normal people?"

"They need work."

"They can become zombies."

"That's–"

"They could self-identify as zombies for employment purposes."

"But that's ridiculous."

"They're not going to get a job otherwise."

"Is this part of future organisational strategies?" Councillor Grant asked.

"Ah yes, thank you Councillor," the minister said. "Item six is future organisational strategies."

"Back to areas then," Bill mumbled.

Fenton-Briggs coughed for attention. His was a deep throaty growl that spoke of importance and expensive cigars.

"The government," he said, "is considering moving the executive decision-making level from a centralised model to a more distributed, countywide command and control template with the oversight in an overseas capacity."

"Overseas!" Bill exclaimed.

"The Seychelles, yes."

"What?"

"Via Zoom."

"But what about going back to the office?" Keith said.

"Oh, that's for everyone else," Fenton-Briggs said. "And one advantage is that we'll only need to decorate the bottom half of rooms."

"Eh?" Dave said.

"Everyone's on their phones, heads down, so no-one looks up anymore."

"But surely the top half of a room is the only half that's seen on Zooms," Bill said.

"Good point," Fenton-Briggs agreed, "if you can only see the top half of rooms on Zoom, then we can save even more money by not decorating the bottom half of rooms as well."

"But that's... words fail me."

"We've been doing government business via Zoom and you can do a Zoom call from anywhere, so there's really no need for the nation's rulers to be actually based in the country. There's no basis for any complaints here. The PM–"

"Via CCTV and window gazing," Bill said.

"Yes, he... eventually agreed, and my fellow cabinet colleagues thought it best to be on an island."

"Britain is an island."

"Though the Seychelles banking is irritatingly regulated, so the exchequer will be based in Panama."

"Panama is not an island."

"Since global warming, you can sail all the way around it."

"Through a narrow strait."

"In a big yacht."

"Gentlemen, please," Councillor Grant said.

"This is rats leaving the sinking ship," Bill replied.

"We are not rats leaving the sinking ship," Fenton-Briggs said. "We're rats *going to* a floating ship."

"So you agree that our ship is sinking?"

"Listen, you!" Fenton-Briggs said, his finger stabbing towards Bill. "I've had about as much as I can stomach of your 'up north' nonsense."

"I'm from Dudley, that's not 'up north'."

"All this will be part of the Northern Partition, once the executive is settled."

"Partition!"

"Yes," Fenton-Briggs said, "the Northern Partition of the UK and then the island retreats of the South. This will be a Year Zero for the United Kingdom's New World Normal."

"I'd like to read the small print," Bill said.

"If you insist."

"I insist!"

"In that case," Fenton-Briggs said, holding the document out for Bill Burton, "you can get it photocopied."

Bill's face went pale.

"Sergeant, make sure he does a copy for each of us."

"Yes, sir."

So, like a man condemned to have his head cut off in triplicate, Bill left the room escorted by the heavily armed sergeant.

"Well, any other business?" Fenton-Briggs said. "No. Good. Now—"

"I think—" Keith began.

"No other business, good," Fenton-Briggs concluded. "Now, I've visited in person and listened. And now you'll all do as outlined in the plan, once Burton brings you a copy. Thank you—"

"Minister, are we skipping items eight to fifteen."

"Yes, thank you, meeting over. You, Knight, are there biscuits?"

"Oh, er..." Dave said.

"I have some ready, minister," Keith said, "from our executive supply."

"Good," and with that, Fenton-Briggs, MP, got up and swept out of the office.

"Typical meeting," Anderson said under his breath. "The Four Horseman of the Emergency Planning Policy – procrastination, distraction, lethargy and meh."

There were biscuits and coffee in the other room along with long-life milk.

When Bill came back, rubbing his arm, the copies of the Future Organisational Strategy (Version 9 – amended) were given to each of them.

Fenton-Briggs finished his coffee.

"Miss Withany-Justday, would you join me?"

"No, it's just Dey, that's Dey," she said. "Not Withany."

The minister's eyes narrowed.

"Of course," Dawn said to clarify.

"Good, Miss Knott-Withany, and I thought we'd have a spot of dinner first."

"Lovely... sorry?"

So, Fenton-Briggs, MP, led the way out with his two security police going ahead.

As she left, Dawn turned to this Dave character.

"Are you..." he said.

"Back to the bunker for dinner."

"Eh?"

"There's a secret nuclear bunker," Dawn explained, "built at the start of the cold war."

"Oh."

"It's under Telephone House in Newhall Street."

"Ah."

"You don't say much."

"Uh?"

"I mean you're quite monosyllabic."

"Eh?"

"For an advertising copywriter."

"Ah... um..."

23

BACK TO WORK
BACK TO THE OFFICE
BACK TO THE WALL

Bill Burton, 1975-0000 (New Calendar)

Dave had made a good impression with this Dawn.

He was sure of it.

Not 100% sure, but pretty sure. Mostly. He'd been sort of articulate, generally, and... well, he hadn't burbled or gone on about himself, football or anything embarrassing. He'd listened – which was what not-talking was really – and who was he kidding? Perhaps he'd only get a yellow card.

But, if he checked his phone, he suspected she'd have swiped left, rating him with 1 star and reported him to the police. That was a red card. How dare he 'um' and 'ah' at her? It was definitely non-PC, unwoke, misogynist and abusive.

Just because she had registered on Matchbox, searched for his profile and swiped right, it did not give him permission *to chat her up.*

Oh god, she was HR as well – he was doomed.

HR got together in little cliques over Prosecco and they talked to each other, every HR department was connected to every other, probably by underground tunnels, with all their secret handshakes and girls' nights out.

And there was that 'dinner' with that minister – what was that about?

And why had she told him in such great detail?

And that comment about being monosyllabic – uh?

The advertising team had gone back across the building in their open-plan office. Eddie had declared it 'a good thing' as no-one did any work from home.

"We're back to a proper team," he said. "In the office. Much better. All together."

So, they all went their separate ways to fix lunch. Dave had forgotten to make sandwiches and he wasn't about to nip out to Greggs, so it would have to be snacks from the vending machine again. Bill made his usual soup, Mandy had a salad, Keith had crisps, Wotsits and Pot Noodle. Eddie had his in his office, so who knew what that was?

"Where are the biscuits?" Dave asked to general shrugs.

"While we eat, let's have a debrief while it's fresh in our minds," Keith suggested. "You know, to quantify just how badly it went."

However, not everyone could fit in the small meeting room, so it was back to their desks in the open-plan office for a Zoom call.

"So?" Eddie said.

"Well," Bill said and then he added, "oh, *ah,* oh, this is hot."

His glasses had steamed up.

No-one said anything, except Keith, but he was still on mute. He mouthed something that looked like something, something, can you hear me?

"I can't really do anything," Dave said.

"Why ever not?" Eddie demanded.

"All my stuff's back at home."

"Didn't you bring the report for quarter two?"

"Yes," Dave replied. He fished it out and held it up to the camera, complete with the YouGov analysis of their slogans' effectiveness, some blood splatter and a lot of smeared ink from when he'd tried to wash his jacket. "We didn't need it for the meeting anyway."

Keith said something.

"You're on mute," Dave said.

Keith unmuted, "I said, what shall we do now?"

There followed an overlapping onslaught of confused interruptions and 'after you' pauses.

Then there was silence as complete as a mute all.

"Zoombies?" Dave suggested.

Unluckily, there were only five of them.

"I'll get Zack to join us," Keith suggested and he started typing an email. Zack was trapped in a shopping mall in California, where he did a night shift. Keith had met him online somehow via Facebook, Twitter or WhatsApp. Zack soon joined by audio and then video.

"Hi."

"Hi."

"Noughts and crosses?"

"Man, you mean tic-tac-toe."

Mandy contacted her friend, Anne, Dave got Dexter his flatmate online, and Keith remembered Barry on the front desk.

While they waited for the full set of nine to join the Zoom, everyone fiddled with their backgrounds and filters until most of them were cute animals or wearing virtual sunglasses.

"You made it then," Dexter said. He was still in his pyjamas.

"Yes," Dave said, "doddle."

"I thought it would be."

"Well, not a doddle exactly."

"You do know that this is being monitored by China," Dexter pointed out.

"Yes."

So, filters off, they each got their piece of paper, A4 folded and stuck together with Pritt stick, ready and...

"Is it on three or after three?" Zack asked.

"On three," they all chorused, out of time because of the inevitable delay.

All together, "One, two, three!" – they flipped their paper up to show an 'X' or a 'O', click-held and dragged the images around, rapidly screenshotted and–

"Line of crosses!" Zack shouted.

Bill dropped his card and then his mug of soup.

"It was a nought, man," Zack insisted. He shared his screen and there was a line of crosses and another of noughts going down. Two points.

"Best of nine, isn't it?" Dexter asked.

"You OK, Bill?" Dave asked.

Bill looked pale, but then everyone looked strange when badly lit on Zoom. The light from Bill's screen, complete with their own faces reflected in his glasses, was green and sickly.

"I got bitten," Bill admitted, "but I'm fine."

"You taking antibiotics?" Dexter asked, "'cos that's a scam by Big Pharma."

"But–"

"Try homeopathics." Dexter held up a jar. "I mix this with a litre of water and take two teaspoons, three times a day."

"You should take three teaspoons and antibiotics," Zack said. "Look at your arm, man."

Bill pulled his arm down out of shot.

Dave caught a quick view of pustulated flesh.

"Bill, mate," Dave said. He glanced across at Bill's cubicle and heard Bill scream.

A moment later, Bill screamed on the Zoom. Phlegm splattered on his camera and seemed to dribble down the inside of the screens of the other eight.

They all flinched back.

Dave double-flinched trying to avoid his computer and the far side of the open-plan.

Magnified by his glasses, the whites of Bill's eyes turned bloodshot. He attacked his screen, trying to maul the others, biting and spitting.

He was turning.

The Bill they knew descended into a monster, less than a beast and nothing more than an animated corpse driven by an unholy power.

"Fuck, man," Zack said.

Mandy and Anne disappeared.

The sound of someone vomiting played over the speakers until Dave turned it down. Suddenly Zoombies seemed silly and pointless.

Dave collected *Brainbiter 2.0* and stalked towards Bill's desk.

Eddie was at his door. "Bill? Bill?"

Bill staggered away from his desk.

"Please, please," Bill begged. He held out his hand. "It's just a rash."

"Oh God," Mandy said, her hand over her mouth.

"Hell," Keith added.

"Shit," Dave added.

"I don't want to – work – die," Bill said, looking from one colleague to another.

"Oh God."

"Hell."

"Shit."

"Could I – work – have a little ointment?"

"What's the policy here?" Mandy asked.

"I don't know," Dave said, because he didn't.

"This always happens in Zoom meetings," Keith complained.

"Does it?" Eddie said. "I always thought it was some video filter."

"Where the hell is HR when you need them," Keith said.

"Work..." Bill started to say.

"She's on the third floor," Mandy said.

"HR's on the third floor!" Dave said, shocked, "but that's... ah. I see."

"Less Human Resources and more Inhuman–"

"Unhuman," Keith automatically corrected Mandy.

192

"Unhuman Resources."

"U. R."

"Oh God."

"Hell."

Dave wondered what to do, so he added, "Shit."

Bill opened his mouth, baring his bloody fangs. "Work, work..." he said. He sprang forward, sprightly considering he was recently deceased, and his bloodshot eyes loomed behind his glasses.

Dave swung his edging tool.

"Triage first!" Mandy shouted.

The metal end struck Bill. The zombie fell back and Dave thrust the sharp edge forward, decapitating the abomination. Bill fell into a puddle of putrid pus and spilt minestrone.

"Oh God, Dave," said Mandy, "you're in so much trouble now."

"Eh?"

"Wait 'til HR finds out."

"You going to the third floor to tell 'em?"

"Yes, I'll... oh."

"You register him," Eddie said, putting a friendly hand on Dave's shoulder, "and we'll say no more."

"I saved your lives," Dave pointed out.

"And we're grateful. Do the paperwork."

"Can I go to the third floor and tell HR instead?"

"There's a good lad."

Dave sighed, stomped off to his desk, but returned to wipe *Brainbiter 2.0* on Bill's expensive suit jacket. The blade looked worse afterwards, if anything.

Back at his desk, Dave leant the great weapon against the filing cabinet, which was within easy arm's reach.

Bill had passed on, forcibly.

There was only Dave, Keith and Bill's blank screen in the meeting, and then Keith ended it for everyone.

All animals auto-destruct.

They have genes, the very genes that a certain Chinese scientist changed more than in his wildest nightmares, that tick away inside. Once the animal reaches a certain age, these genes decide that this experimental version has had long enough to pass them on, and so they hit the overload warp core, light the blue touch paper and flood all tanks.

It's 'game over'.

Is Generation 2.0 ready to play?

Bill was gone, Dawn was gone... well, she wasn't technically gone-gone, but she was gone.

"Oh shit," Dave said aloud. He knew he had to register Bill's turning, but he was not happy about it.

So, Dave turned on his PC, changed his password to what it had been with an added '2' at the end, checked his email by marking all as 'read' and then logged on to the government website. It was a 404, but he found a link to the right place and then, after scrolling, he located the 'Register a Zombie' button.

There were options.

Dave tried the obvious ones to no avail.

If at first you don't succeed, go round the loop again.

Are you registering yourself or someone else?

As if Bill would be capable of registering himself.

Name and surname?

Dave typed in 'Bill' and then paused. 'Underscore 44' didn't seem like a surname, but then he remembered that it meant his real surname.

Something is wrong.

Dave tried again.

Something is wrong.

Something was very wrong.

'William' worked.

Where did the incident happen?

A drop-down menu listed the choices. It was three screens long.

The zombie's corpse was over by the fake rubber tree, but that wasn't an option. Clicking 'Office' didn't work.

According to the website's helpful pop-up, you still weren't allowed to go into the office, so that option wasn't allowed.

Bill should have followed that advice.

So should Dave.

So should everyone.

Dave's next try was 'somewhere else', but that led to street, park, neighbour's, home, place of home working, library, other public building or swimming pool.

He'd been bitten in a place of working, so 'place of home working' it was.

Postcode?

There was a button for manually entering an address, but when he clicked that, Dave realised that he didn't know the office's actual address. It was just a tall building with silver doors and an intercom.

He found it on the company's fancy website and managed to copy it on the third carousel around.

He pasted it in.

Home postcode of victim.

"Oh for..."

Bill's accent had been Yorkshire, so Dave typed 'Yorkshire' realising this was pointless, but it was the least he could do for Bill, the very least.

Eventually, Bill lived at 1 Somewhere Road, Wherever, Yorkshire. YO1... Dave imagined that it was nice up there and that Bill had had a happy childhood. He hadn't been happy at work or at any of their team-building events.

We are experiencing a high level of demand at present, please try again later.

"Oh for..."

He looked out of the window. Down below, a few shamblers worked their way along the road vaguely.

His email pinged.

He'd been promoted to Acting Slogan Manager with no extra pay, privileges or holidays. *Woo hoo*, he thought, but he didn't feel like celebrating.

Bill was undead... dead.

Time to live a little.

Dave took out his phone.

Dawn_372's blue blob was crossing to Newhall Street and then she was gone. Not that they were an item, but they had taken their non-existent relationship to the next level by meeting in person. None of this direct messaging preamble, but in actual real life. In a zombie apocalypse that had to count for something, surely?

No, she was going to 'dinner' and everyone knew what that meant.

Perhaps, he should do something wildly romantic like send a chat request or give her a five-star rating. Instead, Dave texted Frank, 'Fancy a point?', and then he texted, 'Fancy a pint?'

After a moment, his phone pinged – 'Where?'

Dave started to reply and then hit the green symbol.

Frank answered.

"Dave here."

"I know."

"I don't mind."

"Being Dave?"

"No, I don't mind which pub."

"Wellington does real ale."

"There are other pubs before it."

"If we're going to die, let's do it for a decent pint," Frank insisted, not unreasonably.

"Is it still... open?"

'Open' seemed an insane word in the circumstances. It might be closed, derelict, burned to the ground, bombed to bits or infested with zombies, but now the suggestion had been made, it was impossible not to try it. Like a magic spell, saying the word out loud made the very idea cross from utterly impossible to totally reasonable.

"It will be," Frank said.

Dave glanced at the clock on the wall, saw it was still on Greenwich Mean Time, and then said, "Two?"

"Sorted."

"See you."

"See you."

Dave pressed the red symbol, and grabbed his coat and edging tool.

"Where are you going?" Barry asked as he checked the coast was clear as far as the CCTV could see. It was, so he leaned over to buzz Dave out.

"Bill's leaving do."

"Bill? Oh shit."

Dave pulled, then pushed the door and leapt out into the street.

So, he was going to the pub.

The day had been full of firsts since the end of the world: first train trip, first back at the office, first rejection by a girl... and soon, the first time back in a pub.

24

There is no 'I' in 'team', but there is 'tea' in
'team building'.

Anon

Anderson had filched an entire box of tea bags, proper tea
bags with exotic names like English Breakfast, Oolong,
Darjeeling and Earl Grey. Dawn found herself physically
salivating as the kettle, watched by the entire team, gently
scorched the filtered water up to tepid.

They'd all gathered there to mill about looking lost, all
except Mr Matt and–

"I thought that went well," Councillor Grant said.
"Nice to have been out."

The others 'hear-hear'ed.

Dawn could only agree.

Nicer to be safely back inside.

The outside world had been full of wonder – biscuits
that weren't hard tack, people other than those she'd seen
for an eternity, and a proper brew.

What else?

Sunlight, fresh air, screaming terror and that Dave
bloke... and the promise of dinner.

She hoped it wasn't going to be in the canteen as it
smelt of stale cabbage and disinfectant. And the chairs
were hard and, over the, the tables' brash yellow
surfaces had yellowed to an insipid yellow. The concrete
walls had been decorated with warning posters and fire exit
signs.

"Where's the minister?" Dawn asked. He had mentioned something about dinner and that word, 'dinner', had caused the tongue to lick the top of her mouth. It suggested possibilities other than Spam.

"Getting the VIP suite ready, no doubt," Anderson said.

There were smirks and guffaws.

"There's a VIP suite?" Dawn asked.

"Above your clearance," Anderson said.

"But not now," Councillor Grant assured her.

"There'll be a grievance from Matt," Anderson said.

That rather punctured Dawn's exuberance. Even the click of the kettle didn't fix that. Councillor Grant played mother.

Dawn's English Breakfast looked like the caramel of tea rather than the puce of mud that changed to off-bleach when the reconstituted whey was slopped in.

Brown?

Milk!

Anderson had also nicked a plastic two-pinter of actual, real, flowed like silk and not like porridge, milk. Oh, she loved him, and then she felt a little sick. Randy Anderson... hardly worth a drop of milk. Oh, but it tasted good.

"Garibaldi," Anderson said.

He'd snaffled their biscuits. The bravery of the man weighing himself down with all these supplies stuffed into his crumpled jacket pockets, when he'd had to run across Birmingham through the hordes of hell with only two trigger-happy police gunmen for protection! She could just... no, no, that was too disgusting.

"Dawn," Councillor Grant said. He glanced left and right, took Dawn's arm and led her aside. "I'd like to raise a grievance."

For God's sake, what the hell, but Dawn said, "Yes, Councillor."

"Only it's rather delicate."

"Would you like to talk somewhere private?"

"Yes."

"I'm sure I can fit you in."

Grant sniggered, stopped himself and then looked at her strangely.

"The problem is," he said, "is that the problem is... something I can't tell you."

The others were still in the room, but she dropped her volume to a whisper.

"HR is all about confidentiality," she assured him.

"It's above your clearance level."

"You could raise my clearance level."

"I think that the minister has to do that as the senior member of the emergency protocol."

"Well..."

"And I can't tell him."

"He has the highest clearance, surely?"

"Between you and me, it's about him."

Someone with a complaint about a Conservative politician, Dawn thought; join the queue.

"The minister is going to raise your clearance to cover this matter," Councillor Grant continued. "So, when he has, don't do anything until you've talked to me."

"Well..."

"Promise."

"Er..."

"Please."

"All right."

Back at the canteen's serving hatch, Dawn helped herself to another cup of tea, Oolong – the very word suggesting surprise and yearning. They'd have to ration this manna from the heavenly towers of commerce, but not today, tomorrow.

Just then, the sergeant stomped in, snapped to attention and then turned to Dawn.

"Dinner is served," he said.

Dawn put down her mug of tea, brushed down her smart suit and followed the police officer out.

Behind her, the others murmured to each other. The repetition of their grumbling sounded oddly like zombies moaning. The simmering tone of complaint suggested forthcoming forms, investigations, meetings, sobbing into tissues, recriminations, docked privileges and weeks of sour looks.

Well, it was nothing to do with her.

25

Abandon hope all ye who enter here.

Gent's Toilet Wall,
Wembley Stadium

Dave left his office in a rage.

Bill was dead.

Dawn was... and why should that bother him?

Two shamblers working their way out of town stood no chance against the savage swing of his mighty edging tool. Their heads rolled off the pavement like a ball going over the touchline. He stormed down Bennetts Hill more like a thrash metal fan than Bee Gees devotee and more like a man with a death wish than someone with a high-pitched voice.

Stayin' Alive was for losers.

Like Dave.

He found the Wellington closed, of course, and banged on the door until Frank's large frame appeared in the glass window. The bolts ratcheted back and he was inside the dark, gloom of the traditional pub.

"The decked terrace has zombies," Frank said. "I'll, er, have to promote myself to acting-landlord."

"Hmm."

"We've the corner at the back away from the windows."

"Hmm."

"So, what do you fancy? The screen's off, but the handpumps have badges."

"The usual."

"What's that?"

"I don't know."

"I'll... pick something and have the unusual myself."

Dave found the seating with Frank's camouflage jacket dumped beside it and he squeezed behind the table. It didn't matter, plenty more fish in the sea and who cared anyway.

He counted his breaths.

Why was he thinking about that girl?

Ten more and then another ten and he felt calmer.

Bloody public school entitled twats!

Maybe another ten slower breaths.

Presently, Frank put two pints down.

Dave licked his lips – a pint in a pub – and he might as well enjoy it. He tried to remember the last time he had done this, all those years ago (well, two) and he couldn't. A single tear ran down his cheek as the froth dribbled down the tall, straight glass to soak into the beermat. The pint looked magnificent, standing there on its cardboard stage. Narrow beams of light from the boarded-up window shone like spotlights, shimmering through the amber nectar.

"What beer is it?" Dave asked.

"Brains."

"That's...."

"Tactless, I know."

"Still."

"If you can't beat 'em, join 'em."

They both sipped their beer, forcing themselves to savour every drop. After all, when would they get the chance again? Not for at least ten minutes as they'd have to finish this one before another round.

"Anyone else coming?" Dave asked.

"Guy and Lucy said they'd come."

"The one in the red and blue tracksuit and... the other one?"

"In the scarf, yes, that's them," Frank said. "I guess something came up. We rather need them and two others."

"Eh?"

"The rule is you can meet if there are six people or more. Six people if they all have six packs and packs of six beers... something like that."

Dave nodded.

"So, what's the plan?" Frank asked.

"Stay here and get rat-arsed."

It was Frank's turn to nod and he rubbed his broken nose thoughtfully. "They'll get in eventually."

"So?"

"Just saying."

"It'll be a hell of a way to go."

"The beer will run out eventually."

"But it would be a pity to let it go to waste."

They drank further and Frank fetched another round. There were no staff, unless they were on the decked terrace. This time, he came back with a few packets of crisps as well.

"What's the matter?" Frank asked.

"I met a girl."

"Oh."

They drank for a while in silence, although the moaning outside was still audible. But then it was always audible, a constant refrain like the thumping headache they'd committed themselves to drinking towards.

"It's not the end of the world," Frank said.

"Well, it is," Dave said.

"Yes, I suppose it is."

Dave could feel the beer reaching his stomach, its enlightening ambrosia seeping into his veins and arteries to rush up to his brain.

"There's not going to be a happy ending," Dave said.

"No."

"TV has so lied to us."

"Yes."

Frank matched him, sip for sip, pint for pint, Brains for brains.

"Remember those Brains adverts?" Frank said.

On Dave's internal TV of his mind, he saw the image of a few zombies chanting 'brains, brains...' appearing on the screen. They shambled closer and closer filling the 16:9 frame. A caption appeared, read by a trustworthy male voice: *"They don't want brains, they want Brains."* It finished on a freeze-frame of the nearest zombie springing towards the camera.

"Yeah, one of ours," Dave said to Frank. "Shame about Mike and Tod."

"Mike and Tod?"

"Cameraman and sound guy."

"Oh... right," Frank said. "Was it Brains beers and Mr Brain's sausages?"

"Dunno, adverts..." – Dave waved his hand over his head and made a whooshing noise – "...and I'm in advertising."

"The sausages would have been awkward."

"Beer it was then," Dave said, sipping his pint like the victim of the zombie advert. "I seem to remember they'd shot one version and then the producer demanded more attractive zombies?"

"Jeez."

Dave opened a packet of crisps.

"Past their sell-by date," Frank said.

"So is everything," Dave said.

Dave stared into the open packet, the silver interior seemed to shine with promise, but it was only stale crisps.

"You're in advertising then?" Frank asked.

"I write the slogans for the government," Dave said. "You know, 'Be very careful, do not become infected, save everyone's life.' That was one of mine. We have this competition in the office to write 'em as a haiku – five, seven and... er, five syllables."

They munched for a while taking it in turns with the salt'n'vinegar.

"I'm in insurance," Frank said, "since you've not asked."

"Uh?"

"Big changes in insurance."

"Hmm."

"Our slogan is 'not alive is not the same as dead'."

Frank waited for Dave to respond.

"Thing is," Frank continued, warming to his subject, "the definition of 'undead' has become very important. Put simply, we don't pay out on someone's death just because someone's 'not alive'."

"Not alive is dead."

"They're walking about so clearly there's a grey area. The new 'undead' definition industry has been worth billions. And doctors are unwilling to examine the dead, so death certificates are like winning lottery tickets. It's the same with health insurance. That only pays out for living patients and the undead aren't 'living'. It's a bonanza."

Frank ran out of steam.

He finished the salt and vinegar and started on the cheese and onion.

The zombies continued migrating past the window.

Those on the decking continued to demand a particular beer.

"You want to talk about it?" Frank asked eventually. "For your mental health. I saw this podcast about it."

"I'd rather not."

"Thank God."

"It's just that we had this connection."

"Oh, you are going to talk about it."

"But she's gone off with this government minister, who's like old enough to be her grandfather for dinner." Dave shivered. He didn't like the idea of Fenton-Briggs touching her, kissing her, doing things to her.

"Where is she now?" Frank asked.

"She's in some nuclear bunker."

"That'll be secret."

"Telephone House, Newhall Street."

"How do you know that?"

"She said." And why did she tell him, Dave wondered.

"Do you know where that is?" Frank asked.

"Dunno, but I know where Newhall Street is... it'll be some old telephone exchange or where the telephone was invented or founded by Lord Telephone."

"What good's that?"

"It'll be written on the building."

"Oh yeah, loads of zombies thereabouts."

"I know."

Dave wondered about all those zombies thereabouts, and those zombies he'd heard saying 'brains', and those saying 'trains' and 'shiny'. Perhaps there hadn't been a virus or whatever, perhaps it was simply that staring at a phone or a computer screen all day, and a video game all night, had rotted everyone's brains. Maybe people's attention spans had become so low that all they could manage was a single word, one over-riding desire that blotted out everything else.

He wanted to blot everything out... Brains, hmm.

The rat race was all about the shiny, money, beer... brains. It was how you got on now that the human race had invented technology and killed all the mammoths.

But what did Dave want?

What was his one thing?

He didn't know.

"Dawn," he said out loud.

"Not for ages," Frank said. "It's mid-afternoon."

Charles Darwin called it 'Survival of the Fittest' to suggest a great struggle between individuals as if the best would win out. However, no amount of keen eyesight, acute hearing, strong heart, powerful muscles and supple limbs helped if you happened to be at the edge of the herd when the sabre-toothed tiger leapt out of the bushes intent on killing and eating the nearest.

'Survival of the Furthest Away' wasn't catchy.

It ought to be 'Survival of the Survivor' with 'survivor' defined as making it long enough to produce offspring. That's what it was all about. You didn't have to just survive; you had to reproduce.

Dave checked his Matchbox profile again.

He hadn't marked himself down as a survivor or as a hero. He was interested in walks and nights out, because that was what women wanted. In reality, it was football and beer. And women.

There was Dawn, who looked nice with long, dark hair and sultry eyes. She worked in local government, it said.

The window suddenly echoed with a bump, quiet but enough to make them both jump out of their skins and stifle a screaming diatribe of panic.

Zombies shuffled past outside the pub chanting the famous advertising catchphrase.

The two of them waited until their hearts were less likely to explode and sipping their beer wouldn't make them choke.

Frank was the first to break their silence with a whisper. "You remember when the government changed the statistics? You know, they're not a zombie, if they turned more than 28 days ago."

Dave nodded.

"So... that one, or that one," Frank continued pointing at the dark shapes moving past the window, "you know, those two, they're probably not zombies. Officially. There may be millions and millions, but only a few thousand according to those Number 10 briefings."

Three million or so people lived in Birmingham. Dave corrected himself: *had* lived in Birmingham. Many had fled early on taking the infection with them, but others had come to Birmingham to escape elsewhere. There were deaths, both of the living and the undead, but Dave knew that the vast majority had turned and roaming the streets.

"Remember," Frank persisted, "when they told us that, in addition to shamblers and ramblers, there were joggers in the South East. That government spokesperson said it was no cause for alarm, but merely part of the plan."

Dave grunted – there were only shamblers and ramblers outside, although joggers only jogged when they smelt your breath with its promise of brains.

"They said the world wouldn't end," Frank continued. "They said that. Next slide, please. And it didn't, did it? It carried on... lurched on."

Was it Dave's imagination or were all the zombies passing their very pub? There did seem to be a lot and they were all going left to right, up Bennett's Hill towards Newhall Street.

"Only a few thousand, eh?" Dave said.

"Those would be the odds."

Dave knew he needed to do something. He had needed to do something with his life even before the apocalypse. Enough sitting around waiting, he decided. He had swiped right, after all.

And she had told him where she was!

It was obvious, wasn't it? Come here and get me.

"The girl," Dave said. "Dawn."

"Oh, her again."

"I'm going to rescue her."

"That sounds like the beer talking."

"We have to test ourselves," Dave said, "see what we're made of."

"Too much Brains."

"And brawn."

"I meant too much Brains... beer."

"Uh?"

"It'll be dangerous."

"Mildly risky is my middle name."

"Seriously, there's no way you can, what... get across town to—"

"It's only—"

"To defeat all the zombies *and break into a secret nuclear bunker.*"

"No, I guess not."

It was hopeless.

In the Game of Life, Dave wasn't a survivor. He just went through the motions – football, beer, video games... those were his watchwords, the mumbling repetition he'd spout when his luck finally ran out. The walking dead would catch him, but he was dead inside already. They'd turn him into a zombie with his dull office job and there would be no real change.

But he didn't just want to survive, he wanted to live, and he did like walks and nights out.

Dave stood up – dramatically – and downed the rest of the Dutch courage, savouring the hops and malt as if for the first time.

Yes, he felt alive, really alive, like a new-born gulping for air and seeing the transcendental delivery room lights for the first time. He had become empowered, as if he could do anything – leap tall buildings, dodge bullets, fly.

Nothing could stop him.

He was a man of action, who brooked no delays.

He should update his Matchbox profile... no later.

His time was now!

"I am going to save her," Dave promised. "Right after I've had a slash."

26

You are what you eat. If you wish to be
strong, eat meat. If you wish to be healthy,
eat vegetables. If you wish to be intelligent,
eat brains.

Good Advice

Fenton-Briggs bit into his side order of ribs in barbeque
sauce and the bloody juices drizzled out onto his expertly
raised napkin. It reminded Dawn of... and she had to look
away. So many others she'd seen eating flesh.

"Don't be coy," Fenton-Briggs said.

Dawn took her fork and stabbed a French fry.

"Is it all right?" Fenton-Briggs asked.

"Lovely," Dawn replied. She thought the ribs were too
rare, the fries too greasy and the lack of greenery
despairing, but it was candlelit, there was wine in an
enormous delicate glass and she was being fussed over.
And, to be fair, the meat wasn't Spam and the fries hadn't
had to be reconstituted with water.

"Otto's my personal chef," Fenton-Briggs explained.

"I thought he was security."

"Everyone has to double up. Christ, I have to do my
own letters to constituents... did. Fewer now."

"Fewer letters?"

"Fewer constituents."

"Other people don't get to eat like this."

"Of course they do," countered Fenton-Briggs. "And
there are food banks. It's heart-warming, isn't it? Those

people coming together like that. It's the good old British blitz spirit."

"I suppose, but a pity they needed them."

"Well, not anymore," Fenton-Briggs said. "All closed due to the apocalypse. Another government success."

Dawn tried the wine.

"Champers later," the minister informed her.

Wine and fizz, Dawn thought, putting down her glass. It had been tasty, velvety with a hint of fruitiness. She could get used to this. She had been used to gin and tonics and nights out.

Where was all this leading?

"You wanted to talk to me," Dawn hazarded as a way of a leading statement.

"I'm on the rise, Miss Knott-Withany, groomed for PM and greatness." Fenton-Briggs paused to think about this. "Even more greatness. Our recent PMs have been an absolute shower. Our current one, when all this kicked off, said... what was it? Oh yes. Stack the bodies thousands high. Except the bodies didn't stack, they rose from the grave to attack the gullible, foolish and misled."

"Oh yes, er... a pity."

"But I'll be different, buck the trend of the last couple of decades, and really turn things around."

"Oh good."

"And someone who hangs on to my coattails could go far. That's what Councillor Grant is doing. He's not being an obsequious toady, he's being wise. You could do the same."

"I could?"

"That's got to be worth a blow job."

Dawn wasn't sure she'd heard properly.

"A joke, a joke," Fenton-Briggs assured her. "I know you work hard and you're ambitious."

"That was sexist," Dawn said. "It makes you sound like you're a—"

"Misogynist?"

"Yes."

"Nonsense," he said. He focused in the middle distance as if a glass teleprompter hovered in front of him. "I love women. Love them. Why do you think I had Councillor Grant pick you as the liaison down here? Because you are vital to the running of this whole emergency response."

"Why, thank you."

"Exactly, the men trapped down here – and they are trapped – need a sympathetic ear, a kind word, an understanding, empathetic soul... that's HR's function."

"I've always seen it as that, but over the last few years it's been more–"

"And there's no harm in choosing someone to do that vital task – that important and vital task – who's easy on the eye."

"Well, that's... I see."

"So, I thought we should get to know each other first." Fenton-Briggs picked a sinew out of his teeth. He was quite disgusting. "Dawn, I want you to head up a project."

"Oh."

She saw him in a new light. This was both slightly disappointing and wonderfully exciting. The former because there was an ulterior motive to the dinner and the latter because... well, finally some recognition.

"Project Eve fell through – dreadful shame – so we need a replacement," Fenton-Briggs said.

"I don't know that project," Dawn admitted.

"The Emergency Volunteer Employment project?"

"Emergency... Eve, yes, I see. What is it?"

"Above your pay grade."

"And this new project?"

"We could name it Project Dawn," Fenton-Briggs said.

"Dawn!"

"Yes, er... Development Awareness with... something beginning with 'N'. We'll get that Dave chap to come up with the right words."

"Yes."

"It's all about developing our economy in the post-apocalyptic world. We're not scoring well in some important metrics. Not our fault, you understand, the virus, or whatever it is – the science is still undecided – came from abroad. From Europe."

"From China."

"Via Europe."

"But the Europeans–"

"We're not listening to those baguette-waving idiots at FENNEL," Fenton-Briggs said.

"The Federal European North National Emergency Liaison do have some sensible–"

"They can go and screw themselves. We had Brexit so we don't have to listen to them, no matter how sensible they might be."

"I suppose."

"The nation that gets back on its feet quickest will have the advantage."

"I can see that."

"And we don't want that to be some foreigners, do we?"

"No"

"So, best if we increase our workforce, pronto."

"Oh, HR, of course, recruitment, I'd be delighted."

"Excellent, because, between you and me that Eve woman was as whiny as hell about it."

"Oh dear."

"I mean, I'm a government minister, Eton educated, clearly fine material having risen to... well, nearly the top."

"Yes, you've done well."

"I know."

"So what exactly is it?"

"Breeding."

"Sorry?"

"With me."

The candles made a twinkle in the minister's eye. The romantic light cast pretty, swirling patterns on the chequerboard tablecloth and matching napkins. The unused cutlery, the spoon that promised pudding, shone with a red light. The warm bun from the oven lay on her side plate. Her meat was going cold.

"That woman, Eve, for some inexplicable reason objected to having sex with the surviving cabinet," Fenton-Briggs said. He leaned across the table and took her unresisting hand in his. "You're not going to let us down, are you, Dawn? I can call you Dawn, can't I, Miss Knott-Withany? Because I can see you're a fighter, a team player, a responsible adult who can see the need to repopulate the planet, surely?"

"Yes, of course, I mean... pardon?" Dawn said, taking her hand back.

"Good, good, excellent, so Project Dawn is a goer."

"I need to think about this," Dawn said. She could feel the candlelight sparkling in her deer in headlights eyes.

"It's part of your contract," Fenton-Briggs said, and then he added, "you know the clause, 'any other duties commensurate with the post'."

"But..."

"And then, phased in next financial year, with Councillor Grant."

"Councillor Grant!"

"Then Anderson and so on."

"Randy Anderson!"

"Is he? Well, he'll have to wait his turn," Fenton-Briggs said. "You do understand the importance. BASIL went on about spreading the gene pool."

"Basil? As well?"

"BASIL, the British Association for Scientific Intelligence Liaison."

Oh yes, Dawn realised, the thinktank. "I know what BASIL stands for."

"Good, good, that's all settled then."

"No, no, I think we need to discuss this further."

"God, you're not suggesting we set up a sub-committee."

"NO!"

"You see, it's not a pleasure, it's business. Think of it as a transaction."

"I want to go home."

"This is home. For the foreseeable. I'll think of this as my second... no, fourth home, but there's no rent so there's no point in flipping to here, financially speaking."

"Financially?"

"It means a pay raise for you."

"Oh... er..."

"Phased in over three years depending on productivity."

"Oh!"

"And bonuses," Fenton-Briggs said. "I'd put those abroad. Maybe not Panama or the Canary Islands, but Switzerland, that's like a fortress. The whole country is one big vault."

"I'm not sure... that is..."

"You've enjoyed the meal."

"Well, yes."

"Which I paid for out of *my* expenses."

"Er..."

"So, it's time for you to give up and put out."

"But..."

"You'll be saving the world – literally."

"Yes, though–"

"You've had resilience training, so time to be resilient."

"But... it's all rather sudden!"

"Don't fret," Fenton-Briggs said, his oily hand resting on hers again. "I'm not a monster. You've two hours to get your head around this. I've only just taken the Viagra."

27

Nor is Philip's church safer than Philip's
church-yard:
Nay, run from altars with a speedy tread;
For the wise rush off when angels become
undead.

Not Alexander Pope

Right, Dave thought, just a short way up Bennett's Hill
and it turns into Newhall Street... or alternatively, Dave
thought, down Bennett's Hill to avoid all the gathering
zombies, left onto Waterloo Street, along to the cathedral.

*You can tell by the way I run, I'm a woman's man. No
time to waste...*

Coming back along Temple Row West didn't look
good. Dave trotted along Temple Row proper... oh dear.

He'd have to go down Temple Street, but that led to
New Street and the station – the wrong way. He glanced
down the street over the 'Road Ahead Closed' and saw the
barricades.

The cathedral, surrounded by pleasant grounds,
affectionately known as 'Pigeon Park', was on his left.

Could he go all the way around the cathedral?

Nope, he saw a mass of undead office workers over
towards Snow Hill station at the far corner.

So, Needless Alley, the next turning on the right, it
was, he decided, even if it did narrow towards New Street.

Except that was full of zombies.

He was becoming surrounded.

Zombies, shamblers so far thankfully, massed in loose lines across the alley, row and streets.

There was no becoming about it, he was surrounded.

He came to a halt and raised his edging tool, the ever-dependable *Brainbiter 2.0,* but he knew that wasn't going to cut it.

There was another gateway leading to a path that ambled up to St Philip's cathedral, but it too was blocked by a burnt-out car.

There was no other choice.

He sprinted to the black railings, javelined his edging tool over the gold-painted spikes, and leapt up. He caught the spikes – *oww* – and clambered – *woah, careful* – to drop gingerly down into the graveyard that made up the wide-open space around the cathedral.

Fingers grabbed him through the wrought iron.

He struggled to get free.

Evil, rotting teeth snapped at his neck.

He wriggled out of his jacket and stumbled forward.

His mask slipped down.

Hang on, Dave realised, that car blocking the gate had been put there to keep zombies in, not out. Taking refuge in a graveyard during a zombie apocalypse was perhaps not the most sensible thing he'd ever done.

As he tried to get his breath back, the ground trembled, the soil split and the gravestones rent asunder as the dead rose all around. They had been, but sleeping, cosy in their tombs and now they smelt the gasps of life – Dave's life... Dave's soon-to-be ex-life.

This wasn't a virus!

It wasn't, 'Avoid contact, don't get bitten, save lives' – it was hell giving back its dead. The government had lied to him *using his own slogans!*

Dave searched for his edging tool.

There, but before he could reach it, a hand burst from the ground to grasp its fine, FSC-certified hardwood handle.

"Shit!"

All around him, through every gap in the railings, clawed hands reached and grasped.

He jumped onto a tomb.

Fists punched upwards through the crumbling stone.

Everywhere the ground heaved as it spewed forth a multitude of crawling corpses. Dressed in tatters from Victorian and Georgian times, they lurched towards Dave's precarious position.

"Headmeat, headmeat..." they chanted.

Dave jumped down, hared off as fast as he could. There was no escape, but terror and desperation had given him wings, although unlike Red Bull's variety, it did not mean he could actually fly.

And he needed to fly.

Around the small cathedral – why did Birmingham, the second city for heaven's sake, have such a small cathedral? – and he nearly collided with the back of the ravenous mob of undead chasing him.

"Oh..."

He slowed down, not *Stayin' Alive,* but more *God Save Our Gracious King.* He let those ahead move around the cathedral while keeping a pace or two ahead of those behind him. These zombies were slow, very slow, 17th and 18th century slow. Even some of their chants were slow.

"Head... meat... head... meat..."

But all it needed was for one to catch him and there were a lot of them, a growing lot of them.

Round again, walking now.

It was like some weird pitch invasion were they'd all decided to do endless laps of honour around the hallowed grounds. Perhaps Headmeat had scored the winning goal. The stories these undead could tell if only their vocabulary extended beyond a single expression.

And round again.

He even managed to collect his edging tool on his... he'd lost count, circuit. It felt better to be armed, but he knew he wouldn't be able to kill them all. He'd take some with him, but then he'd be one of them.

The zombies bunched up.

Dave found that if he went outwards, then in, the ones at the front zig-zagged, and those behind did not, so the zombies became a bunched, condensed herd. The ones coming out of the ground, attracted by his breath, took a couple of circuits to emerge properly and then they joined their brethren.

If only he could keep this up forever, he'd be fine.

The zombies outside the graveyard were more... 'lively', being modern, 21st-century undead. They chanted as if Dave's pursuers belonged not to Birmingham City or Aston Villa, but Brains FC.

"Brains, brains..."

Dave paused to check the escape routes – none – and the old zombies were closer.

"Head... meat... head... meat..."

"Oi!"

"Eh?" Dave said, but he'd already moved on.

When he came around again and spied someone peeking out of a side door into the cathedral, Dave sprinted over and slipped inside through the solid doorway.

It took a few moments for Dave's eyes to become accustomed to the darkness.

"My son," said a clergyman, "you are saved by the good Grace of the Lord."

"Thank you," Dave said.

"Come, join our congregation."

"Oh, is there a service on?"

"There's always a service on."

The man led the way into the main hall. It was light and airy with white plaster walls, square columns and fancier, Greek columns at the altar end. In the main area, a group of people sat on wooden chairs arranged in a wide circle.

"Ah, Brother John, I see you have a new convert," said another clergyman. He stood and came over to Dave. "Welcome, brother, welcome."

"Thank you."

"And you are?"

"Dave."

"Ah, Brother Dave, join us. We are sending our thoughts and prayers to all those in peril. I am Brother Mike. Please, sit, sit, here between Brother Paul and Sister Jordan."

"Thank you."

Dave sat, comfortable with the blue upholstery of the beech chair, and his presence brought the number of attendees up to a round dozen. He'd just sit a while, mouth the words and then... sit some more and sit some more.

How was he going to get out?

"The... er..."

"Our wondrous graveyard," Brother John said, "was used from 1711 to 1859, and has, in these glorious times, given up its dead."

"Oh."

"60,000 of them, apparently."

"There seemed less than that," Dave said, although there had been far too many.

"Buried deep."

"Ah."

Dave smiled in response to Brother John's grin. They all seemed to be beaming with peaceful beatification, their faces as serene as the heavenly light shining through the stained-glass windows.

"Let us have a reading from the Book of New Revelation," Brother Mike said.

Dave raised his finger.

"Yes, Brother Dave," said Brother Mike.

"Excuse me," said another man in the circle.

"Yes, Brother Other Dave."

"He can't be Brother Dave," Brother Other Dave said, "I should be Brother Dave, now that the first Brother Dave is no longer with us."

"Good point," Brother Mike agreed. "Let him from this moment onwards be known as Brother Third Dave."

The man opposite Dave coughed theatrically.

"Sorry, Brother Also Dave, he shall be known henceforth as Brother Fourth Dave."

Brother Also Dave nodded.

So, Dave thought, Mike and John were in charge, Paul, Jordan, Dave and Dave, five others and himself.

"You had a question, Brother Fourth Dave."

"Did I? Oh, yes, the Book of New Revelation?"

"Ah, yes," Brother Mike boomed and the large space echoed his words. "This is the End of Days, when Death and Hades have given up their dead and they've been judged as clearly evil, but not thrown into the lake of fire and the faithful... well, we've not been raptured."

"Raptured?"

"We've not been taken up by the Lord to save us from the final battle between good and evil. Disappointing, really."

"The problem is Armageddon," Brother Paul said.

"The final battle between good and evil," Dave said. He knew all about this as his ex-flatmate, Clarkie, had been a heavy metal fan.

"It doesn't quite work," Brother Paul continued. "If the good are raptured – that's taken up – to heaven to save them from the awful battle between the forces of evil, then... well, you see the problem?"

"One team's a no-show."

"Exactly."

"So," Brother Mike said, taking over, "we needed a new book, the Book of New Revelation, one that makes sense."

"Right," Dave said slowly.

"So, gone are lakes of fire and riders on pale horses and six, six, six, and instead, we have concepts like... well, that's what we've been discussing. You could help! You've been outside. Any lakes of fire, any Jerusalems materializing from thin air, any great cracks in the very Earth opening up or any springs of magical water appearing?"

"In Birmingham?"

"Yes."

"Not that I've seen."

"Anything else?"

"Apart from the dead rising to feast off the living?"

"Yes, apart from that. We already covered that in the Book of New Revelation, beginning at chapter one, verse one."

"Right, and how far have you got?"

"We're discussing verse three."

"Oh."

"We hadn't expected to write much, it being the End of Days, but they have gone on a bit."

"What's verse two?"

"Oh, Brother Also Dave, if you would."

"Of course, Brother Mike."

"Perhaps all of it," Dave asked.

Also Dave looked to Brother Mike, who nodded, so Also Dave coughed to clear his throat, took out a Moleskine notebook and began to read:

"The Book of New Revelation, chapter one, verses one to two," Brother Also Dave began. "Verily, forsooth, in the terrible End of Days, the dead rose from the ground to feast upon the living."

"Verse one," Mike whispered helpfully.

"Gathered together were the Lord's servants, Mike, John, Declan and his sister, Jordan, Paul, Clifford, Xander, Chester, Kaylee, Zelda, Joey, the two Andys, the four Daves, the quiet one and the screaming one."

"That's us," Mike added. "And that was verse two."

"And that's as far as you've got?" Dave said.

"We do need divine guidance, Brother Fourth Dave."

"Ah. Yes. I see."

"Oh," Brother Other Dave said, interrupting, "he can't be the fourth Dave as we originally had four Daves."

"Henceforth, let him be Brother Fifth Dave," Brother Mike pronounced.

Brother Other Dave nodded, approving.

"And that's it?" Dave asked.

"Yes, Brother Fifth Dave," Brother Also Dave said.

"What about the others?"

"Others?"

"The other servants," Dave said, indicating the circle.

"Oh," Brother Mike said, "we ate them."

"Right. What!"

"They have given of their bodies so that we faithful might continue."

"Apart from Clifford, who came back to life and ate Kaylee's brain," Brother Paul said.

"Oh yes," Brother Mike said.

"But that's cannibalism!" Dave said.

"We couldn't get a supermarket delivery slot," Sister Jordan added.

"And it's not as if it's against any of the ten commandments," Brother Mike pointed out.

"I think it's probably mentioned somewhere else in the Bible," Dave said. "And it's murder."

"Not if they commit suicide for the greater good," Brother Mike said.

"Or if we kill them to stop them killing us," Brother John added. "That's self-defence."

"Oh yes, Xander did start the cannibalism and we couldn't let that carry on, could we?"

"Without us, we mean."

"I see," Dave said. Carrots cooked to resemble tagliatelle and cabbage disguised as toast suddenly seemed so much more appetising.

"So," Brother John said, looking at Dave, "any thoughts on verse three?"

– Apocrypha –

Any sufficiently advanced pseudoscience is indistinguishable from superstition.

Anon

"I represent Water," the wizard said. He knew he should be helping the others, those that would wear the mantle of Fire, Earth and Air, but it was in this plane that he had lost his love.

He dribbled from the sacred chalice the water of life from the secret spring hidden in the grounds of Eden. The conjuring circle's chalk outline, so complex and intricate, smudged.

"Fire and brimstone," he intoned.

He cast within the cauldron the feather of a raven plucked in the Tower of London.

"Blood and sand," he chanted.

He added a cloakroom ticket from the inner sanctum of the Vatican.

"Life and death," he cantillated.

The final item for the spell was the nameless thing.

It burst into flames!

His offering was accepted.

Lucifer himself, the dark angel, appeared within the binding spell.

"Oh Black Prince of Hell, I command you."

"Ask."

"Oh Evil Lord–"

"Ask then, I haven't got all night."

"Dread Bringer of Light and–"

"YES, YES."

"Sorry, thou defiler of–"

"I AM ON A TIGHT SCHEDULE HERE."

"Etcetera," the wizard added. "I, the Great Magi, Euronymos Daibolus Azazel, ask for nothing less than immortality."

"NO NEED TO BE SO MELODRAMATIC ABOUT IT."

"Sorry."

"ARE YOU REALLY CALLED EURONYMOS DAIBOLUS AZAZEL?"

"I am, oh Great Dark Lord."

"SERIOUSLY?"

"I changed it by deed poll."

"FAIR ENOUGH," said the Devil. "AND YOU WANT TO MAKE A PACT WITH THE DEVIL FOR IMMORTALITY."

"Yes, oh Evil One."

"ARE YOU SURE?"

"Yes, oh Despoiler of All that is Good."

"REALLY SURE?"

"Yes, yes, of course, I was sure the moment I found Eden and I was even more sure after consulting the hidden texts."

"BUT IT'S A PACT WITH THE DEVIL."

"Which you must honour."

"YES, BUT, YOU KNOW, 'PACT', 'DEVIL'."

"Yes, yes, grant me my wish."

"EVERLASTING LIFE."

"Yes."

"DID I MENTION THE DEVIL PACT BUSINESS?"

"Yes."

"OH, VERY WELL."

"Thank you."

"IF YOU ARE SURE?"

"Yes, I am sure."

"REALLY, REALLY SURE?"

"Good God, yes, I... sorry. Oh Ruler of Hell, yes, I'm sure!"

"WELL, FINE THEN... 'TIS DONE," Satan said as he made the wish come true.

"I'm immortal!"

"INDEED."

"And I shall live forever."

"THAT'S WHAT IT MEANS."

"And ever and ever with eternal youth."

"FOR AS LONG AS THE WORLD LASTS, YES."

"Sorry, what was that?"

"FOR AS LONG AS THE WORLD LASTS," Lucifer the Bringer of Light said.

"For an infinity of ages."

"OR A DAY OR TWO."

"What was that, Dark Lord?"

"OH NOTHING. I'LL BE OFF THEN."

"Yes, yes, thank you, oh Lord of etcetera, etcetera."

"MUST GET ON. LOADS OF THE DEAD TO KICK OUT OF HELL. WORLDS DON'T END THEMSELVES."

"I'm sorry, Satan, but what... Lucifer?"

But Lucifer had flapped his wings and was gone.

"Lucifer?"

28

Use the appropriate amount of panic and
keep going.

Government advice

Dawn was back in the Ladies. She was just going to
powder her nose, she'd said. However, instead of dabbing
some long-lasting shine control natural glow on her pale
complexion, she'd put her shaking hand over her mouth to
stop herself from screaming.

Her other hand reached for the panic cord.

She wanted to curl up on the sofa with Snookums
purring on her lap, a big box of chocolates and a glass of
Prosecco within easy reach and Hugh Grant being cute in
a romantic comedy. She did not want to be trapped in a
concrete catacomb with every randy sod still alive.

She checked her bag: a packet of tissues, purse, lipstick,
compact, mask, sunglasses, bottle of hand sanitiser, attack
alarm, a screwed-up copy of the agenda and a ticket for
Symphony Hall. Not much to show for a lifetime. She
wondered if the Strauss concert had taken place and
whether to take her attack alarm – it seemed superfluous
give the circumstances. Although the agenda point hadn't
been debated and hadn't gone to a vote, it was obviously
being actioned. Item 12 *Project Eve replacement* – that's
all she was, a replacement.

She hadn't always wanted to go into HR.

She'd wanted to be a vet.

Or a princess. The sort that lives in an impregnable tower and heals cute, talking animals – bunnies and deer, perhaps even the occasional piece of animated furniture that had come to life–

She sobbed.

Couldn't help herself.

No knight with floppy hair and shining armour was coming to save her.

She was to be the Mother of a Brave New Normal, a second Eve... no, that was the other Eve. Dawn was to be the third Eve, Eve 3.0.

She hadn't really expected grand romantic gestures, flowers, witty one-liners and handsome men falling for her, but she'd never dreamed that her love life would become an item in a government policy document.

Damn this zombie apocalypse!

There were millions dead and millions undead, and she was expected to replace them. A baby every nine months until she reached 67 and retirement age was... a lot.

And they'd no doubt raise the retirement age... again.

But wasn't it better to be in the bunker pissing out?

There had always been Us and Them. Better to be one of Them, surely?

Then Them would be Us and Us would be Them, everyone else – the plebs, the zombies. Yes, zombies even before the virus. They'd tell Us utter nonsense, nonsense you could see was utter nonsense, and somehow it would be believed. Not by individuals, but by the masses. No wonder They think of Us as plebs. We are plebeians, give Us our sport, our headline to be angry about – bread and circuses. Even if it makes no sense and the next day's headline contradicts the chip wrappers of yesterday – and then we'll be righteously outraged about that common enemy – Us's Them that wasn't Them, but Them's other Them.

And we'd let the leaders, those Tory Eton boys, get away with anything. Even Dawn.

And she realised that she still thought of Them as Them, which meant she was still part of Us.

She held her head in her hands and stared down the sink's plug hole, her thoughts going round and round making her more and more drained.

Why not just give in, lie back and think of the Northern Sector?

It was her sacred duty, just as Cain and Abel had been the first Eve's sacred duty.

How had it gone in the Bible?

God had taken one of Adam's spare ribs, probably dunked in barbeque sauce, and made Eve.

And God said, "Adam, this is Eve; Eve, Adam."

And Adam said, "Phwoar, look at the tits on her."

For women had smooth bodywork, all curves and sleek lines, and – this is the important bit – all their reproductive organs neatly tucked away as part of the design. Clearly, homo sapiens 2.0. Whereas God made man chunky and lumpy, a first draft, originally with no sexual organs as he didn't need them.

Dawn realised she was going mad.

Obviously, when the first woman arrived, the male variety needed a little extra. So, God realised His omission and so He had simply tacked the extra appendage on at the front, ready to stick out when needed.

Dawn decided to silently scream.

Eventually, Anderson banged on the door.

"Are you all right?" he asked.

"Yes."

"It's just that I heard screaming."

"I'm fine."

She wasn't, but her nose would have to do, she realised.

– 29 –

To be announced.

Book of New Revelation, 1.3

"Well, verse three," Dave said, carefully.

Everyone leaned forward.

A hush descended as the saints and apostles stood motionless in the stained-glass windows. The candles in their golden sticks flickered less, and instead, burned upright and attentive. Even the tapping on the underside of the gravestones paused.

"How about, er... Verily forsooth, a fifth Dave came from outside... to guide the faithful."

"Oh, that's quite radical."

"And it's a haiku."

"But how does this fifth Dave guide us?"

"Well, verily, the fifth Dave suggested less of the cannibalism and more of the 'how do I get out of here?'"

"Is that verse four?" Brother Mike asked.

"You could catch a bus," Brother John suggested.

"Bus?" Dave asked.

"Colmore Row, loads of 'em."

"Still?"

Brother John nodded.

"Why don't you all... you know?" Dave looked around the circle.

"Oh no," Brother John said.

"Why not?"

"It's not written in the New Book."

"Surely, you could just scribble down, 'Verily, they all legged it for the bus.'"

"Is that verse five?" Brother Also Dave asked.

"These buses," Dave said, musing as he spoke, "do any go to Dudley?"

"The 12A and the 87, I think, but they're not running," Brother John said.

"Bugger."

"Oh, I don't think we should have rude words in the Book of New Revelation," Brother Also Dave said.

"But they have laid on an armoured convoyed replacement service," Brother John said, kindly. He was a mine of information.

"But you wouldn't want to go to Dudley," Sister Jordan said. "That's got a zoo."

"But the Dudley buses go down Newhall Street," Dave pointed out.

"Not all the way," Brother John said.

But the idea was there, fully formed in Dave's brain – the very brain all the zombies wanted to eat – and all he had to do... no, best not list all he had to do as it would be depressing.

Instead, he said "When's the next one due?"

"You can't leave," Brother John said.

"Yes, stay," Sister Jordan said, "please stay."

"Yes, do stay," Brother Also Dave added. "What if we get peckish,"

"I think..." Dave began, but then he stood, strolled over to Brother Also Dave and took the Book of New Revelation from him. He flicked the spirally-bound Moleskine notebook to the first page.

He skimmed the first two verses taking in the ornate and stylish way that the 'V' of 'Verily, forsooth, in the terrible End of Days, the dead rose from the ground to feast upon the living' had been swirled. The calligraphy was excellent.

"Beautiful penmanship," Dave said.

Brother Also Dave blushed. "Thank you."

"May I?" And Dave snatched the biro off him and scrawled to the sound of gasps and severe tutting. He handed it back.

"Brother Also Dave," Dave said.

Brother Also Dave looked confused and then read aloud, "Verily, the dreth... leth..."

"It's a 'bee'."

"Ah, yes... verily, the brethren helped fifth Dave with the correct time of the next bus."

"Oh," Brother John said, "well, if it is so written, then... er... 2:25 or thereabouts, depending on traffic."

"Best write down what Brother John just said," Dave advised.

"Oh, yes, that would be verse five," Brother Also Dave said. "What was that again, Brother John?"

"Oh, well, if it is written... or did I say, 'verily'?" Brother John said.

And with that, the group descended into a theological debate, while Dave checked his watch, collected *Brainbiter 2.0* and sauntered back to the side door.

He peered through the diamond-shaped windows to check the zombie situation. It was calmer. Verily, he thought, this was... forsooth, they'd got him doing the 'verily' nonsense too.

Best to escape before any verse six put him back on the menu, so certain death outside it was.

Dave pulled up his mask and slipped out. He closed the door behind him and sneaked around the cathedral to the Colmore Road side.

"Head... meat..."

Ignoring the first burnt-out car at the first exit, he went left and scrambled up the barricade. Standing on top of an SUV meant he could see the bus stops clearly. He could even make out the timetable display with its pasted-over new schedule and he couldn't miss all the zombies waiting for the next ride.

They saw him.

"Bus, bus..."

Dave checked his watch.

Five minutes.

By the time he'd waited fifteen minutes, and had struck down a few zombies, a horde of hell surrounded him with modern ones on one side and the ancient variety on the other. The car began to rock and Dave had to kneel down to hold on.

After twenty minutes, three armoured vehicles all arrived at once.

The nearest armoured truck belched diesel fumes as it stopped, firing machine gun rounds from its forward and rear turrets.

Du-du-du-du-du-du-*ping*-du-du-du. Du-du-du.

Those zombies on the pavement jerked and fell. Bullets even went through the overturned car Dave was standing on and hacked lumps out of the graveyard zombies.

Dave waved his edging tool aloft.

"Oi! Careful! Bus! Bus!"

"Waaaa," a voice shouted, muffled by a mask and an armoured truck.

Dave jumped down and made it to the bus stop's pillbox.

A man stepped out of the truck via the metal side door. He wore a West Midlands Travel uniform complete with gas mask, breathing apparatus, stab vest, hi-vis vest and a dangling name badge. He took out his equipment from a bum bag.

"Yeah?" shouted the bus conductor.

Nice to see bus conductors back on armoured trucks, Dave thought. "Newhall Street?"

"That's just round the corner."

"Yes, Newhall Street, please."

"We don't stop there."

"Ah."

"We've not stopped there since the third emergency timetable."

"Oh."

"You could get a cab."

There were cabs strewn across the road, slammed aside by passing armoured trucks.

"I'll, er... can I walk alongside."

"Alongside?"

"Please."

"Suit yourself." The bus conductor put away his ticket machine, portable credit card reader and his West Midlands Travel sidearm, and reboarded the truck.

The vehicle belched fumes causing Dave to cough and his eyes to water. It would not pass the city's Clean Air Zone criteria.

Dave stayed in the smoke until the vehicle lurched forward, slowly because it was a 20mph speed limit and because it needed to crush dead zombies under its thick tyres.

There was a spot of bother as they passed the Temple Row West turning as a clutch of undead office workers formed a 4-4-too many formation. The forward turret spat fire – **du-du-du-du-du-du-du-du-du** – tearing the away team into bits.

And then the truck turned right into Newhall Street.

Dave crouched at the back checking each building on both sides for some sign of Telephone House. At the crossroads, the armoured truck turned left onto Great Charles Street Queensway, and roared off at speed.

Dave was left alone standing in the middle of the major dual carriageway.

There were still zombies staggering in his direction, but they were some distance away, spread out over the wide roads of Queensway and Newhall Street. He could hear their different cries. Perhaps he was more attuned to their words having spotted it earlier, but in amongst the mumbles for "Brains, brains...", there were other words.

Maybe "Heart, heart..." and "Courage, courage..." Each wanted something and that somehow drove them to rise up from the grave and hunt the living.

Just as Dave had wanted... what?

He'd risen up each morning for what?

His brain told him to run and hide, but he followed his heart and plucked up his courage to keep going.

Further down Newhall Street, he passed the intersection with Lionel Street. In one direction, he could see a slice of the fancy cake that was the new library and, in the other, it was down a long way to a dark, brick railway bridge. There were zombies in both directions sensing his passing presence and reacted.

He went on.

They followed.

Yet again, there were zombies in a line across the road like rows and rows of defensive players.

His brain had been right, stuff his heart and his courage. There was no real hope, but if Sunday league football had taught him anything, it was to play to the whistle.

Wait!

The big building on his left, brick on top of grey stone and occupying the length of a block, looked promising. In the middle was a large opening, with carvings of lions and an intertwined snake above. Next to it, on a wooden sign and written in two rows with black lettering, was the legend, 'Telephone House'.

He'd made it.

The grand old building had been constructed from dependable, solid stone for the first storey and then good old-fashioned red brick for four storeys and a modern level above that. There were even windows for a basement level. The door was beautiful, art deco with an elegant design above that boasted 'GR' and '1935'.

The solid wooden doors were invitingly open and the glass doors beyond were broken. However, further in, filing cabinets had been piled across the entrance.

It looked formidable.

He pressed the doorbell – what else could he do?

– 30 –

God grant me the patience to change the
things I can and the bloody-mindedness to
rail against the things I can't.

Anon

Councillor Grant intercepted her on her long walk along
the narrow path of the main corridor.

"You've been told... about... you know?" he asked.

Dawn stopped.

The man was in the way and perhaps he was also in the
way of her climbing the ladder of success. Stuck here in
Birmingham's deep underground, there had been few
opportunities for career development, let alone promotion.
All those training days – even one involving crying while
being shot by paintballs – had been something for her CV.
She could almost hear the interview panels asking what
she'd done in the past three years.

"I have," she said.

She had seen the light.

"Then... you know... my grievance?"

Dawn did not know his grievance. There didn't seem
to be anything the man could complain about given that
he was the most important person in the brand-new
Midlands Sector. Or was it area? Or zone? She didn't
shed a tear for tiers.

"Perhaps you could submit it in an email?"

"I can't, it's urgent," Councillor Grant said. "You...
you know."

238

"I know?"

"It should be me. I'm in charge here. I've been slaving away down here for years, and then that southern twat swans in and takes over. Just because his parents could afford to send him to the right school."

"He is the minister."

"Oh, you would side with him, wouldn't you, now he's given you a cushy number?"

"Councillor!"

"Project Eve, Midlands, would have been you and me."

"Well, I... pardon!"

"You and me, repopulating the Midlands."

"Councillor!"

Did repopulating the Midlands Sector with a councillor sound better than repopulating the UK with a minister? Well, no, it didn't, just as stubbing your toe was not better than repeatedly bashing your head against the wall.

"There's no gratitude," Councillor Grant said. He pointed an accusing finger. "I saved your life."

He walked away as Dawn remembered dragging the man's suitcase across Birmingham all those years ago when it went pear-shaped.

Did they all want to get into her knickers? The minister, the councillor, Anderson and then what? The police officers, Ahmed and Rob, and then all those people at the advertising company, Bill Burton and that Dave.

"P'ah!"

To hell with them all.

Why shouldn't she use her sex for proper tea and biscuits? She had been given certain gifts that men wanted and she had needs. She needed chocolate for starters. So, why not? It was a fair exchange. There was an apocalypse on, after all.

She straightened her clothing. She might as well look her best. However, she knew she looked fraught and her hair needed a proper £65 wash, massage, haircut, styling, a long conversation about where she was going on holiday this year and hairspray in her eye.

That wasn't going to happen.

Although, maybe in London, a hairdresser might have survived.

She set off along the straight and narrow corridor again. It is a far better thing I do, etcetera, she thought, and for whom the bell tolls.

If at first you don't succeed, perhaps you
shouldn't have started.

Anon

Dave pressed the button again.

Nothing.

Zombies staggered towards him from both directions.

He looked for another doorbell, an intercom, a large cat
flap – anything.

"Brains, brains..."

"Yes, yes," Dave replied, "I'm thinking."

There was an intercom at the side of the door. Dave
pressed it, and again, and even harder still.

Nothing.

"Oh, for..."

There was a window that led into the basement... lower
level as Newhall Street sloped. The safety glass had failed
and the iron bars damaged as if they'd burst outwards from
the inside.

Only one zombie in the way.

Dave sliced the head clean off.

He dived in, head first, got stuck, wriggled and felt
hands grabbing at his shoes. His middle came free and he
fell, badly, bumping his shoulder and arm on a table before
he hit the floor. He'd never felt happier.

"Brains..."

The zombies were trying the same manoeuvre, let them. Dave was on his feet, running or rather lurching to a limp. He'd bumped his ankle as well.

It was gloomy, the light shifting as the zombies piled against the window, but Dave saw the door and it was *locked!*

"Oh for–"

Wait, there was a latch.

Dave unlocked it.

Why was it locked from the inside?

On the other side was a corridor, the yellow walls obscured by walking corpses. He took them by surprise, and weaved around and through them like Maradona dribbling through the entire England team in the Mexico '86 World Cup quarter final.

Stairs.

Up, two – *ow!* – hurt shin, one at a time until he reached the next floor.

Zombies rose from the down direction – wasn't Dawn in some bunker? That meant he was going in the wrong way – the story of his life – and, sooner or later, he'd run out of stairs.

But what could he do?

He ran up.

Holy cow! He was unfit.

Saturday league games were a long time ago and they'd been replaced by playing FIFA on his PlayStation. If only he could climb the stairs on his thumbs or by hitting triangle, square, triangle.

He made it round a corner and piled straight into a shambling figure. They tumbled together as they fell on the square of lino that made up the turn.

Dave shrieked.

The other man shrieked, then he held his chest, jittery and shivering.

"You nearly gave me a heart attack," he said. He pulled at his thinning hair.

"Sorry."

"What are you doing sneaking around like that?"

"The place is full of zombies," Dave pointed out.

"That's no excuse... maybe it is, but please, be careful in future."

"Like I said, sorry."

"Who are you anyway?"

"Dave."

"Dave?"

"Dave... Knight."

"Are you with the minister?"

"Er... yes."

"You utter bastard!"

"Sorry?"

"You left me on the roof!"

"Oh, I'm not with the minister, I'm er... advertising."

The man looked at him suspiciously. "Well," he said, "you can help me with this stupid case."

"OK... who are you?"

"George Matt, Acting Senior Logistics Advisor."

"Acting..."

"Mr Jackson is Senior... oh, he's dead now."

"Promotion then."

"I must have a word with HR."

Dave nodded and took over wheeling the suitcase.

"This way," George said.

"Zombies down there," Dave informed him.

"That way then."

He led the way up to the second floor and then along a corridor to another set of stairs. The case bumped along, occasionally acting like a supermarket trolley when the carpet went from threadbare to luxurious.

"Down here," George said when they reached the far stairs, servants' if the decoration was anything to go by.

Dave nodded and then hefted the case, but it slipped, narrowly missing George as it bumped and bounced down. It stayed upright for a remarkably long time, but inevitably it keeled over and rolled down as inelegantly as a rectangular object could down square steps. It crunched to the bottom, slid a little and then started bleeding liquid from its seams hissing as it did so.

"Bugger," Dave said.

They went down.

The clear liquid spreading over the concrete fizzed.

Dave and George looked at each other with the same guilty expression. George knelt down and opened the case. In amongst the sodden clothes, a broken bottles glugged and spat.

"Champagne," George said. "Expensive champagne."

"That one's all right."

"I'm not taking the blame for this."

"I wouldn't expect you to," Dave said.

"I've a faultless record."

"I'm sure you have."

"I've brought thirty-five grievances to ensure that."

"Thirty-five, excellent."

"Just so long as we understand one another."

"Let's take that bottle out just in case of another little mishap."

Dave bent over and hauled up the bottle, which was surprisingly heavy. It was a long time since Dave had seen posh booze. This was like fizzy single malt wine compared to the rubbish thieves hadn't even felt like looting from the local offie. He marvelled at the deep ocean, green colour of the glass, the golden foil neck and the understated...

"Dave!"

"In a moment."

...fancy label that boasted Moet & Chandon, imperial and brut. It was a thing of beauty like a ten-pin bowling skittle and as solid as a club for battering seals.

Just as Dave stood upright, a zombie lurched out at the end of the corridor. It wasn't a problem at that distance unless it was...

"Jogger!" Dave shouted. He fumbled with his edging tool, but the champagne bottle was in his right hand. George dived behind the suitcase with his hands over his head.

Dave dropped the bottle, it landed heavily with a dull thud, poised on its edge and then toppled.

The zombie was nearly upon him.

Dave retreated backwards.

Uncharitably, he thought he only needed to get further away than George Whoever, but the zombie ignored the cowering, newly appointable senior logistics advisor and thrust its claws towards Dave.

"Noooooo..." Dave explained as the second stretched towards a freeze frame.

"Brains..." said the zombie as it put its foot on the bottle, did a high kick, and then keeled over backwards.

Dave got the edging tool into a two-handed grip and hacked it down like an axe, again and again, over and over, *thwack* and *thwack* and *splot*, until the bloody pulp was splashed all over the floor, sprayed on the ceiling, splatted on the walls and pollocked on the suitcase.

George emerged, shaking. "Thank you."

"Ah... ha..."

George picked up the champagne bottle and wiped the fancy label with his sleeve. The man giggled, his safe brains unhinged, as he yanked an entire tuft of hair out. Mental health was important in these trying times, so Dave said, "You OK, mate?"

"Yes, yes, oh yes, yes, yes-yes."

"Good to hear it."

"Yes, yes, let's..."

"Good idea."

"Yes."

Dave carefully recovered the precious bottle from George's shaking hands, making sure he held it in his left hand with *Brainbiter 2.0* in his right.

George led the way, endlessly explaining that 'yes', it was the right route.

Down they went, the stairs transforming from wallpaper luxury to functional concrete. Along a passage, they came to a huge round door like the final test on a major bank heist. It even had a security access panel.

George keyed in a four-digit access code, while Dave stood guard with his edging tool and the blunt instrument of the '07 vintage.

"Come on," Dave suggested.

"I am going as fast as I can," George said, carefully articulating each word to avoid misunderstanding.

The door finally breathed a sigh of relief as the pressure between the inside and outside equalized.

"Made it," Dave said as they stepped inside.

"Not yet," George replied. He went to manhandle the door, but before he could close it, another man in a crumpled suit marched up.

"Matt, where the hell have you been?" he said. "Who's he?"

George abandoned the heavy door to reply. "Hugh Anderson, this is Dave, Dave... meet Hugh Anderson."

"I've bought a bottle," Dave said, helpfully, and he showed the chateaux '07 to the Anderson bloke. He'd been at the meeting with the minister, Dave realised.

"He doesn't have clearance!" Hugh Anderson yelled.

"There's an apocalypse on, if you hadn't noticed."

"Matt, this is a high security, top secret, government facility. We can't have just anyone strolling in."

George rallied. "You left me to die."

"Where's the minister's suitcase."

"I'm going to talk to Dawn and start an official grievance."

"The minister's case?"

"His champagne–"

"Vital champagne."

"Is leaking all over the place."

"My God, Matt, you fool."

"There's this," Dave said, holding up the bottle again.

"Where's your clearance?" Anderson said, twisting the hatred into every syllable.

"This is my clearance," Dave said, switching from showing the bottle to brandishing the edging tool.

A gun cocked. "And this is mine!"

Dave turned to face an Asian man in a security uniform pointing a Glock 17M, the nasty type issued to the Metropolitan police, in Dave's face. For his part, Dave dropped his edging tool. It clattered, echoing in the vast tunnel network.

"Who are you?" the security guard said.

"Dave."

"Shoot him," Anderson suggested.

"He saved my life!" George said.

"More fool him."

"I was at the meeting with the minister," Dave said. "With you, Hugh."

Anderson looked at Dave, eyes narrowing.

"It still doesn't give you clearance to come down here," Anderson said. "Ahmed, hold him here, while I get Rob and Pete... oh, while I get Rob."

Anderson stormed off, disappearing into what looked to Dave like a labyrinth. He wasn't going to find Dawn down here without help.

"Ahmed, is it?" Dave said, carefully holding up his hand as he bent his knees, bowing to this security guard. He put the champagne bottle down. "I came here to save Dawn–"

"How do you know Dawn?"

"She asked me to come here."

"How do you know she needs saving?"

"She... well, it seemed obvious."

And she did, Dave realised, otherwise why had she told him the precise location of the secret bunker.

Ahmed shifted his head back and narrowed his eyes.

"I have proof," Dave added. "Clearance of a sort."

Theatrically, he reached into his jacket, very slowly, and produced his phone held between his index finger and thumb.

Ahmed nodded.

Dave turned it on, made the shape on the dots and the screen lit up... eventually. He tapped the Matchbox app and up came Dawn's picture.

Ahmed squinted at it. "You fancy her, so what? We all do."

"No look, we're compatible," Dave said. "I swiped right *and so did she.*"

"Hmm... OK," Ahmed said and he lowered his gun.

"So, Dawn needs saving," Dave hazarded.

"She's in the VIP suite."

"That sounds... good?"

"With Fenton-Briggs," George said. His hand went to his head, but there was no hair left. "I mean, we ought to draw lots or go by–"

"Lots?"

"To see who sleeps with her to repopulate the planet."

Dave's eyes widened until his pupils were surrounded by white. He tried to speak, but his jaw had dropped down.

George and Ahmed waited.

Eventually, Dave said, "Excuse me?"

– 32 –

BETTER TO BE SAFE
FOLLOW GOVERNMENT ADVICE
DO NOT BE SORRY

Government Advice (unused)

The VIP suite turned out to have its lighting low, not to save energy, but to create a romantic atmosphere. Dawn wouldn't have found it, except for the two police officers on guard outside the anonymous door.

Fenton-Briggs, MP, stood looking like a statesman in his black dressing gown. He smiled, one hand in his pocket with a thumb peeking out. He was suave, sophisticated, savvy and shrewd, and other words beginning with 'S'. So far away from those schoolboys pretending to yawn in the cinema to put their arms around you.

The rest of the room – why had she never been told about it? – consisted of a large double bed, a chest of drawers and a wardrobe, an en suite bathroom and a drinks cabinet.

"Help yourself, Dawn," Fenton-Briggs said. He waved his hand to the collection of fancy bottles.

"I'd prefer us to be professional, Mr Fenton-Briggs," Dawn said.

"I can role-play, Miss Knott-Withany."

Dawn let that one go – although she should insist on 'Ms' – as she had reached the well-stocked drinks cabinet with all its shiny, colourful delights. It should be shared with everyone or kept in storage for emergencies, Dawn thought, as she poured herself a gin so massive that it burnt all the passages down to her quivering stomach when she knocked it back.

She burped, silently.

Fenton-Briggs came over, sniffed. "Are you wearing gin as a perfume?"

"Eau de Gordons."

"Suits you." He topped up a whiskey. "When you're ready."

"Yes, er... I'll just powder... I mean slip into something more comfortable."

Dawn fled to the en suite, locked the door and stared at herself framed in gold leaf. There were marble surfaces and the floor was tiled. A black furry rug lurked by the toilet. She opened the wall cabinet and saw brands of cologne that hadn't existed for decades – Old Spice and Hai Karate. There was even a tube of Avon Smoker's Toothpaste.

Who was the last woman lured into this den?

Dawn had never smoked, but she wanted a cigarette, something to hold to stop her fingers jittering. Would she have to stand outside to smoke it?

A sharp rap sounded on the door.

"Miss Knott-Withany–"

"Just Withany! No, no."

"My apologies, Miss Just-Withany-Knowno?"

"There's no 'Just'."

"Withany-Nojust?"

"No, it's just... not just."

"Withany-Knottjust?"

"My name is Withany... no, no."

"Miss Withany-Knowno."

"No, no!"

"That's what I said, 'No-no'."

Dawn tried to explain by silently screaming.

"I mean," Fenton-Briggs said, his tone becoming disgruntled. "Make your mind up, woman."

"It's fine." She was going to be called 'Dawn Fine' next, she knew it.

"Are you all right?"

"Yes."

"It's just that you've been in there a long time and I'm... keen to get on. The pill doesn't last forever even when I've taken three."

"Yes, of course."

Dawn flushed the toilet. The water gushed forth and churned in the bowl before gurgling down the closet bend and out to sea.

Right, Dawn thought.

She stepped out of the en suite and found the VIP suite empty. Where was the minister?

He was lying on the bed.

He sat up, leant on one elbow such that his dressing gown slid up to reveal his chubby thighs and fell open to his waist. His chest was covered in discrete, wiry hairs and the skin was a pale pink colour contrasting with the brandy blush of his cheeks and neck.

"I thought you were going to slip into something more comfortable," he said.

"I forgot to pack it."

"Never mind, you can take off your work suit, sexily."

He smiled and patted the bed beside him. There was a wide, comfortable-looking space ready to envelop her in the covers and quilt. After three years sleeping in a camp bed, it was inviting.

"Er... no," she said.

"Now, now, don't play hard to get."

"I'm not sleeping with you," Dawn said, emphatically.

"Oh, come on," Fenton-Briggs said.

"No."

Dawn knew that she didn't want to sleep with the minister or any of them. She was fed up with taking orders from those promoted above their ability with their eye-wateringly huge salaries and massive bonuses. What she wanted, above all, was to find someone she could talk to.

"So," Fenton-Briggs said, "it's 'Withany-Knowno' by name and it's 'no-no' by nature."

"Yes, I mean, no. It's not 'no-no'."

"No-no, no, no, nono, nonnie-nonnie, it doesn't matter how it's pronounced – it's always 'no' with your type."

"My type?"

"Women."

"Well, honestly, this is cause for a grievance."

"Nonsense."

"Yes, it's... all this is distinctly suggestive and could be construed as a sexual context."

"That's the idea."

"No," Dawn said. "I am on strike!"

"You can't go on strike, we made it illegal."

"I protest."

"And to protest."

"The law banning strikes only applies to essential services."

"Every service is essential in an emergency."

"That's ludicrous."

"And I declare that you servicing me is essential."

"No!"

"Look, Miss Whatever-Knowno, according to the Civil Contingencies Act, 2004, part 1, section 5." – The minister made air-quotes – "A minister of the crown may by order require a person or body to perform a function of that person or body, blah-blah, subsection b, reducing, controlling or mitigating the effects of an emergency."

"So?"

"It's an emergency, and breeding with me will reduce the effects and mitigate the death toll."

"That's–"

"Look, woman, we declared a state of emergency, so I can do whatever I like."

"You've been doing whatever you like for the whole time you've been in government."

"And now it's legal."

Dawn stepped back, her mouth open and her eyes wide.

"So," he continued, "get your sweet butt over here before I have to take matters further."

Dawn became acutely aware of the presence of the two police officers standing guard outside the door. They were there to enforce the law, the minister's law, by force if necessary.

"I..." she said, but her mouth wouldn't work properly.

"Now," Fenton-Briggs said, "I'm a minister of the crown and, by order, come and perform a certain function on my person with your body."

STAY ALERT
RUN QUICKLY
SAVE LIVES.

Government advice

There was no time to lose!

Dave sprinted down the tunnel. Before he and his team started making haikus out of the advice, it was all 'run', 'run fast', 'run quickly', 'run away' and–

"Not that way," Ahmed shouted after him.

Dave ran back.

"And you won't get to her," Ahmed added. "The minister brought two Rasps."

"Eh?"

"Royalty and Specialist Protection officers," Ahmed said. "Mean buggers too."

"Oh."

"That's it then," George said.

Dave stood helpless. The concrete of the tunnels seemed to close in, while the open blast door beckoned with the threat of utter failure and the hope of a few pints to take his mind off things.

"I have to try," he mumbled.

He picked up his *Brainbiter 2.0* and the bottle of champagne.

"I can't let you take that," Ahmed said. "Security and all that."

"Oh." Dave dropped the edging tool. He kept the bottle. "So, which way?"

Ahmed pointed and then added, "left, red door."

"Thanks." Dave nodded and then sloped off like someone going to a friend's party.

Down where Ahmed had pointed and left, he came across two security guards. They did look like mean buggers too. They checked him over as if he was something that the cat had dragged in, played with, chewed up and spat out.

"Champagne... for the minister," Dave said.

"We've not been told," the sergeant said.

"Oh... shall I take it away and tell him you wouldn't let me bring it to him?"

"Er... no, you... where are the glasses?"

"Glasses? Oh, he said he had some... this is the third bottle."

"Oh."

"We didn't see anyone bring a second bottle," said the other guard.

"Or a first," said the sergeant.

Dave shrugged. "I dunno, I didn't bring either. You know what it's like, no-one tells anyone a damn thing."

The guard nodded.

"OK?" Dave said.

"OK."

Dave went past and approached the first door, green. He knocked, turned and smiled at the guards.

"It's the other door," the guard said.

"Oh, right."

Dave knocked on that one, a red one, and pretended to hear a shout from within. He heard something, as it were, and went in.

Inside, it was dark, candle-lit and gloomy.

Dave blinked, trying to get used to the low light.

"Who the fuck are you?" said a powerful, male voice.

And the extremely important minister up from London was on the bed struggling with Dawn Dey.

"Champagne?" Dave hazarded, showing the '07.

"I didn't order room service."

"Help," Dawn added. She tried to pull her torn blouse back on and adjust her half-worn jacket.

Fenton-Briggs slid off the bed, straightened his silk dressing gown and sauntered over.

Dave backed away and held his palms out.

"Hey," Fenton-Briggs said, "you're that advertising pleb, Dave the–"

Dave punched Fenton-Briggs as hard as he could.

"You little shit," Fenton-Briggs said. "That hurt."

"Sorry."

"Dave," Dawn said, "duck!"

"Eh?"

But Fenton-Briggs had already hit him back.

And down Dave went.

– 34 –

To avoid contamination, use a wet wipe and
hand sanitiser. Avoid touching anything and
at all costs, keep your distance from
everything.

Government advice

Fenton-Briggs dragged the unconscious Dave to the exit,
flung him out, locked the door and then rubbed his hands
together in satisfaction.

"Right, Miss Whatever Name Namey Name Name,"
he said with a smile, "where were we?"

Dawn smiled too, a sweet innocent smile that promised
so much, and then she kneed him in the bollocks – hard.

"Oooofff," Fenton-Briggs said as he crumpled into a
ball.

She kicked him.

"Ahhh," she cried out, and then she kicked him with
the foot that still had a shoe on.

After that, she found a waste paper bin, held her loose
hair back and threw up into it. The barbeque ribs and
French fries came back with a vengeance.

In the en suite, she found some toothpaste and a
toothbrush still sealed in its packaging. She ripped it open
and brushed the vile taste (and any tobacco stains) from
her mouth. She even considered brushing her eyeballs to
clean them, but the image of the beastly minister was
etched through her optic nerve right to the back of her
brain where she stored her darkest nightmares.

Back in the VIP suite, Fenton-Briggs still writhed on the floor.

"B... bitch," he managed.

"Mr Fenton-Briggs, we'll have none of that sexist language."

"You're one of those honey-trap spies sent by the Left-Wing Economic Establishment to destroy me."

Dawn kicked him again, found her shoe and then, once it was back on, she kicked him with that too.

Outside, back in the corridor, she found Dave sitting on the floor, holding his head and remonstrating with the sergeant and the officer.

"What's going on?" the sergeant demanded to know.

"Zombie!" Dawn screamed. "Zombie! There! He's a zombie."

She pulled Dave to his feet as the perplexed police officers looked about for advice.

"The minister," Dawn explained, "is a zombie."

"He didn't show any signs," the sergeant said.

"Did he take a test?"

"Well, he... er... refused to take it. Thought it stupid. Oh fuck!"

"There you go," Dawn said. "Come on, Dave."

"Eh?" Dave said.

"Run."

"Eh?" Dave asked.

"Run!"

Hand in hand, they fled as the two guards fumbled into action with their weapons. They cocked the evil things and readied themselves for combat, each mouthing a prayer or personal pep talk. They opened the door, but Dave and Dawn were well round the corner by then and legging it towards the blast doors.

An automated female voice came over the tannoy.

"Attention please, attention please." – the voice was calm and soothing – *"A situation has arisen in the building. Please listen for further instructions."*

"What did it say?" Dave asked.

"It doesn't matter," Dawn explained. "It's the female voice, so it's only the warning."

"I see."

"If the male voice speaks, we're in trouble."

"Oh... isn't that sexist?"

"Yes."

On cue, the message changed and the deeper tones of a male voice sounded from the speakers. If anything, he was even more soothing and calm than the woman's had been.

"Attention please, attention please," he said, politely. *"A situation has arisen in the building."*

"That was–" Dave said.

"Attention please, attention please. Please evacuate the building."

"That was the male–"

"Yes."

"So..."

"Yes."

"Right."

"At least it's not the alarms," Dawn said.

"Why, what would they mean?"

"Well, for starters, we wouldn't–"

Boop-boop, boop-boop, boop-boop...

"Shit," Dave said.

"I know what that one means," Dawn yelled. "They've found the minister."

"And he's a zombie?"

"No, he's just... winded."

"Then–"

But another alarm went off.

Wa-wa-wa-wa-wa-wa-wa-wa...

The two alarms mixed together.

boWA-boWA, wa, WAoop, Waoop, wa...

"It's the zombie alarm," Dawn shouted. "Some idiot must have left the main door open!"

Dave looked towards the distant exit.

259

"Eh?"

"The zombie alarm."

Dave glanced at her and then looked at the distant exit in terror. "EH?"

Dawn felt calm. She felt like she was in control at last. The moment she'd kneed the minister in the bollocks, she had been free of it. She had her whole life ahead of her to enjoy, savour and live – if only she could hear herself think.

"Why," she said, "is it that when you're trying to cope with a real emergency, does that THING take away all your ABILITY to CONCENTRATE?"

"What!"

"I said... never mind."

"What?"

"NEVER MIND."

"WHAT?"

"WHAT?"

"WHAT?"

Above the cacophony, gunshots sounded – deep bangs that added percussion to the wailing, synthetic racket of the alarms.

It mixed together.

boWA-boWA, wa, **BANG**, *Waoop,* **BANG**, *wa...*

"WHAT!"

"WHAT?"

Ahmed sprinted past them.

Zombies jogged after him.

"RUN!"

"RUN!"

They ran, this way and sadly that.

"Dave... Dave..."

He'd disappeared.

Dawn kept going, and her feet took her along a familiar route. She reached the Ladies and instinctively nipped in for her usual snatched solace. She locked the door behind her.

The muffled alarms didn't penetrate too much – they'd not thought it important enough to put a speaker in the Ladies – and so, finally, she could almost start to get a grip.

Zombies hunted on sound and scent. Hearing would be useless in the circumstances, but smell would be easy, given that everyone was panicking and, therefore, reeking of adrenaline and fear.

Her blouse had lost a few buttons.

She felt like crying.

But she wasn't going to, even though she'd wasted her old life and her lovely new life was soon to be cut short.

The lock on the Ladies would keep the likes of Randy Anderson out, reinforced by the man's innate worry about disciplinary action, but that wouldn't work on the hordes of the undead.

Or Fenton-Briggs.

She had to get out of the bunker.

She found her bag and used the last of the tissue to dab her eyes – oh, she had cried. She knew she was going to face all the zombies, actual zombies, with a mask, sunglasses, a bottle of hand sanitiser, a attack alarm and a lipstick.

She went back into the corridor.

And screamed!

"Aaaaaaaaaaaaaaaaaaaarrrrrrggghhhhhhh!"

It added to the cacophony.

Aabo WA-bo WAaawaaa WAoopaa Waooph!wa...

It was Dave.

He'd screamed too.

Now he shouted pointlessly behind the racket, "Don't sneak up on people like that!"

"What?" Dawn said.

"WHAT?"

"WHAT?"

A roar of authority and entitlement split through the noise. "OI, YOU FUCKING BITCH!"

No words reached them, but the tone of anger hit home. Fenton-Briggs, still in his silk dressing gown stormed down the corridor towards them. Behind him, came the two police officers hurrying to keep up.

"Dawn! Zombies," Dave shouted, pointing the other way.

"What?" Dawn said, but there was no time to work out what he'd said. "Never mind. This way."

"WHAT?"

Dawn grabbed him and pulled him towards the Ladies.

"I can't go in here," Dave said as he stumbled through the door.

"What!" Dawn replied.

"I SAID... oh!"

The precious doors kept some of the noise out and the lock slammed home making Dawn feel safer.

Until the door almost jumped off its hinges.

"It's all right," Dawn said, but then she added, "EEK!"

Bullet holes appeared around the lock.

BANG! BANG-BANG! BANG!

Perhaps they could hide in a cubicle.

A combat boot kicked the door open.

Dawn fumbled for her attack alarm.

The other alarms jumped in volume as Fenton-Briggs pushed the sergeant aside.

Panicked, Dave tugged at the panic cord and yanked it down. Even though it hang limply in his hand, it had been enough.

Outside, the speakers above the door blurted.

Riiiiiiiiiiiiiiiiiiiiiiiiiiiiiiiiiiiiiiiiiiiiiiiiiiiiiiiing.

It added to everything.

iiboWA-boWAiiwaiiWAoopiiWaoopiiwa...

Feeling attacked, Dawn activated her attack alarm.

It went, WAAAAAAAAAAAAAAAAAAAAAAAAAAAAAA...

And it all merged into a Spector-like wall of sound.

IIBOWA-BOWAIIWAIIWAOOPIIWAOOPIIWA...

Fenton-Briggs started shouting, his face red and his words lost in the audio avalanche.

IIBOWA-BOWAII-"Bitch"-OOPIIWAOOPIIWA...

Zombies fell on the two police officers from behind tearing at their necks and faces. One of the bigger guns fired destroying all the polystyrene tiles in the ceiling.

RAT-A-TAT-TAT-TAT-TAT-TAT-TAT-TAT!!!

Dawn screamed, but even she couldn't hear that.

Dave pushed Fenton-Briggs away – he wasn't strong enough to shift the man's huge, bloated frame, but it was enough for the zombies to fall upon him from behind.

For a moment, the zombies each had a living person to occupy them. Soon, there would be more zombies and only Dawn and Dave left alive... and not for long.

Dave opened his mouth to shout, but Dawn had seen the opportunity herself.

She led the way.

They jumped over the flailing bodies into the corridor beyond, and scarpered, buffeted by the constant hooting horns of the sirens and reached the blast doors. Fresh blood stains smeared the floor, but there was no-one about, living or undead.

Ahmed, Matt, Anderson and Rob must have changed sides, no longer Us, but Them.

Dave paused to pick up a gardening tool. "Let's get out of here," he said.

"What?"

"WHAT?"

"LOOK, LET'S JUST GET OUT OF HERE," Dawn yelled.

Dave motioned. He'd not heard her, Dawn realised, but at least he'd come up with the same idea.

They went through the huge metal protective door, along the passage and up the stairs. The alarms became the screams of those from Hell far below, it seemed.

On the ground floor, Dawn stopped them at the lift, fire point and vending machine.

"Mr Knight, could you?" Dawn said.

"Sure," Dave replied and he used his edging tool to smash the glass over the fire equipment. He levered out a fire axe and gave it to Dawn.

"I meant the chocolate."

"Oh, right."

He smashed the glass and they shared a Twix, and she had a dark chocolate, a Dairy Milk and a Fruit and Nut.

"Mmmmm mmm," she said. She loved him already.

"You know, we could... you know."

"Yes... Dave, I'd like that."

"Good."

"NAMES!!! NAMES!!!"

The corpse of Fenton-Briggs, MP, jerked towards them. His hands like claws, his teeth bloodied and sharp, and his eyes were bloodshot and furious. Rancid spittle sprayed from his mouth.

Dawn and Dave struck together.

And they kept going cutting him to pieces with their weapons – spine severed, brain smashed in and body mashed to a pulp.

Afterwards, gasping, Dawn led the way through the corridors of the ground floor to the side exit. They paused before the door to collect their breath, wits and sanity. It took a while.

"We'll forget about this," Dawn said.

"I won't forget you," Dave replied.

"No. I mean, us... the human race."

"Oh."

"If we survive this and if they find a cure, then everything will go back to normal."

"Another new normal?"

"A better normal," Dawn said. "And it'll be like it never happened. Even those of us who lived through it will forget about it."

"A lot of 'if's at the start of that."

"You know what I mean."

"Yes," Dave said, "but I for one would welcome it."

"After all these people have died."

"That's the point."

"Then they died for nothing," Dawn said.

"There was nothing they were trying to die for," Dave said. "It's like the First World War. You know, lest we forget and, in the morning, we'll remember them. Well, if we do forget, if war, zombies, plague, hornets, climate change, whatever, do become such a thing of the past that's forgotten, then those lost will have won. They will have died to make war or whatever so much a thing of the past that it is gone and forgotten."

"And then we'll repeat history."

"Not if the curriculum includes History again as well as Maths."

"But that won't happen if people like Fenton-Briggs have anything to do with it," Dawn said.

"Then that's the next war we need to fight and we must remember that."

"The zombies aren't the zombies," Dawn said.

"Eh?"

"Those shufflers, ramblers and joggers out there, the walking dead – they aren't the zombies, we are," Dawn said and then, warming to her subject, she went on, "We're the ones who sleepwalked into this world and let men like Fenton-Briggs, Johnson, May, Rees-Mogg, Gove, Sunak and the rest – and, good heavens, Trump and Putin, take over and turn everything to shit. The greedy exploit the needy and we let them. We knuckled down to our spreadsheets and our reports, working all hours to give them a better return, so they could buy heated swimming pools, ludicrous yachts and wars."

"And we have to stop being zombies."

"Yes."

"Should we stop yakking and get on?"

"It would be for the best."

"Dawn, I like you with your hair down."

"Oh... thanks."

Dave nodded. "Are you ready?"

"Are you ready, Dave?"

"I was born ready. Well, reddish... pinkie-red, I guess."

"Your place or mine?" Dawn asked.

"Well, er..." Dave looked good when he smiled.

"I'd like you to be an apocalypse keeper."

"I'd like that too."

"So, yours or mine?"

"I'm Cotteridge."

"Mine's closer then," Dawn said.

"Is it a green tier?"

"All the way. And it's sectors now."

"OK, yours then," Dave agreed. "Mine's not very tidy to be honest."

"Ha."

"OK?"

"OK."

"You have a mask?"

"Yes," Dawn said. She did and it was home-made with flowery material.

"Lovely," Dave said. "Not everyone wears them nowadays."

"Who would they be?"

"Zombies."

So, they pulled their masks on and readied their weapons. Dave had his edging tool; Dawn had her fire axe. They'd go out into the world once more and not trust the government ever again.

And so, after a couple of deep breaths, a kiss for luck through their non-woven, layered filtration fabric, Dave opened the door and they rushed out screaming into the daylight, swinging wildly and happily ever after.

Or at least until the next variant.

The En

266

David Wake often resembles a zombie in the morning. This is his 13th novel, appropriately enough for a zombie apocalypse tale. The others include the *Derring-Do Club* adventures and the *Thinkersphere* SF series as well as stand-alone novels.

Thank you for reading *Dawn and Dave of the Dead*. If you enjoyed it, please leave a review.

TAKE CARE AND STAY SAFE
DO NOT TRUST CONSERVATIVES
SAVE EVERYONE'S LIVES

For more information, and to join the mailing list for news of forthcoming releases, see www.davidwake.com.

Many thanks to:–
Dawn Abigail, Helen Blenkinsop, Steve Bond, Andy Conway, Guy Etchells, Jill Griffin, David Muir, Mike Roberts and Prudence S Thomas.

Mystery, clues and danger with tea and cake

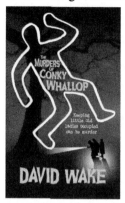

The Vicar lies dead – Murdered!

Three budding Miss Marples, Pat, Diane and Annabelle, swing into action and they want answers: Why would anyone want to kill the vicar? Where does Mrs Entwistle go every night? What was Sir Victor up to at the warden's? And how will so many murders affect the circulation of the parish magazine?

The truth will be uncovered: once they've had a nice cup of tea and a biscuit.

Includes a FREE scone recipe.

"Enjoyed the whole thing and absolutely loved some of the touches both clever and amusing. No spoilers – no details. Read it yourself!"

"...all kinds of red herrings thrown in to confuse the reader. Unlike many crime thrillers or cosy crime stories when I have usually sussed out who the killer is, in this case I really hadn't a clue."

Available as an ebook and paperback.

A bloke-lit tale of political intrigue and beer

Guy Wilson lives in the past.
Every year, he and his friends re-enact rebellion.
Every year, they celebrate the Jacobite's retreat.
Every year, they have a few drinks and go home...
                    ...except this year, they go too far.

An unstoppable boozing session meets an unbreakable wall
of riot police in this satirical thriller. Guy struggles against
corrupt politicians, murderous security forces and his own
girlfriend in a desperate bid to stop a modern uprising.

And it's all his fault.

Will any of his friends survive to last orders?

*"Witty, warm and well-written, "Crossing The Bridge" was
so enjoyable that I didn't want to finish it."*
★ ★ ★ ★ ★

*"My sort of book. Couldn't put it down. Comedy, tension
and an uncanny resemblance to the moral fibre of some of
our elected representatives."*
★ ★ ★ ★ ★

Available as an ebook and a paperback.

A ripping yarn of cliff-hangers, desperate chases, romance and deadly danger.

Earnestine, Georgina and Charlotte are trapped in the Eden College for Young Ladies suffering deportment, etiquette and Latin. So, when the British Empire is threatened by an army of zombies, the Deering-Dolittle sisters are eager to save the day. Unfortunately, they are under strict instructions not to have any adventures...

...but when did that ever stop them?

"Think 'Indiana Jones pace'. It's fast and dangerous and does not involve embroidery!"

★ ★ ★ ★ ★

"A brilliant, fast paced steampunk adventure, trains zombies and zeppelins, what more could you want?"

★ ★ ★ ★ ★

THE DERRING-DO CLUB

Putting their best foot forward, without showing an ankle, since 1896.

The first novel in the adventure series available as an ebook and a paperback.

A ripping yarn of time-travel, rocket-packs, conspiracy and *sword fighting!*

The plucky Deering-Dolittle sisters, Earnestine, Georgina and Charlotte, are put to the test as mysterious Time Travellers appear in Victorian London to avert the destruction of the world...

...but just whose side should they be on?

"Loved it! [...] Fast paced and exciting another great adventure for three Victorian Young Ladies."
★ ★ ★ ★ ★
"...if I had been wearing a hat, I would have taken it off to David Wake."
★ ★ ★ ★ ★

THE DERRING-DO CLUB
Putting their best foot forward, without showing an ankle, since 1896.

The second novel in the adventure series available as an ebook and a paperback.

A ripping yarn of strange creatures, aerial dog-fights, espionage and *pirates!*

Strange lights hover over Dartmoor and alien beings abduct the unwary as the plucky Deering-Dolittle sisters, Earnestine, Georgina and Charlotte, race to discover the truth before the conquest begins...

...but betrayal is never far away.

"Well-written, fast-paced, and dangerously addictive – but with some extra thinking in there, too, should you choose to read it that way."

★ ★ ★ ★ ★

"As with previous adventures I really enjoyed the imaginative scene setting, building intrigue into unexpected twists and a spectacular ending."

★ ★ ★ ★ ★

THE DERRING-DO CLUB
Putting their best foot forward, without showing an ankle, since 1896.

The third novel in the adventure series available as an ebook and a paperback.

An Arabian tale of murder, Egyptian gods, mummies, temple raiding and *flying carpets!*

Nine suspects trapped on the SS *Karnak* with a killer! As the Deering-Dolittle sisters, Earnestine, Georgina and Charlotte investigate, mummies rise from the dead, ancient gods send messages and plots turn like cogs.

Their journey is far from straight even on the Suez Canal.

> *"Well-written and witty, this is a gloriously over the top pastiche of Agatha Christie's 'Death on the Nile' – and much, much more."*
> ★ ★ ★ ★ ★
> *"You will not put this book down. [...] a quirky funny enjoyable Victorian tale and the last 300 pages fly by."*
> ★ ★ ★ ★ ★

THE DERRING-DO CLUB
Putting their best foot forward, without showing an ankle, since 1896.
The fourth novel in the adventure series available as an ebook and a paperback.

A ripping yarn set in the British Raj with handsome officers, vile thuggees, diabolical plans, a terrifying death-goddess and *a fate worse than death!*

It's soon to be the happiest day of Miss Deering-Dolittle's life, but abandonment, betrayal and an old foe stand to ruin everything – and destroy the British Empire.

All roads lead to the temple of Kali and a desperate last stand against impossible odds.

Can our plucky young heroines, Earnestine, Georgina and Charlotte save the day?

"Think 'Indiana Jones pace'. It's fast and dangerous. My kind of Adventure! MORE PLEASE."

THE DERRING-DO CLUB

Putting their best foot forward, without showing an ankle, since 1896.

The fifth novel in the adventure series available as an ebook and a paperback.

Think *Black Mirror* with a Scandi-crime feel

Twenty years from now, everyone's thoughts are shared on social media: the Thinkersphere. Privacy is dead and buried. Pre-mediated crime is history. So who killed the woman in Chedding car park?

Detective Oliver Braddon is plunged into an investigation to track down the impossible: a murderer who can kill without thinking.

Hashtag is a gritty, dystopian neo-noir that poses uncomfortable questions about our obsession with social media and presents a mind-bending picture of what life might be like when our very thoughts are no longer our own.

"Superb futuristic scenario – good story
and touches of dark humour."
★ ★ ★ ★ ★

"Oh my God what a fantastic concept!"
★ ★ ★ ★ ★

"...and suddenly you need to tell everyone else
to go away and let you finish this book!"
★ ★ ★ ★ ★

Book One of the Thinkersphere series
available as an ebook and a paperback.

The dark sequel to Hashtag

Black Mirror meets Scandi-crime in a mind-bending dystopia where 'likes' matter more than lives.

Detective Oliver Braddon's investigation into an apparent suicide leads him to a powerful media mogul. Is he the killer?

In this alarming vision of the near-future, everyone's thoughts are shared on social media. With privacy consigned to history, a new breed of celebrity influences billions.

But who controls who?

A gritty, neo-noir delving into a conflict between those connected and those with secrets to hide.

"Darker in tone than the previous book, which fits with our now slightly older Braddon's move from new and enthusiastic PC to somewhat more careworn Detective, there's a Scandi-noir feel to this one."
★ ★ ★ ★ ★

Book Two of the Thinkersphere series
available as an ebook and a paperback.

The mind-bending future continues

Another mass suicide. Or is it murder?

The case drops into Inspector Oliver Braddon's inbox. The world demands answers. With everyone's thoughts shared, liked and monitored, why haven't the police solved the case in the usual 20 seconds?

Braddon's suspicions focus on a disturbing cult, the Church of the Transcendent Cloud, and tech-billionaire, Jacob Lamb, the creator of the Thinkersphere app, *After Life* – except that he's dead.

Plus Sign is a gritty, dystopian neo-noir.

"...crackles with humour and tension as the reader is drawn into a world dominated by the all-embracing Thinkersphere and its tantalising app offering the promise of an After Life. Plus Sign is intriguing and alarming in equal measure [...] Thoroughly recommend."
★ ★ ★ ★ ★

Book Three of the Thinkersphere series
available as an ebook and a paperback.

A tonic for the Xmas Spirit

Being Santa's daughter would be a dream come true for any child, but for Carol Christmas, the fairy tale is about to end. Evil forces threaten the festive season, and only Carol can save the day...

A grim fairy tale told as a children's book, but perhaps not just for children.

"This starts out as a delightfully childlike modern take on the Christmas myth – the kind of Pixar-esque story that can play to the kids and give the adults a knowing wink or two, but it gets dark. Very dark."
★ ★ ★ ★ ★

Available as an ebook, a paperback and an audiobook.

Do you fear technology? We have an App for that.

Your phone is your life. But what if it kept secrets from you? What if it accidentally framed you for murder? And what if it was the only thing that could save you?

In a world where phones are more intelligent than humans, but are still thrown away like yesterday's fashions, one particular piece of plastic lies helpless as its owner, Alice Wooster, is about to be murdered...

In this darkly comic near-future tale, a very smart phone tells its own story as events build to a climactic battle. Can it save all the virtual and augmented worlds? Can it save the real one? Can it order Alice some proper clothes?

"Excellent novel – by turns strikingly original, laugh-out-loud funny and thought provoking."
★ ★ ★ ★ ★

"Want to read it again soon..."
★ ★ ★ ★ ★

"A thoughtful, tense and funny look at a future that seems to be already upon us."
★ ★ ★ ★ ★

Available as an ebook and a paperback.

An epic tale set in Japan's Samurai era

In the days of the sword, a girl disguised as a boy turns killer to avenge her Samurai master, murdered by a brotherhood of ruthless and powerful men. Following the trail of blood, a brilliant detective – an Emperor's Watcher – searches for answers only to come face-to-face with an old enemy, a man honour dictates he must protect.

As the death toll rises, and the hunter closes in on the hunted, truth-seeker and ninja assassin find themselves at odds, not only with each other, but also with their fundamental beliefs:

Honour or truth? Instinct or intellect? Justice or revenge?

Roninko is a bloody, action-packed revenge thriller steeped in ancient wisdom. A philosophical and breathtaking story of Bushido, 'the Way of the Warriors'.

> *"This is a beautifully written, atmospheric adventure through ancient Japan. Lovingly researched and with nuanced and interesting characters, I enjoyed this greatly."*
> ★ ★ ★ ★ ★

Available as an ebook and paperback.

Printed in Great Britain
by Amazon

39490991R00162